SUN DANCE

SunDance

S.W. BROUWER

 VICTOR BOOKS

A DIVISION OF SCRIPTURE PRESS PUBLICATIONS INC.
USA CANADA ENGLAND

Editors: Liz Duckworth, Barbara Williams
Designer: Paul Higdon
Cover Illustration: Chris Cocozza

ISBN: 1-56476-427-3

1 2 3 4 5 6 7 8 9 10 Printing/Year 99 98 97 96 95

To K.S.
(and to Nick)

I've always loved the glories of the old Wild West, and I would like to express my gratitude to the historians whose dedication has preserved that era, allowing the rest of us to cherish its spirit of freedom.

To them, and to you who may be reading this as more than a mystery, I would like to apologize for any of my research mistakes which I may have passed on to you in my attempts to make the fiction as historically accurate as possible.

SWB

SUN DANCE

Wyoming Territory, Laramie, April 1875

ONE

AT THE FRACTURED, ECHOING THUNDER of a single gunshot somewhere ahead in the night air, I threw aside my tin mug of coffee and began to sprint.

It was coffee I didn't need anyway; I had an enamel pot of my own stewing on the stove in the marshal's office, and the only reason I'd wandered a few streets over to the Chinaman's cafe was to take a rest from the letter I'd been composing at my desk.

I'd stayed at the Chinaman's a half hour, enjoying some of his fine apple pie, reading this week's copy of the *Laramie Sentinel,* and watching for Doc Harper to return from a sick call which had taken him to a ranch at the feet of the Medicine Bow mountains some twenty miles southwest. It wasn't that I fretted for Doc and his travel through the open plains at night. With the kindness of this year's spring, weather wasn't a concern, and Doc's horse was trustworthy to the point where Doc often slept in the carriage on his return trips to Laramie. Instead, my concerns were selfish. I could have used some of Doc's considerable conversation skills to take my mind off the letter waiting for me on my desk.

The Chinaman had insisted on pouring a final cup of coffee into the mug I'd brought with me, smiling and nodding with his usual cheerfulness as he shooed me out and secured the door locks behind me. I'd made it almost to Main Street, newspaper now tucked in the back of my pants, occasionally stopping to sip at my coffee, when that single gunshot rocked me from my thoughts.

It wasn't hard to discern which direction I should run. Although, along with the lights of the Red Rose Saloon to my left, the strains of dance hall music seeped into Main Street, I plainly heard the spreading clamor of dogs excited by their rude awakening. Others too had heard the shot and the dogs. The first gawkers had already stepped outside the saloon, yellow light from inside on their backs as they stood with the swinging doors held open.

As I ran, my boots clattered on the wooden sidewalk on my side of the street, and I decided I'd fare better on dirt. Both for comfort and for silence. The single gunshot told me this was one of the few occasions I'd earn the pay I accepted for wearing a marshal's badge. After all, a harmless cowboy in a drinking mood would have been firing pistols like a boy banging a toy drum. No, a single gunshot without return fire usually meant the first cartridge had done its job. Somewhere ahead, I'd probably find murder. Last thing I needed to do was give ample warning of my arrival.

I hopped over a railing onto the street and pushed hard, taking my Colt .44-40 from my holster. The Colt, however, gave me little comfort. The night air had not been ripped by the snap explosion of a pistol, but by the booming roar of a shotgun. Only fools or stubborn marshals continue in the face of those uneven odds.

From a side street twenty-five yards ahead to my right, a big, black horse cantered onto Main, turning in my direction. I skidded to a stop, brought my gun up, and turned sideways to make myself a smaller target.

"Off the horse!" I shouted. "Wyoming marshal!"

If he was innocent, we could sort out the explanations

later. If not innocent, I wanted as much notice as possible.

His outline, a shade darker than the night sky, shifted in the saddle, and I saw him reach toward a gun stock protruding from his saddle scabbard.

Notice enough.

I fired twice, hoping for little, but knowing if he got any closer, his shotgun would shred me into bloody pulp.

My scare tactics worked. The rider yanked his reins and pivoted his horse into the opposite direction, leaning forward to surge away in a gallop. The horse kicked clumps of dirt backward at me and became a fleeing shadow.

I straightened and sucked in air, conscious of the sidewalk suddenly alive with more spectators drawn from the Red Rose. I also became conscious of a more compelling fact. The rider and his horse had bolted from the side street which held the marshal's office.

Before moving ahead, I pulled two cartridges from my gun belt and replaced my spent shells.

I walked slowly.

From behind me and to my left came the thump of fast, heavy steps.

I didn't turn, but continued my slow walk, eyes ahead for any other movement.

The steps reached my side, then slowed. I took a quick glance to confirm my guess. The man was broad-shouldered, his crippled right arm hanging uselessly at his side.

"You're slowing considerable, Jake," I said to my deputy, my eyes again sweeping the street. "Saloon's barely twenty steps back of us."

"My pace is fine, Sam," my deputy replied. "It's my start that was lacking. Vexing decision, when a man's got a chance to draw to a straight flush on the biggest pot of the night."

We were almost to the corner.

"Who's watching the ante?" I asked, thinking of the usual crowded confusion around the poker tables in the Red Rose. "Suzanne?"

"Nope," he said, "money's in my pocket. I made my straight flush."

"Nice to know you had priorities."

"I already allowed as it was a vexing decision."

"Yup," I said. "That you did."

"Only heard one shot," he said. "Say it was you in the gunplay: you were dead or the other was. Either way, another minute wasn't going to matter much."

I grunted agreement.

We reached the corner, moved up onto the wooden boardwalk, and hugged the edge of the building. My shoulder pressed solidly against the large window pane, lettered to read OVERBAY'S DRESSMAKING & FITTING. Inside, an inch away from my face, a broad corset covered a dummy.

"I don't figure there was more than one horseman," I said. "Should be fine to move out from here."

"Probably."

Neither of us moved anyway. It's easy enough to talk about gunplay. But once you're in it, with time to think about what you're doing, you discover how real fear can be. Bullets punch messy holes in skin and muscle and bone, and if you've ever seen a man shot dead, you don't mock those who prefer caution to heroics.

A couple more seconds passed. The dogs' barking had begun to subside.

"You care much what the crowd behind us thinks?"

"Nope," I said.

"Then how 'bout I try the old trick of a hat on a gun?"

I did it for him. Took my hat off my head, hung it on the end of my pistol barrel, and extended the target past the corner. No jumpy, panic-crazed gunman fired a hasty shot.

"Looking better," I said.

"Yup," he said.

Neither of us moved.

A horse reined to the railing behind us swished its tail.

"We could be here all night," I finally said, jamming my

hat into place. "Got a match?"

He told me he did.

"Take the newspaper from my waistband, will you? Light it and throw it into the street."

I didn't want to light it myself and destroy my night vision. I preferred instead it would grab the eyes of anybody waiting around the corner.

Jake tossed the lit paper over my shoulder, and I swung into the open, facing sideways down the street to the marshal's office, my Colt extended shoulder high in my right hand. No showboating with one-handed firing from my hip.

The street was empty; the building fronts were unmoving shadows.

I didn't need to beckon Jake. He was beside me, his back to my back, his gun extended shoulder high in his left hand. The newspaper burned itself to char in the dirt as we stared at the empty street.

"A lot of sweat for nothing," I said.

"Yup. A waste of good whiskey." Jake paused. "Sam, I'd say our window's been shot."

He was right.

The marshal's office was a few doors down the street. While the street was dark, light from a lamp within clearly showed the jagged edges of broken glass.

I frowned. Despite my preoccupation over the letter I'd been writing, I would not have left the office with the wick of the lamp still lit. The danger of fire was too great for such carelessness.

"We might want to check it slow," I said.

We moved past the door, the note still plain where I had left it pinned to the frame: *Back Shortly.* We did our best to keep our steps soft, and we had our guns ready for any movement.

Again, our caution was wasted effort.

The dead man slumped in his own gore across my desk posed no immediate threat to anyone.

TWO

FROM WHERE I STOOD outside the window, I had no doubt the man was dead. A shotgun at close range can blow away half the trunk of a thick tree; this man had been shot from a distance of less than four walking paces.

I bit my tongue against sudden nausea. The sight of blood can't bring any memories except bad ones, and for me, it always puts my dying brother back into my arms, coughing blood onto my shirt sleeve.

I stepped back from the window to get some clear air.

"Jake, we got time to look at this man later."

"Sure."

"What I'm saying is—he ain't gonna move. But it'd be nice to get a look at some fresh horse tracks before anyone muddies them up."

"The fella you shot at?" he asked.

I nodded. "Long odds of tracking him down tonight. Least we can do is make a few guesses about his horse."

I was using the word "we" lightly. Jake also ran a livery and knew as much about horseflesh as anyone alive. Whatever judgment he rendered was judgment I'd wager upon.

"I'll grab a lantern from the stable," Jake said. "Meet you

back on Main Street."

He left me with the dead man at my desk.

****

"The horse has got an interesting kick to the side," Jake said. He was leaning over the tracks in the center of the street, with me beside him holding the lantern knee-high. "See how the right rear track pushes the dirt uneven?"

I nodded. Some horses do lift and circle their feet outward as they walk. Others inward. This one had an exaggerated push.

"Let's backtrack," he said, "to where you saw him come out at a canter. Chances are, you ever see these tracks again, it won't be at a gallop like this."

He was right, of course. Few were the occasions a man pushed his horse into a gallop. Not only did it tire the horse badly, it greatly increased the chance of a fall. No amount of riding skill can prevent a horse in full gallop from stepping into an animal burrow, snapping its leg, and pitching the rider.

We followed the tracks backward.

The street was now clear of spectators, as there was little excitement in watching two grown men peer through a lantern's light at the ground. And earlier, while Jake had gone to the stable for his lantern, I'd hurried back to the Red Rose and managed to head off a crowd from gathering at my busted office window by telling folks we'd found little to interest them.

Jake and I found the point where the rider had first turned toward me.

Jake studied these tracks for several minutes.

"I'd say he gets around," Jake said.

"Why's that?"

"Look for yourself. Not one horseshoe matches another."

I looked for myself. Where the horse had stopped and the

impressions were clearly stamped into the soft soil, I could easily see the truth of Jake's statement. Horseshoes are as individual as the blacksmith who forges them, and these were definitely mixed.

"It's like he's replaced each one right when it needed doing."

I nodded. A horse might drop a shoe occasionally, or have a shoe break, especially as it wore down. Either way, you made do on the trail.

"What you're saying," I said, "is if the rider was more settled, he'd get them all changed on a regular basis. And they'd match."

"It's exactly what I'm saying. Only I'm not sure it helps much."

Jake shuffled further down, his eyes still on the ground.

"He was here when you shot?" Jake asked.

"Only hoping to let him know I meant business," I said. "You know how I load my pistol. From where I stood, I'd be lucky to break skin."

Which was true. When I carried in town, my cartridges held a load of lead no bigger than chunks of unground pepper. It guaranteed accuracy at close range, and as the shot lost all power more than a stone's throw away, it ensured innocent bystanders stood little chance of dying to any of my stray bullets.

"Then it appears you had some luck," Jake said. He squatted. "Hold the lantern closer."

I did.

In the light, we both saw a delicate ruby of gleaming black-red.

"He's hardly more than stung," I said. "You'll notice we saw no sign of blood further ahead. I doubt we'll find him dead at the edge of town come morning."

"Would be convenient, wouldn't it?"

I left his comment unanswered as we continued to follow the tracks back toward the marshal's office. I was glad for the chance to concentrate on finding the story told by those tracks. It took my mind off the shredded body across my desk.

"Still got that outward swing," Jake said, "gentled down without the gallop, but it plainly shows. Trouble is, I'm not sure it's enough to hang a man."

It wasn't, even if we could match the horse to these tracks. I'd spent much of the winter reading up on law procedures. It wasn't necessary for my job; plenty of towns are grateful if the hired marshal is sober more than four days a week and manages not to shoot himself when he draws. But it passed time, and I always figured a man couldn't have too much knowledge. From what I'd learned, the man who'd rode the horse from here could ably defend himself by claiming another man had been on his horse. On the other hand, since all I had to go on was the dark outline of his profile, finding the man's horse would be a good start to finding proof which would link the man to this scene.

"Jake, what do these tracks here tell you?"

He studied the ground and came up with a conclusion which matched mine.

"You see his bootprints where he was leading his horse in," Jake said. "He reined the horse to a post, and stepped up to the sidewalk. See where his bootprints disappear? Just to the left of where the horse stood. He stepped onto the sidewalk well clear of the window. He could move up to the window, look inside, shoot, then mount the horse and leave. That's where the tracks moved into the canter you saw."

I nodded, grateful we'd had a chance to check the tracks before weather or carriage traffic robbed us of the opportunity.

"Get the light closer down," Jake said. "Maybe his boots will tell us something."

The left heel print was deeper than the right. Both heel marks were sharp—new boots?—and his feet were roughly the size of mine. Nothing else to set them apart though—no distinctive bootmaker's stamp impressed into the soft soil.

All we knew was that a man had walked his horse down

this street, looped the reins of his horse to a railing, snuck up to the window, and fired a shotgun at a man sitting at my desk.

It left me with a host more questions than answers. The murderer's careful approach told me he expected someone to be in the marshal's office. How? Why? And who was the person he had brutally murdered?

"Well," I said to Jake with a sigh, "we'd best learn what we can from what's inside."

****

I'd never taken to the habit of smoking. I'd also never taken to the copper smell of fresh blood.

"Jake," I said in the confines of my office, "you might want to reach behind the top books of my bookshelf. You'll find some cigars I've been saving for a special occasion."

He raised his eyebrows. "A dead man at your desk is something to celebrate?"

"Nope. You drawing to a straight flush. How about you light up a couple."

He might have read my face correctly, for he didn't protest at my weak excuse and, instead, began to search for the cigars as I studied the scene without moving closer to the dead man.

Opposite the shattered window and desk, where Jake stood on his toes to find the cigars, was the bookshelf—a luxury here in the Territories. Beside the bookshelf stood a locked rifle rack. At the back of this moderately sized room was a single jail cell, usually empty except for the evenings I couldn't convince drunks to undertake a journey homeward or to the nearest available hotel room. In the center, standing on floorboards of warped and knotholed planks, sat my potbellied stove.

The planks were now covered with shards of glass and pooled blood. The potbellied stove had taken the bulk of whatever shotgun pellets had passed by the dead man. My coffeepot lay on the floor, dotted with holes, and glints of silver showed on the heavy iron of the stove where the pellets had smeared lead before bouncing to the floor.

All of this showed too clearly in the steady light of the oil lamp on the desk corner nearest the door. The lamp had been spared the shotgun's blast only because the shooter had stood so near the window; the pellet pattern hadn't been given the necessary distance to expand.

Cigar smoke filled my nostrils. Jake handed me mine and lit his.

"Good idea," Jake said, inhaling deep. "My stomach was feeling a mite greasy."

I finally turned my attention to my desk.

Only briefly.

The blast had pushed the dead man away from the window toward the edge of the desk. His shoulders had twisted sideways; his cheek would have been resting on my desk, had there been enough of his face remaining.

Brief as that glance was, not even my cigar helped.

"Jake," I said, "why don't you give me a minute?"

I stepped outside again and saw the angular figure of an approaching man.

His face was lost in the shadows of his hat, but his stiff-legged, bone-grating gait left me no doubt about his identity.

"Evening, Doc," I said, as he closed the gap between us.

"Heard there was a shooting," Doc Harper replied. "Folks said it hadn't amounted to much."

"They'll find out different in the morning, I imagine." I jerked my thumb over my shoulder. "It ain't pretty."

Doc stepped past me through the doorway. He was a no-nonsense man, so I didn't expect the whistle of surprise I heard.

Several moments later, he joined me again. Jake stepped outside too.

"Wouldn't hurt to take a closer look at the man," Doc said.

"Yup," I said. "I'm working up to it."

Jake stepped around us and moved to the window, staring inside from near the same spot where the murderer might have fired the shotgun.

"Sam," Doc said, in the soft voice which never failed to surprise me when he gentled himself around folks who needed his help, "how about you wander to my office. You know where I keep my bottle of medicine whiskey. I'll be up shortly to tell you what I find out."

Doc knew I didn't smoke much. Doc also knew as much as anyone about the long road which had brought me to Laramie. I didn't even try to fool him with a halfhearted protest.

"Thanks, Doc."

He nodded, then stepped back inside.

A half hour later, Doc and Jake joined me in the sparsely furnished waiting room outside Doc's office. I'd barely touched Doc's whiskey, thinking my own sad thoughts about blood and memories.

I didn't rise.

Each man remained standing, looking down on me.

In daylight, I knew exactly what I'd be seeing.

Doctor Cornelius Harper would be dressed in the same dull-brown suit he wore in his office, at funerals, and as he set out in his horse and buggy—a dull-brown suit well short of his wrists and his ankles, giving him the appearance of an awkward schoolboy. Except Cornelius Harper was at least forty years beyond school, his age obvious in thatched hair almost white, obvious in his eyes deeply sunk into a worn, narrow face, and obvious in the slow, crooked way he walked. We'd made acquaintance the previous fall during the only pressure I'd faced as marshal here in Laramie, a double murder in the bank vault of the First National Bank.*

I'd met Jake Wilson during the same weeks. He was a

_____
*Moon Basket

broad-chested man of medium height with straw-filled blond hair and a blocky face. Nothing remarkable about his appearance. Except for his arms. His left arm was massive, his right arm limp and useless. Marbled scars, I knew, covered the skin on the upper half of that right arm like ugly, red worms. He'd once made the mistake of standing too near a mean-tempered stallion. The stallion had reached around, clamped its teeth into Jake's right biceps and ripped the entire muscle off the bone. When I'd heard that, I'd been impressed Jake had the presence of mind to escape the stallion; most men would have fallen, leaving themselves helpless to be stomped to death. Nothing since then had changed my original impression of Jake, nor had anything showed me wrong for hiring him on as the town's only and part-time deputy.

I could not read either of their expressions as they stared down on me.

I pulled myself out of what had come dangerously close to self-pity. I felt a spasm of disgust. At least I was still alive, not draped in blood over a stranger's desk.

I shortly discovered how well the disgust was deserved.

"Samuel," Doc began, "you been chasing after another man's wife?"

"Doc!" I sat forward sharply. "You know better."

"It's a poor joke," Doc said. "I know full well where your heart lies."

"What Doc is getting at," Jake said, "is whether you made some fresh enemies."

"Jake?"

Jake shook his head at my puzzlement. "Sam, think about it. If you were going to shoot someone from outside the window, would you stand there long? Or would you step into view and pull the trigger as quick as you could?"

"You know the answer. It'd be quick."

"So quick you might not get a good look at the person's face?"

I had a bad feeling about his line of inquiry.

"I'm afraid Jake makes a good case, Samuel." Doc Harper spoke slowly, almost reluctantly. "He had me stand outside the window and look in against the light of the lamp. Where that lamp was perched, it would have caused the man's face to be no more than a shadow. And isn't that desk where you spend long hours writing your letters to Rebecca?"

I nodded with an unwanted comprehension.

"You understand, don't you, Sam." Jake didn't say it as a question. "Whoever pulled the trigger thought he was murdering you."

THREE

THERE IS AN UGLINESS to the gash of an open
grave, especially a grave with an unmarked slab of
wood for a tombstone. The gash of raw earth is even
uglier beneath a gray sky.

I braced against a cold, north wind and blinked my eyes at
the scattered rain driven not downward, but sideways across
the plains. Despite my knit jersey and a buttoned, heavy
duster with tail flaps swirling in the wind against my boots, I
shivered.

Probably not from cold.

It was a bleak day made more bleak by my self-imposed
duty here at the east bank of the Laramie River. The man
had died in my place. I didn't even know his name. The least
I could contribute was stoic endurance as the only mourner
keeping company with a weary undertaker's assistant.

Earlier, I'd been led to understand God's grace, and since,
death had held much less for me to fear. Still, each hollow
thump of dirt hitting the cheap coffin seemed like a blow to
my own chest. Save for an urge for the Chinaman's coffee to
take me from my office, it could just as easily been me rigid
and blind to the eternal blanket of soil.

Doc Harper had instructed me not to dwell on it, had said I should not take blame for my habit of leaving the office door open to visitors. He'd said the blame rested on the man who'd pulled the trigger of the shotgun.

I wondered. Somewhere in my past, knowingly or not, it had been an act of mine—and thus my responsibility—which had driven someone to eventually commit last night's act of savage revenge. A drifter I'd escorted to the town limits, perhaps. A drunken cowboy who'd thrown ineffectual punches at me and had taken great insult at the laughing response of his friends. Or more likely—since the winter had been a quiet one with only drunks and drifters my greatest problems—it had happened before my marshaling days. The previous summer I'd busted up a buffalo skinners' camp. Maybe the survivors had tracked me down. And before that, long before that, there'd been the bounty-hunting days with my brother Jed. Of those outlaws we'd tracked down, more than a few had faced jail terms instead of the noose. Years had passed, more than enough time to serve sentence. Maybe one of them had found me here in Laramie.

The wind gusted, sending plumes of rain-splattered dirt downwind.

The undertaker's assistant jabbed his shovel into the ground. He reached into his jacket pocket for a flask. He offered it to me, shrugged as I declined, and tilted a shot into his mouth.

After a ceremonial gasp at the whiskey's potency, he half-shouted to be heard above the wind. "Harry says town's paying for this one."

I nodded agreement with what the undertaker had told his assistant. Jake had gone through the man's bloodied clothes, finding nothing, not even the money to pay for this funeral. All Jake found was an old, antler-bone handled jackknife tucked in the man's left boot.

The assistant took another slug of whiskey. He was fat-faced, sweating, and bleary-eyed, with rubbery lips which folded around the flask's neck.

"So who you figure it was?" he said as he put the flask away. "Harry said weren't enough face left for the man's own mama to recognize him."

I did not feel like speaking, but if the assistant hadn't realized it by now, he wasn't going to tumble onto that fact in the foreseeable future, either.

"I imagine I'll find out as soon as someone comes looking for him," I said. We hadn't yet found the dead man's horse, and I was hoping it might hold a clue to his identity. Otherwise I would be waiting until someone came looking. I didn't, however, care to continue conversation, so I decided to find an escape. "You need help with the shovel?"

He didn't reply. Instead, he found his flask again and pointed it at the shovel as an invitation. I stepped around him and, as he tilted the flask again, I began to push dirt onto the coffin. If I kept my back to the assistant as I shoveled, I could pretend not to hear anything else he might say or ask.

I did not enjoy looking down at the cheap wood of the coffin. It was too vivid a reminder of what might soon become my own resting place. After all, the murderer's need for revenge had not been satisfied.

Because I was still alive.

I had also proven that by shouting at the murderer, announcing my identity as a marshal, and shooting at him.

He knew, then, that his attempt had failed and that I was still alive.

Part of my guilt arose from the relief that it was me shoveling dirt onto the unknown man who'd died in my place.

I wanted to remain alive.

It did my spirits little good to know I stood no chance against a man who could callously pull a trigger from ambush—anywhere, anytime.

FOUR

A *FULL DAY PASSED* in which I did not die.

In the middle of the morning of the second day after the funeral, I was in the marshal's office at my desk — now moved away from street window exposure to the corner of the opposite wall. I was attempting again to find a way to write my troublesome letter, when the door was pushed open.

I dropped my left hand from my desk onto my lap, leaving my right hand poised with pen beside the ink bottle.

Although the man stepping into the cramped marshal's office wore full military uniform, I did not relax my left-hand grip on the stock of the shotgun hanging from a strap beneath the desk.

"Morning, Marshal," he said. He held his gauntlet gloves in his left hand, anticipating a handshake of greeting from me.

I squinted at the the stripes on his arm. "Morning, Lieutenant," I said. His cuff edging, sleeve stripes, hat cords, and trousers side seams were yellow. Cavalry, then.

The shotgun's cut-down barrel faced him squarely from its hiding spot. Jake had insisted on rigging it, and I had protested neither long nor hard.

The lieutenant frowned slightly at my lack of courtesy in

failing to rise. It was a naive frown—not censure, but puzzlement—for this officer hardly seemed more than a kid. His
flattop cap was perched on tight, fine coils of red hair. His
face was heavily freckled, round, and unlined. Slight wisps of
fuzz served as sideburns. I guessed him to be a military
school graduate, leap-frogged ahead of the old-time campaigners because of education or politics or both.

I also guessed it was probably not the military wanting me
dead. I moved away from my desk and extended a handshake.

"You're welcome to sit down," I said, pointing at a
caneback chair opposite my desk.

He backed into the chair, fumbling with his saber scabbard as he sat. After finally setting it in a position which
didn't distract him, he took off his cap and rested it in his lap.

I was perched on the edge of my desk, waiting.

"Marshal, I'm Lieutenant Grimshaw. Fifth Cavalry, here
at Fort Sanders."

I knew of the fort, of course. Just south, alongside the
Laramie River. First established as Fort John Buford then
renamed for a brigadier general who died from wounds suffered during battle in the Civil War. The fort had first protected the emigrants on the Overland Trail, then this part of the
stagecoach route from Salt Lake City to Denver, and more
recently, protected the construction of the Union Pacific railroad during the late '60s, a time when my own contribution to
laying the tracks had been scouting and hunting for work
crews. Fort Sanders accommodated six companies—some
500 men—and had its own military reservation of nine square
miles. My only dealings with Fort Sanders occurred when the
soldiers celebrated too hard here in Laramie—not a difficult
job, because the enlisted men were so fearful of punishment
back at the fort, they themselves helped me tame any individ-
uals who got too whiskeyed.

"Samuel Keaton," I said as return introduction. "Call me
Sam."

He probably wouldn't. I was his senior by at least a dozen

years and every inch of his posture showed awkward shyness.

He took a breath.

"Mr. Keaton, I—"

"Sam. I prefer not to be reminded about the age of my hide."

He tried a grin, then resumed his earnestness. "I'm here to offer you a scouting job."

I opened my vest to show the badge I had pinned on the inside. "I'm already employed. And to tell the truth, you could do lots better when it comes to hiring scouts."

He shook his head. "No scout in the territory has Red Cloud's promise of safe passage."

Whatever Red Cloud had promised, he'd promised to me, not to the military. My face probably lost some of its friendliness.

"I'm here at the colonel's request, Mr. Keaton," Grimshaw said in apologetic tones. "He's the one who told me about Red Cloud and the . . . rest."

"What do you know?"

Grimshaw's face scrunched. He recognized my tension, and he wanted to tread softly. I told myself to ease up on the poor kid.

"Last summer you helped Red Cloud's granddaughter return to the Sioux." Grimshaw lifted his eyes to stare at me in such a way I had cause to wonder how much the story had been exaggerated. "You and her sorted out who was behind the Rawhide River massacre of '52."*

Morning Star. The passage of an entire winter had not eased the ache of missing her.

I waited to hear if he was going to pass on whatever gossip had accumulated over the winter. He wisely did not.

"That must have been something, Mr. Keaton, right on the heels of Custer, going alone into the Black Hills among all the Sioux he riled."

---

*Morning Star

"Is that why you're here?" I asked. "On account of what Custer's stirred up in the territory?"

"Yes, Sir."

The sacred Black Hills belong to the Sioux, much in part because of Red Cloud's wily warfare, which had forced the government to grant it in the treaty of '68. Custer's assignment last summer, six years later, had been to lay to rest rumors of gold in those very same Black Hills. Instead, he'd told newspaper reporters about finding nuggets among grass stems, and the trickle of prospectors had become a flood. The army was now either unable or unwilling to stop these prospectors, and the government was to the point where it might offer as high as six million dollars to buy from the Sioux these ancestral lands.

I'd heard, both through official reports and in the occasional letter from Morning Star that Red Cloud wanted peace—ironic considering how effectively he'd forced the army into the '68 stalemate along the Bozeman Trail. Unfortunately, his influence was beginning to wane, and among those who angrily refused any government appeasement were the Sioux war chiefs Sitting Bull, Gall, and a rising young chief named Crazy Horse. It meant the Sioux were drifting onto the warpath.

On the opposing side I knew Custer chomped at the bit for a military campaign; without the Civil War he had no other way of creating headlines and remaining the heroic darling of the Washington elite.

My feeling, then, was that the tinder was well set for any spark to flame the unrest into full-fledged war.

Grimshaw was waiting for my response. It took little thought on my part.

"Not interested," I said. "I will not insult Red Cloud by returning with a military expedition."

"This is a survey expedition," Grimshaw said. "My detachment of soldiers will be on a reconnaissance assignment."

"Survey? Move soldiers into Sioux territory and you're begging for battle."

He shook his head. It seemed to embarrass him to disagree, and I wondered how effective he was as an officer.

"We want to establish a route which stays out of their territory," he said. "If we do, it will take travelers off the Bozeman Trail, maybe cool down the troubles. We'll be helping peace, not hindering it."

Hesitant and embarrassed or not, Grimshaw did have a point. The Bozeman Trail, running northward along the eastern slopes of the Bighorn Mountains, through the basin of the Powder River, cut through prime Sioux hunting grounds. It had been fought over for decades, usually with the Sioux victorious. Another route into the Montana gold fields would indeed ease the pressure.

"You're talking about Bridger's Trail," I said.

He nodded. "You're as knowledgeable as I've heard."

It didn't take much knowledge to be familiar with mountain man Jim Bridger, already a legend and not yet dead. He'd been the first white man to see the Great Salt Lake and to explore the Yellowstone. This was a man, I'd heard, whose storytelling once held a party of Sioux and Cheyenne spellbound for an hour — using only silent sign language. If I recalled correctly, he'd guided a few wagons up to the Yellowstone River by following the western slopes of the Bighorns, but the trail had never become popular because of lack of water.

I said as much.

"If some permanent outposts with wells were established," Grimshaw said, "water would no longer be a problem."

"Sorry," I said, "still not interested." I did intend to go north, but by myself.

"The colonel thought you'd see it that way," Grimshaw said, embarrassment again beginning to flush his freckled skin. He looked downward, fumbled with his saber. "Colonel

Crozier told me to remind you of your debt to the military."

I raised my eyebrows.

"Please remember, sir, it isn't me saying it, but Colonel Crozier."

"I'll remember."

"He said it was his friend, Colonel Braude at Fort Laramie, who gave you enough slack last summer to prove how you and Red Cloud's granddaughter were innocent of the murder charges. He also mentioned it was his friend Colonel Braude who made sure you were cleared of the bounty on your head for the Colorado bank robbery."

I sighed. Calling in markers was something I took seriously. "How long do you expect this expedition to take?"

"A month to six weeks. We're to go no farther north than the Yellowstone."

"I'll think on it," I said. "But if I go, don't be expecting me to salute everytime you blow your nose."

Grimshaw grinned. "It would ease my mind, knowing you'll be along on my first expedition."

First expedition. I didn't comment on how little my mind was eased at the prospect of enduring whatever mistakes he was bound to make.

Grimshaw stood, replaced his cap, and marched through the doorway and onto the street.

I put the ink bottle away and set my unstarted letter back into the top drawer of my desk. Little consolation, but travel northward would save me writing the letter to Morning Star.

FIVE

"**S**AMUEL V. KEATON,**"** Doc Harper began, "I want you to sit there, real quiet for a spell."

"Why in—"

"Shush," he commanded. "You sit quiet and study on something humorous to tell me. When you're ready with your story, then flap your jaws. But I want it to be a good one, the best you got and one I haven't heard before."

His stern features told me there was no room for argument. And it was him buying me supper at the Chinaman's. I'd taken advantage of it too, ordering a steak as thick as a Bible, along with brown beans baked in molasses.

I had a lot on my mind, and I'd eaten quiet, finishing just in time for Doc to declare his strange command. I pushed aside my scraped clean plate, wrapped my hands around a cup of coffee, and thought.

Doc had near finished his own coffee when I took in a lungful of air.

"Alright," I said, "it happened back East, before my folks took me and Jed onto the Oregon Trail. I was five, Jed a couple years older. I remember it clear because it was Christmas Day. We had plenty of visitors, as I recall. Aunts, uncles and such."

"Christmas," Doc repeated, to show he was listening.

"Ma had given me a pair of fur mittens. White rabbit fur, warm as toast."

"Samuel," Doc said, "there's an alarming smile growing on that face of yours."

"Sometime that afternoon, I went out back to the outhouse. Proud as I was of those mitts, I wore them, admiring them every step of the way. Naturally, once inside the privy, I had to take them off. You might guess what happened next."

"You dropped one."

"Both," I said. "Straight down. To a five-year-old boy, it seemed a drop as deep as a water well. And all I could think about was the whupping I'd get for being so careless."

Doc was smiling too, imagining as I was the look of fear on a boy's face as he peered into the depths.

I paused to slurp at my coffee.

"Doc, I ran and got brother Jed. He joined me in the privy and assessed the situation. Jed pointed out how it was winter and weren't it lucky everything down there was frozen hard as rock. He said quickest thing to do was go right down and retrieve them. He also pointed out how, being as it were my mitts, I should be the one going down. It made so much sense—and him promising to stand up top and pull me out when I needed it—I did exactly that."

Doc snorted.

"Doc. I started crying. Got too scared to move. So Jed began to figure how much trouble he'd be in for sending me below. He climbed right down there with me, expecting to push me up high enough I could grab the edge of the seat with my hands. Now there's two of us down there, neither of us big enough to look over a grasshopper's shoulder. And then. . . ."

Doc had removed his wire frame glasses, and was rubbing his face as he tried to hold back his laughter.

"Privy door creaked open, Doc."

"Samuel, tell me this isn't true."

"True as that skinny beak of a nose plugged onto your face, Doc. Now Jed and me faced a dilemma. Do we shout out and get a double whupping, one for losing the mitts and two for going down there? Jed made the decision. He pushed me to the side and we hoped for the best. Only Jed lost nerve. I think it was the petticoats."

Doc was laughing out loud now, pounding the table, with the Chinaman giving us nervous looks.

"Doc. It was Aunt Ethel, a woman so big her petticoats were like a circus tent. Them floorboards above us were groaning with her weight, Doc. Her petticoats came into view and we squinted our eyes shut. Did I tell you Jed lost *his* nerve?"

Doc just nodded, short of air as he was.

"Yup," I said. "Jed reached up with one of my fur mitts and tickled her hind end."

Doc howled.

"Light hit us again, so sudden it hurt our eyes, followed by a crashing and thundering. That woman was built so big it hardly slowed her at all, knocking the door off the hinges. Her screaming faded as she gained speed."

I stopped to enjoy the sight of Doc clutching his stomach. He whooped and gasped and each time he'd almost settled down again, he whooped and gasped some more.

"Much later, Pa told us what it was like in the sitting room, seeing out the window as Ethel plowed through the snow, bellowing like a shot moose, holding her petticoat up around her hips and calling for the menfolk to grab their guns."

"Guns?" Doc managed to ask. He was back to clutching his stomach.

"Guns. To shoot the varmint that had laid in wait just to get her. Jed and I were too scared to run. Next thing we knew, the barrel of Pa's shotgun is poking right in our faces. Doc, I can still hear it, Jed saying in a squeaky scared voice, 'Pa, don't shoot. It's only your boys.'"

Tears streamed from Doc's face, and I have to admit it was hard on me, trying to keep a straight face.

"We should have got whupped good," I said. "And Pa did give it a manful try, pressured as he was by Ethel screaming and hollering at what spiteful creatures me and Jed were. Except every time Pa raised the belt to whup us, he'd commence to laughing again, and he never did get a good lick in."

Doc wiped at the corner of his eyes with his shirt sleeves, left arm going across the right side of his face, right arm going across his left side.

"Thank you, Marshal," he said when he could finally breathe straight, "I do believe that was worth the price of steak and beans."

"Sure, Doc," I said. "Now what was the real reason you made such a strange request?"

He gave me a steady look. "Wanted to see if you had any sense of humor left."

"Doc?"

"I got to wondering when was the last time I caught you smiling your crooked grin and realized I couldn't remember."

"*You* try smiling with someone skulking about Laramie, waiting to gun you down."

Doc grinned triumph. "See, there's the Sam Keaton I know. Feisty, grumbling, and not taking the world so serious."

I stared at my empty coffee cup. "I guess I have been quiet over the last while."

"Since February."

"That obvious?"

"Even Jake noticed."

"I've been troubled," I said. "You'll remember I've been waiting for spring."

"It was what you and Rebecca agreed," Doc said with a nod. "To give her time among the Sioux."

"Yes." *She was Rebecca Montcalm in the white man's world. But now she lived as Morning Star with the Sioux.*

"I've often thought it must be difficult on her," Doc added. "Pulled one way, then the other."

"With me right in the middle, Doc."

"You fear she'll choose to stay among the Sioux?"

"There's that. But more."

Doc didn't say anything, giving me the chance to decide if I wanted to explain. I took my time choosing my words.

"Doc," I finally said, "I spent most of my adult life drifting. Bounty hunting with Jed before he died, hunting buffalo for the railway, riding range, busting horses from spread to spread. 'Twas easy to grin and spit life in the eye. All I had at risk was my horse, my wages, or my life. What I'm saying is . . ."

It was difficult, trying to put into words the thoughts which had been gnawing at me for a while.

" . . . it's easy to be carefree if you ain't got nothing to care about. Now I do. There's you and Jake and the folks here in Laramie to thank for it. All winter long I was busting inside for the chance to leave, and now that spring's here, I ain't so sure anymore. What if something happens, and I lose what I've gained here?"

The Chinaman interrupted by stopping by with some more of his black coffee.

Doc put up his hand to stop me from what I was trying to say next. "Worse," Doc guessed, "you're wondering if you really love Rebecca the way your memory tells you you should."

"Something like that."

"And what if when you see her again, you discover, or she discovers, or you both discover it's not the way you, or her, or you both imagined it would be like."

"Something like that. Even though right now I believe I want to marry that woman. And then what if she says no, she wants to stay with the Sioux?"

Doc studied my face. "You got plenty to fear."

"Yup."

"You're not accustomed to fear."

I hadn't thought of it that way before. Slowly, I nodded agreement.

Doc grinned. "You want some easy advice, Sam?"

"Yes, sir."

He grinned wider. "There ain't none."

"Thanks, Doc."

"Life is tough," he said, "always will be. Drifting all those years kept you from knowing that. Sure, you had your share of scrapes and hardships, but nothing a fast gun or extra wages couldn't cure. Until now, when for the first time you're facing a situation a bullet won't solve."

"So?"

"Don't be disappointed in yourself. Much as I believe in God's goodness, life truly is tough, and that will never change. Realize it and you can ease off being so hard on yourself. Once you accept how tough life is, your expectations change, life becomes easier."

It was my turn to study Doc. He didn't say anything more. Just smiled a small smile and sipped on his coffee.

"All right," I told him, "I'll think through what you said."

I took a deep breath. "And it looks like I'll have plenty of time to do it. Day after next, I leave with a cavalry detachment on an expedition into Sioux territory."

SIX

DAY AFTER NEXT ARRIVED without a stranger's shotgun blasting me from ambush. It bothered me to have to sit back and wait for his next attempt—skin prickling at unexpected noises or footsteps behind me—but I had so little to go on, I could not even begin to look for the man on the big, black horse. While there was some relief in knowing the survey expedition would be taking me out of Laramie, I could not forget the same problem waited for me on my return. Nor could I forget that this unknown man bent on revenge seemed the patient sort.

I used those two days to settle what affairs needed settling. I arranged for Jake to take over full-time marshaling in my absence. Jake, in turn, hired a hand to tend to his stable.

I paid my account at the Chinaman's, at the Red Rose Saloon, and at the general store, adding to my bill a good supply of .44-40 cartridges which fit both my Colt and my Winchester rifle. While I had a good saddle horse, I also purchased three more and supplies to pack, including two full water bags on each; regardless of what Lieutenant Grimshaw and the military might supply, I intended to be self-sufficient.

In fact, these horses were Grimshaw's first item of comment upon wheeling his horse from his detachment to greet me near the train station at the prearranged hour shortly after dawn.

"Mr. Keaton," Grimshaw protested as he drew near, "our quartermaster has released all necessary provisions. And I'm afraid the payroll authorized on your behalf does not include nonmilitary purchases."

I looked past him at the line of soldiers on horseback and the string of packhorses at the rear, all waiting for the arrival of the western-bound Union Pacific locomotive.

"You do appear to be adequately supplied, Lieutenant. However, you might recall my reluctance to join your expedition." I jerked my thumb over my shoulders to indicate my own packhorses held by rope to my saddle horse. "This way, should you and I disagree over terms of employment, you needn't be concerned over my return to Laramie."

He blinked a few times. "In short," he finally said, "you're telling me I should think twice before asking you to salute every time I blow my nose."

If I thought he was capable of making a joke, I would have smiled.

****

Our point of disembarkment from the freight car was Fort Steele, some hundred miles north and west down the Union Pacific track. I spent the rolling journey atop the freight car, enjoying the contrast of the Medicine Bow mountains blue-green to my left against the wide sweeping brown of the Laramie Plains to my right.

Fort Steele was built where the railroad crossed the North Platte River. As I understood it, we would follow the Platte downstream—north—to where it was joined by the Sweetwater, then we'd move upstream on the Sweetwater until we reached Independence Rock on the Oregon Trail. From there, we would cut north, along the western slopes of the Bighorn Mountains. We weren't likely to get lost, so my job was to serve as peacemaker should we run into Sioux hunting parties at the northern end of the trail on the Yellowstone River in Montana Territory. That was also where I hoped to find Morning Star.

We moved the horses down the ramp and without ceremony began the expedition.

It was my first chance to evaluate the soldiers of Detachment E, Fifth Cavalry. Including myself, Grimshaw, and the other scout, the expedition consisted of an even dozen.

Two, I discovered, did not speak English — not uncommon in the army. They were German immigrants and had enlisted for the $13 a month because other jobs were so scarce back East. Three of the soldiers were Negroes, a fact which gave me great comfort. The Sioux called them "buffalo soldiers," because they'd earned a fighting reputation for being as hard to bring down as the revered, hard-charging buffalo. My experience had confirmed what was generally known about the buffalo soldiers: the military was one of the few places they could prove themselves away from the bigotry elsewhere, and few troops were better.

Of the remaining four men, three appeared to be veteran campaigners, and the fourth was a smooth-faced boy who rode apart from them. Otherwise, I saw nothing striking about them.

What did strike me was the other scout's horse. Big and rangy and brown. For the first miles of our journey, I followed behind the brown, and eventually it caught my eye that the horse kicked outward with its rear feet as it walked.

I told myself I was imagining too much.

I tried to absorb myself in the passing countryside. The plains' basins are stark and treeless, yet they have their own beauty, especially with the wide sky a changing picture each passing hour.

Yet the countryside did not distract me.

My eyes kept returning to the outward kick of the big,

brown horse. Nighttime would transform its brown hide to black, the color of the horse which had cantered out onto Main from the side street of the marshal's office. I also knew a scout's traveling habits would lead to a mix of horseshoes, much like the tracks Jake and I had examined in front of the marshal's office.

As a result, I studied as closely as I could the scout upon the big brown. The scout was obviously half-breed. He wore a buckskin jacket and buckskin boots. No hat. Instead, a red cloth wrapped over his skull and knotted at the back. The hair which curled out was as black as his thick beard. From the weather lines around his eyes, he looked to be in his fourth decade. Because he was on horseback, I couldn't judge his height, but by his broad shoulders and short arms, I didn't guess him to be a tall drink of water. What wasn't short was the Bowie knife tucked in his belt.

I noticed too, his saddle scabbard. Only the stock of the gun showed, giving me no clue as to whether it was a shotgun.

I watched too, the first time he swung off the horse.

I had that chance a half hour later when Lieutenant Grimshaw called out orders to halt and dismount, customary procedure to check packs and tighten girths.

This scout stepped onto the ground. As he walked, he limped, favoring his left knee.

I didn't like that. Not at all.

His walk had the exact stiff-legged heaviness which would leave a heel imprint deeper on the left track than on the right, the exact sort of heaviness in the bootprints Jake and I had examined in front of the marshal's office.

Chances were I hadn't left the murderer behind in Laramie after all.

SEVEN

FOR SOMEONE I THOUGHT wanted me dead, the scout wasted no time in saving my life.

By then, I knew from Lieutenant Grimshaw his name was Mick Burns, assigned to the detachment by Grimshaw's commanding officer. Burns had scouted for Custer and would probably return to Custer and the Seventh Cavalry at Fort Abe Lincoln when this expedition ended, and Burns was reputed to be a silent, miserable, ornery cuss—attributes highly typical of all scouts.

I could not justify any action at this point, simply because all I had were suspicions. It left me with two choices—continue with resolved great caution, or turn back. And with only suspicions, I could hardly justify turning back.

My resolution to take great caution lasted less than an hour.

Our group was some twenty miles downstream of Fort Steele, traveling along the west bank of the North Platte beneath a glorious, clear blue sky. We rode near the edge of the high bank; the flats of the river below, while smooth, tended toward mud this time of year and only gave illusion of easier travel.

I was at the head of the expedition. Just behind me was the smooth-faced soldier, whistling and riding with a jaunty eagerness as if this were a great adventure. The rest of the men were scattered in a line to our rear.

We approached the shallow gully of a creek trickling into the North Platte. Tangles of shrubs filled the gully, their green, leafy tops almost as high as the gully banks. I paused, then noticed the easy way down. As we were far enough south for ranchers to have no fear of Sioux raids, over the years range cattle had worn a path down the bank to the water. I swung my horse to follow the rutted tracks.

The path meandered into the thick, newly green shrubs. Past the shrubs, I saw where it continued up the other side of the gully. The cattle path saved us the effort of cutting through the shrubs or finding a way around them.

The smooth-faced soldier and I moved down the path, at least twenty yards ahead of the horses closest to us. As a result, he and I were the only riders in the gully when it happened.

I can only blame myself for ignoring the flicking of my horse's ears and its short snorts of fear. My only excuse is that I was leaning back in my saddle, concentrating on balance as we moved down the cut in the bank.

My next warning, just before reaching the dense shrubs, was a low woof, a sound which chilled my neck despite the late spring heat.

Before I could react to my surge of fear, the woof repeated itself, louder and closer. Shrubs snapped and popped.

I did not have to see the huge shadow bursting into the outer fringes of the shrubs to know what was charging upon us.

Grizzly.

The Medicine Bow mountains were still large on the horizon behind us, still snow clad, still short of game. This grizzly had probably wandered down the river looking for easy feeding upon cattle. We discovered later we had interrupted it fresh upon a kill, the steer's blood still forming pools in the sand near the creek.

My horse reared in panic as I fought to reach my rifle in its scabbard. Behind me, the horse belonging to the smooth-faced boy had spun with equal terror. It turned and lunged into my packhorses.

The grizzly, dark and the size of a small horse, roaring fury now, cleared the shrubs and moved with dizzying speed toward us.

My horse reared again, screaming shrilly, but tangled with the lines and the other rearing horses, it had no chance to bolt. My world shrank to a blur of motion, noise, and confusion.

The grizzly reached us as my horse landed on all four hoofs. For a moment that hung like the dying notes of a bugle in clear, night air, the confusion fell away and all motion froze. My horse had landed facing the grizzly. The bear was on its hind legs, roaring and pawing against the air. Astride my horse, I still looked into the teeth and jaws of the massive animal. Then it brought a paw down and across, swiping my horse across the neck with such force I was rocked in my saddle. My horse staggered sideways, then toppled.

The other horses were bucking and lunging behind me. My horse fell into them but threw me clear of their scrambling hooves. My right shoulder bounced off the soft ground, and momentum tumbled me into the base of one of the shrubs.

From there, dazed, I saw the grizzly among the other horses, bellowing immense rage and throwing those sledge-hammer swipes of razored claws, raking horseflesh with every blow.

I was pulling my Colt loose from my holster when the smooth-faced soldier fell from his own horse. I clicked my first shot dry, revolving the empty cylinder I always keep beneath the hammer as safety. It left me with five shots.

The soldier didn't have the good fortune to fall into a

bush. Instead, he landed on the open, trampled grass. Two of the horses had broken their lines and were galloping back up the cut bank. My horse was down and motionless. The soldier's horse was kicking and bucking.

The young soldier made the mistake of trying to rise and drew the attention of the grizzly. It dropped to four legs and turned toward him.

I shot once from my hip.

The grizzly snarled and bit at its own shoulder.

I got to my knees and raised my arm through the branches. I shot again, aiming at its broad head.

The grizzly roared and shook its head.

Then I remembered. I wasn't shooting bullets, but pepper spray chunks of lead. A wagon guide had once told me about his encounter with a grizzly. There'd been ten of them, down from their wagons, firing musket balls at the beast. It had taken five minutes of shooting, and the guide told me when they skinned the bear, they discovered only three balls had penetrated the tough hide to strike at the bear's vitals. Another twenty shots had barely torn holes to reach blood. Without the punching power of a single bullet, my shooting would do little more than irritate the beast.

I shot anyway. The grizzly rose and roared anger again, a sound which shook through me.

"Run!" I shouted at the soldier. "Run!"

I shot a fourth time. The grizzly finally located me screened by the bush. It dropped and charged.

I could see the fine details in such clear horror. Hump on its back etched against the sky. Paws lifting and falling as it galloped at me. Fur matted with sweat and blood. Saliva flying from its jaws. I had nowhere to run and commanded myself to wait until the last possible heartbeat to fire my final bullet. Maybe by a miracle I could blind it, find a way to escape those teeth and claws.

Twenty feet away. Fifteen feet. Ten.

I squeezed the trigger. And watched in disbelief as the

bear rolled sideways, flopping into a motionless heap of fur and blood, so close I could have poked it with the barrel of my revolver.

Then my mind put it together.

The final explosion of noise had not come from my Colt, but from a shotgun. Held in the unwavering hands of Mick Burns, some ten yards up the draw, where he stood among the fallen horses.

I pushed through the branches and wobbled to my feet, taking several shaky steps in his direction.

He watched me, but showed no expression.

I tried to say thanks, but discovered my throat was too dry, and all that came out was a croak.

He nodded once, then walked toward me with his noticeable limp. The top of his head reached my shoulders. Without looking up, he handed me his shotgun, the weapon I thought he had already once used to try to kill me.

Mick Burns whipped out his Bowie knife and continued to advance upon the bear.

"Hot, raw, bear's liver," he said with some satisfaction, wiping the knife blade briskly against his leg. "Ain't nothing to give a man strength like a bear's liver."

EIGHT

FOR THE FIRST NIGHT'S CAMP, Mick Burns chose a wind-protected pocket cut into the bluffs of a low hill. I believed he had chosen well. Remote as the chance was this far south, we had the high ground in the event of a raiding party. Burns supervised the tethering of the horses and insisted upon the posting of three guards, two with the horses and one near camp.

As dusk deepened into night, the arrangement of the small campfires showed clearly the makeup of our expedition. Both German soldiers gathered around one fire, talking in soft, serious voices as they stared at the low flames, with the smooth-faced soldier quiet beside them. The buffalo soldiers had their own fire, set just downhill from the remaining three rough-looking enlisted men, whose efficient movements showed them to be old hands at campaign camps. I had shared my meal with Lieutenant Grimshaw and Burns, setting us as much apart from the others as them from us. Our meal of hardtack, bacon, and hot coffee had been quiet — Grimshaw too shy to speak, Burns too intent on eating, and me in my own thoughts.

Burns left to check on the horses, Grimshaw to arrange

the change of guard throughout the night.

The smooth-faced soldier might have been waiting for the chance to catch me alone, for barely seconds after Grimshaw's departure, a shadow approached from the flickering light of the campfires below. He didn't speak until his face was clearly lit by the fire in front of me.

"May I join you?" he asked.

"Sure," I said, though I felt a need for solitude. Rebecca was somewhere north of us, and I had memories I wanted to revisit as I thought of her.

"My name is Nathaniel Hawkthorne," he said. "I'm from Boston."

I heard in his voice a world of tea parties, frocked coats, and dark, somber paintings of ancestors staring down on him from velvet-lined walls.

"Samuel Keaton," I said in return. "Please sit. I hear Boston is a fine city."

"Yes, Sir," he said, taking the log bench which Burns had recently vacated.

Sir? Was I that grizzled? I hoped I was just being overly sensitive from my weary attempts to cure Lieutenant Grimshaw of his habit of calling me Mister Keaton.

"How old are you?" I asked Nathaniel Hawkthorne.

"Eighteen, Sir."

I hadn't studied him closely before—the tendency to attribute insignificance to someone much younger showed even more clearly that age was sneaking up on me. Here, despite the low light of the fire, I could plainly see what I'd ignored before.

Nathaniel Hawkthorne in his buttoned-down uniform was slightly chubby, but not enough to take away from an earnest sort of appeal. He wore his straight, blonde hair trimmed as an upside-down bowl atop his round skull. He had even features and a big grin, a grown-up version of a five-year-old boy with a blue ribbon in his hair and doting aunts to stuff him with chocolates and gushing compliments.

"Eighteen," I repeated. "Long ways from home."

"Yes, Sir. I ran away." He grinned triumph. I remembered his early jauntiness, as if the expedition were a great adventure.

It was a triumph, however, I did not share. "Your folks are probably fretting themselves."

Inwardly, I groaned. Had I just said that? Doc Harper was right. I'd become a little serious over the last while.

My elderly admonishment didn't dim his smile at all.

"No, Sir," he said. "Once I was enlisted, I sent them a letter informing them of my whereabouts."

I nodded.

"By then," he continued, "there was nothing my family could do. Not even they can interfere with the military machine."

It was there, hanging open to question, what his family did, and I left it there, untouched.

"Have some coffee," I said.

"No thank you, Sir. I am trying to eschew bad habits."

Eschew?

"Glad to see you've left mother and father so far behind."

"Sir?"

"Ignore me, Nathaniel. I'm just a grumpy old-timer."

"Yes, Sir," he said, disturbingly quick to agree. "Anyway, I'm here because I'd like to pay you for your horse."

"I need it to ride."

"I mean your dead horse, Sir. The one killed by the grizzly."

"You didn't kill it," I said. "The grizzly did."

"I know Sir, but you saved my life," Nathaniel said, leaning forward. "That other scout, he must have froze up or something, waiting so long. You're the only one who was shooting. Buying your dead horse is the only way I can think to repay you."

"I see." I opened my mouth to say more, then shut it again. Who was I to teach him the code of living out here, when much of the code itself was meant to be unspoken?

He had taken my silence as agreement. I looked up from the fire to see him counting bills from a roll thicker than an ice block.

"Tarnation!" I exploded. "Put that back before you start a war right in this camp."

"Sir?" he said as he shoved it into his boot.

"How long you been in the military?"

"Since January."

He must have had a guardian angel to guide him past months of pickpockets, poker sharks, and loose women.

"Take some advice," I said. "Make sure that money stays hidden. And forget about my horse."

His hurt at my sharpness was obvious in the firelight.

"Instead," I told him, trying to take impatience out of my voice, "you keep your eyes sharp. Best way to repay me is return the favor some day."

His grin returned. "Yes, Sir."

I expected him to rise now, return to his own fire, and leave me with cherished memories and fond hopes.

He did not.

I cut short a sigh. "Nathaniel?"

"Is it true what they say about you?"

"If you've heard bad, I expect so."

He shook his head vigorously. "No, Sir. It was about how you outgunned John Harrison last summer."

I laughed a laugh he could not hope to understand. John Harrison's gunfighting reputation had been exceeded only by men like Wild Bill Hickok, John Wesley Hardin, and Wyatt Earp. For a while, I had fully believed my bullets had cut him down. But if Nathaniel Hawkthorne wanted the entire story, he'd have to hear it from Rebecca.

"Stories get exaggerated," I told the boy.

"You cleared Laramie of a crooked marshal," he said. "I heard that too. Then there was a double murder in the bank vault and—"

"Like I said, stories get exaggerated. Who's been feeding you all this?"

"Miss Suzanne. At the Red Rose. She certainly seems trustworthy."

I rocked with laughter. Suzanne might be trustworthy, but in the low-bodiced, swelled-tight red dress she sported, trustworthiness would be the last thing a man might remember her for. If this boy had spent time in earnest conversation with Suzanne and still had that wad of bills, he was either exceptionally more experienced than he appeared, or his guardian angel was about to expire from overwork.

I laughed good and hard and enjoyed the chance to do so.

"Thank you, Nathaniel," I said when I finished. "You have certainly brightened up my evening."

"You're welcome, Sir," he said, puzzled, but too polite to push me.

I stood.

He took the hint and stood too.

"Remember, Sir," he said. "Should I ever have the chance, I'll return the favor."

At first, I couldn't place what he meant.

"Your life, Sir," he explained. "I'll do what it takes to save your life."

NINE

YOUNG LIEUTENANT GRIMSHAW followed cavalry regulations as doggedly as if he carried a manual, which I suspected did flop in one of his saddlebags.

One of the enlisted men — at Grimshaw's insistence — blew a bugle for reveille as first light whitened the horizon. My feeling was Grimshaw would have better accomplished wake-up through good-morning greetings during a walk from the dew-darkened canvas of one half-tent shelter to the next.

Fifteen minutes later — with Grimshaw, quirt in hand, pacing unnecessary supervision among the campsites — the bugle blew for assembly. I made a note to talk to him later about the undesirable qualities of such noise in upcoming Sioux territory.

Grimshaw insisted too, upon roll call. As if facing three hundred men instead of nine, he sent them off to their obvious duties — to water, groom, and feed their horses. After that, he had them bugled back again to assembly, simply to dismiss them for breakfast.

During all this, Mick Burns and I squatted near our own fire, tending to the day's first coffee as we observed the ridiculous formalities.

"Hope he runs out of energy soon," I said. "It wearies me just to watch."

Mick Burns grunted. "Fresh from West Point," he said. Which explained everything. "I suspect some of the boys will take the starch out of him soon enough."

Mick stood, yawned, stretched, cleared his throat, and hawked phlegm onto the dirt. "Holler when coffee's done. I swear a skunk crawled into my mouth and died."

He hitched his pants and wandered in the direction of his horse, something for which I was grateful, because his presence tended to cloud the air. I doubted Mick Burns had changed his long johns since before winter.

And I believed I knew how the skunk had found its way into his mouth. For much of the night Burns had been at the campfire belonging to the three rough-looking, enlisted men, and none had been particularly careful about hiding the bottle passed from hand to hand.

Mick Burns was not a man for whom I'd cultivate any degree of affection, nor of dislike. On a campaign like this, he would do his job, I mine, and we would each follow our separate paths during the times of relaxation. Were it not for my questions about his limp and the big, dark horse he rode, I'd tend to give him no thought at all, save for customary wariness around a man who obviously lived life hard.

Now, however, he would be part of my consciousness.

His horse, the tracks I'd had a chance to examine, and his use of the shotgun all seemed more than coincidence in light of the man murdered at my desk.

On the other hand, had Mick Burns truly wanted me dead, he could have stayed his shot on the charging grizzly, and had the satisfaction of watching me die in spectacular fashion.

Or did he want the satisfaction of murdering me himself?

Falling asleep last night, I'd convinced myself no. I'd also told myself an act of murder here on the expedition would leave him to open to investigation, and Mick Burns did not strike me as stupid, but, rather, cunning in the way of a long-lived coyote. Without those thoughts to satisfy me, sleep would have been impossible, especially with memories of how easily he'd carved the dead grizzly with his big Bowie knife.

It still left me much to puzzle over. Because the one thing I knew for certain was that a man had been shot at my desk in my stead. Had Mick Burns wanted me dead one day, only to change his mind later? If so, why? Or was there another man with a similar limp and horse and shotgun still waiting for me in Laramie? If so, who and why?

My prospects for peace of mind had not improved over the last day either. Our short stretch of travel had shown the obvious inexperience of Grimshaw and the military ineptitude of his unit as a whole. This was not a solid fighting detachment forged through shared days of survival, but soldiers who mixed like oil and water, whose only common bond was their inability to rise to officer status. Nathaniel Hawkthorne, naive romantic. Hardened buffalo soldiers, clinging to their self-imposed solitude. A couple of confused, German-born immigrants. Whiskey-sucking veterans. And me, half-fearful of a murderer at my back and filled with disgust at my helplessness to resist wild dreams of joy along with alternating worries of despair about an upcoming reunion with a half-breed Sioux woman who might or might not choose to accept my proposal of marriage.

Fortunately, I was diverted from an urge to feel sorry for myself by Lieutenant Grimshaw's almost pathetic attempts to establish his authority by rigorous enforcement of regulations.

Through the sparse trees on our hillside, I saw him approach the bugler yet again, one of the buffalo soldiers, a tall, strongly-built soldier who did not sigh or sag his shoulders at the lieutenant's persistence.

Moments later the bugler sounded "boots and saddles," giving the men a half hour to break camp. Naturally, Grimshaw was punctual in announcing the next command by bugle, and with "stand to horse" he called for another roll, as if any absences or sickness might have occurred unnoticed within the tiny confines of camp.

Satisfied he still had nine soldiers under his command, Grimshaw barked out another order, his attempt at military dignity vastly offset by the youthful breaking of his voice.

"Soldiers, prepare to mount."

All duly did so, failing to salute.

"Companeeee . . . mount," he finished.

Grimshaw placed a foot in the stirrups and swung atop his horse. As if whipped across the eyes, his mount stutter-stepped backward and reared high in the air on its hind legs. Grimshaw dropped his quirt and grabbed the saddle horn with both hands to keep his balance.

While instinctive, it was the wrong move. Had he leaned forward into the horse's neck, it would have kept his weight centered. Instead, the shift of weight jerked the horse farther backward and, still on its hind two feet, it staggered and swung around to keep its balance. Worse for Grimshaw, he no longer held the reins of the horse.

Out of control, the horse plunged down. Then it kicked backward and bucked, trying to throw Grimshaw from the saddle.

The soldiers all pulled their horses back, away from the flying hoofs of Grimshaw's horse.

It bucked again, screaming anger. Again it bucked, landing stiff-legged. Then it bucked and twisted sideways.

Grimshaw's hat had long been thrown. His saber scabbard flailed with each successive buck, and still Grimshaw held onto the horn with both hands, so rigid that his body absorbed every heavy jolt thrown by the horse.

The horse grew more frenzied. I'd seen this happen once to a man whose feet had gotten caught in the stirrups. The horse's bucking made it impossible to pull his feet loose. The horse's bucking had been so violent, the impact of repeated landing had broken the man's pelvis.

This horse was so crazed and kicking so hard, I worried the same might happen to Grimshaw. In fact I had my gun drawn—cartridges loaded with bullets instead of pepper spray—and from the saddle of my horse, I attempted to take bead so my shot would hit horse, not rider. Before I could squeeze the trigger, however, Mick Burns rode up beside me and pushed my arm down.

Before I could ask him why, the cinch of Grimshaw's saddle snapped, and the next bucking of the horse threw Grimshaw and saddle high into the air.

Grimshaw landed, still sitting in the saddle, still clutching the horn with both hands. I winced at the thud of body and saddle against earth. Grimshaw looked over at his soldiers, grinned weakly, opened his mouth to speak, then slumped over sideways.

The horse quieted immediately, and stood with sides heaving, blowing spray from its nostrils with occasional snorts. Wasn't hard to guess someone had placed a burr or something equally sharp under Grimshaw's saddle; with the goading pain now gone, the horse had no reason to continue bucking.

Private Nathaniel Hawkthorne dropped from his saddle and ran to his fallen lieutenant with a canteen of water, which he poured over the fallen man's head.

Grimshaw woke sputtering.

Mick Burns, horse near mine, spoke softly for my benefit.

"If that don't take the starch out of him," Burns said, "at least it's a good start."

I glanced over at Burns. And felt my heart jump.

Burns was cutting tobacco from a thick plug with a jack-knife. It was a practiced, one-handed movement, and he popped the chunk of tobacco into his mouth straight from the knife blade. He worked the tobacco chaw into one cheek, and grinned at me from a lumpy face.

I grinned back, but to me, my grin felt as weak as Grimshaw's had been.

The jackknife Burns was now folding to place in a side pocket was antler-bone handled. Identical to the old antler-bone jackknife Jake had found tucked in the left boot of the man killed at my desk.

I didn't like my conclusion. Burns was tied in to the man's death. Or Burns had missed me the first time, and was not only on my trail, but sharing it in a way which didn't help my nerves at all.

TEN

LATER IN THE DAY, when the line of plodding horses had separated enough to give our conversation privacy, I moved my horse alongside Grimshaw's.

Our direction was northwest, for we had cut from the North Platte to angle across a broad, treeless, and sparsely grassed basin toward the Sweetwater River, our next watering point. High, reddish bluffs guarded the east and west sides of the basin, each side so distant the edges of the hills blurred against the haze of the horizon.

Grimshaw said nothing as I settled my horse to match the pace of his. He concentrated on staring straight ahead but failed to remain expressionless, for each step of his horse brought twinges of pain around his eyes. He showed great fortitude to be sitting in the saddle again; I could only imagine how badly the bucking of the horse had punished his inner thighs and private parts.

"Lieutenant Grimshaw," I said.

"Mr. Keaton."

I wanted to be careful in this conversation. His command of this detachment was not my business. He also deserved to be able to hold onto his dignity. Humiliation is easy for no person of any age, yet it seems young men are particularly susceptible to the pain of pride.

"Unfortunate incident this morning," I said neutrally.

"If you are referring to the nail heads placed beneath my saddle, you are correct." He said it with tight lips. Nasty prank, nail heads. It was no wonder the horse had gone berserk. With Grimshaw's weight on the saddle, those nail heads had gouged into the horse's hide, and after it had thrown Grimshaw and the saddle, we'd all plainly seen the resulting rivulets of blood run down the horse's ribs.

"It definitely was no accident," I said. I paused, hoping Grimshaw himself would broach the subject.

He didn't.

"Safe bet, I guess, one of the enlisted men did it," I finally continued.

"I can assure you, I did not do it myself." He spat out each word.

"All of them know the same thing," I said.

"Thank you for informing me of that," Grimshaw said, gaze firmly on the horizon ahead.

I waited several minutes. The only sounds were that of horses' hoofs on hard ground, and the light keening of a wind which moved unobstructed across the open land.

I did not want to ask, but saw no choice. Not only did I have a great deal of sympathy for this young officer, I did not want to be part of an expedition with internal problems. The plains themselves presented enough danger as it was.

"How long have you been a lieutenant?" I asked.

I saw his shoulders stiffen. He knew where I was leading.

"Three weeks," he said. "I believe I informed you this would be my first field expedition."

"During officer training, did the instructors spend any time discussing insubordination?"

"I fail to see how this is your concern, Mr. Keaton. You were hired to scout for this detachment."

"Yes, Lieutenant." I understood his prickliness as a defense, and I would not respond in kind. Neither did I move on to leave young Lieutenant Grimshaw alone.

"All right, then," he said after a few more minutes of silence. "What would you have done?"

"Forced all of the men to carry their saddle packs and made them walk ahead of their horses for a half day."

"Not all of them are guilty."

"Yes, Lieutenant." I made sure he heard good humor and patience in my answer. I also waited again, believing it would seem much less like unoffered advice if he was forced to ask me to explain.

"Why would you punish them all?" he asked after a couple hundred more yards of trail.

"Well, Lieutenant," I said, "no one would have admitted to placing the nail heads beneath your saddle. You did well not to ask, for you would have appeared ineffectual."

"*Ineffectual again,* you mean."

Although he was right, I saw no reason to confirm it for him, so I moved on. "Yet the enlisted men probably know who among their ranks did it. By punishing them all, they in turn would have found a way to punish the one who caused their grief. Or at the very least discouraged the prankster from boasting about it or trying something similar again."

What I didn't add was that he also badly needed to establish his authority.

"I do not see it that way," Grimshaw said. "Justice is important to me. It doesn't seem right to punish the innocent."

I wanted to shake him and his idealistic young head. Justice mattered little with his untried leadership at stake. It frustrated me so much, I did what I'd warned myself not to do.

"Lieutenant, if I were you, I'd ease up on the regulations. At the same time, I'd watch real close for the next challenge. The slightest challenge at all. Then I'd use the full authority of the United States military to punish that soldier ten times more than he deserves. And if he protests, add to the punishment."

"That is not justice," he insisted.

"No," I said, "it is intimidation. If they can't respect—"

I snapped my mouth shut, knowing I'd made a mistake.

He did not respond with anger, but with bitterness, as if he'd been thinking the same thing long and hard.

"Go on," he said woodenly. "If they can't respect me. . . ."

I sighed. "Then you can at least force them to respect your stripes. The tradition, structure, and force of the entire U.S. military stands behind you."

"Yes, Mr. Keaton." He'd retreated to coldness.

I had pushed too far and was furious with myself for doing so. At least, until I'd spoken, he would have been able to believe the problem was apparent only to himself. Instead, I'd rubbed his face in it.

"Lieutenant," I said a few moments later, "what do you know about Mick Burns?"

"Is this leading to another lecture, Mr. Keaton?"

I did not blame him for his tone.

"No, Lieutenant, it is a necessary curiosity. And I'd rather he didn't know I asked."

"I know nothing beyond that Corporal Crozier assigned him to this detachment. As to not passing along your curiosity, I hardly expect such an experienced scout like Mick Burns to lower himself to casual conversation with someone he doesn't respect." Now Grimshaw turned his head to look me directly in the eyes. "Don't you agree?"

I had no answer.

ELEVEN

PLAINS TRAVEL—despite what dime novels written by Easterners would have you believe—consists of endless plodding, hour upon hour, day upon day. The grizzly bear attack earlier had been one of those brief deadly moments of terror for which the lull of plodding leaves you unprepared—deadlier danger because it is unanticipated.

Our expedition reached the Sweetwater River and followed it a half day westward. For those miles, our horses stayed along the deeply rutted wagon tracks of the Oregon Trail. We saw both Independence Rock and Devil's Gate, two of the famous landmarks, covered as high as a man could reach with hundreds of names scratched into the rock by passersby. In our solitude, I found it difficult to believe barely a dozen years had passed since the trail was alive with thousands of wagons each summer, an undying path of dust wide and high and visible from miles away. The railroad, of course, had brought change, and all we had for company now were sage grouse, occasional curious pronghorn antelope, and jackrabbits which spurted away for short bursts before stopping to stare back at us.

We were specks in this vastness of rolling hills and gullies and basin flats, and somehow my own smallness gave me a sense of freedom, in the same way I imagined it was for the hawks as they wheeled graceful circles in the wide sky around them. Most times on horseback, undistracted by the puny, constricting barriers of civilization which we accept in our efforts to feel secure against the universe, I was best able to consider the glories of God and the mysteries of spirit.

Now, however, I did not enjoy all the luxury of time to contemplate as we moved north from the Sweetwater River toward the valley of the Bighorn.

Mick Burns, of course, was a disturbing puzzlement. If Burns had wanted me dead in my office, why had he spared me from the grizzly and foregone nightly opportunities to slit my throat as I slept? Perhaps he was waiting for a moment when he and I were alone.

Despite my concern over Mick Burns, more of my thoughts were devoted to Morning Star, somewhere ahead of me among Sioux camps.

Morning Star had been born in London to a Sioux woman traveling in a Wild West show. When her mother died, she was raised among nuns as Rebecca Montcalm. At her coming of age, she had returned to America, determined to find her family. It had been my good fortune — although then I had not seen it as such — to be the guide she chose for her search. She was a contrary woman fearing unwanted advances from me. During the first days of shared hardship I had seen her as merely an irritating impediment to travel. Angry with her at yet another disagreement, my sudden realization of her beauty came as a total surprise. That first real introduction to her — alongside a Nebraska creek the previous summer — was a favorite and well-visited memory of mine.

Considering our travel urgency back then, she had taken far too long for bathing privacy, and I had returned to find her in long johns, the red material wet, her upper body covered by her shirt, also wet. Draped over a nearby branch were her pants, dripping dry. It explained why it had taken so long for her to call me. She'd washed her clothes too.

She was standing in bare feet at the side of the creek, leaning sideways to squeeze dry her unbraided hair. She smiled at my approach, leaned the other direction, and repeated the squeezing with her hands. Water streamed down her wrists and dripped from her elbows.

"Would it be a great inconvenience if we waited here for the breeze to—" She broke off.

I hadn't returned her smile. The time she'd taken to wash was time that had let me grow even more angry at our earlier disagreement.

"You, Ma'am, have been a great inconvenience," I said. "Furthermore, you've played me for a fool."

"Have I?" She studied me. The muscles around her eyes tightened, and her voice lost its light happiness. "My understanding of fools is that generally they only have themselves to blame for their foolishness."

I snapped my mouth shut. She certainly had a way of getting a man's attention. I found myself looking closely at her, which became, in truth, my first occasion to truly see her as she was.

She returned my gaze with a calm dignity that defied the essential absurdity of a barefooted woman in saggy, wet, red long johns. In that moment, my cloud of anger dropped to be replaced by an awareness of Rebecca Montcalm as the woman she was, and my breathing developed a hitch.

For she was beautiful. Definitely Sioux, but beautiful.

Strands of her black hair danced against her forehead and high curved cheekbones. Her face showed a haunting, untamable wildness, yet to me, her half smile promised joy and long shared nights. Her features were unblemished and perfect, yet the duskiness of her skin stayed any porcelain fragility.

I'd seen beauty before, the outward moldings of flesh that cause men to pant and follow, and seen enough of that hollow beauty not to trust it. But I thought of her long, uncomplaining hours in the saddle. How she'd shared the chores I'd thrown upon her. All the other hardships she'd endured with me. Whatever magnificence this woman showed on the out-side—and it matched anything I'd ever seen—she had double on the inside, as hinted by the softness of her smile and happiness of her voice when I'd first returned to this pool to confront her with my anger. And as more than hinted by the steel of her own answering coolness and sharp reply to my rudeness.

Unaccountably at least to me, for I felt like a tongue-tied boy—she averted her eyes to look downward.

I took my hat from my head, held it humbly against my chest, and searched for any words to break our awkward silence.

"Ma'am, what say I go back to my horses, turn around, and come up here just like before. Except this time when you smile and ask about inconveniences, I won't say anything that gives you the opportunity to rightfully accuse me of being selfish or foolish."

It had been enough of an apology for us to start fresh as a man and a woman thrown together in travel. Fitting in with her contrariness, she would never have decided to love me if I had tried to impress her earlier. Instead she took it into her head to love me for all the things I'd done during our first days of travel, uncaring of her watching eyes and unaware of the beauty she hid.

Although we were both stubborn—and at times it seemed against both our wills—our love had grown from that day along the Nebraska creek.

We'd chosen to separate for the winter because it seemed the only solution. She was looking for her Sioux family, and if she joined me in my world—the world of white men deter-mined to conquer these territories—she would always won-der, maybe even begin to hate herself or me for the reason she turned her back on a people who needed her. We did not want to sour our love in that manner.

On the other hand, I could not travel with her and live

among the Sioux as she made her decision about which life to choose. The Sioux life was not mine, and I would always be the stranger, my presence making it impossible for her to fully explore and understand what she needed to discover about herself and her people.

We had hoped one winter—a winter during which I fiercely ached for her—would be enough time among the Sioux for her to choose who she should be. Morning Star. Or Rebecca Montcalm.

Or Mrs. Rebecca Keaton.

To propose marriage, I planned to leave this detachment as soon as it was headed safely homeward. I'd depart no earlier, for I did believe I owed the military for the chance a corporal had taken on my innocence last summer. I believed too, that outposts along the neglected Bridger Trail would contribute greatly to peace by keeping settlers out of the Sioux ancestral grounds on the other side of the Bighorn Mountains.

Yet my allegiance did not extend to accompanying the detachment back through these safer territories on their return to Laramie. I would take a week alone to search for the summer camp which held Morning Star and ask her then for her decision.

As the cavalry detachment rode beneath blue skies dusted by high, drifting strands of cloud, I played out her answer again and again in my mind. No sooner would I convince myself that she was waiting breathlessly for my return, than I would find a way to plague my certainty with doubts. She loved me, perhaps, but loved life among the Sioux even more. Or had found comfort on lonely, cold nights with a handsome and daring brave. Or. . . .

Yet I could not retreat from love. Far better to hope and risk, than to shut myself off from my greatest joy by pretending I did not care. So I endured the agonies of fruitless speculation and plodded northward with the detachment.

Day by day we followed the Old Bridger Trail, with Lieu-

tenant Grimshaw diligently making notes about road conditions, water holes, and possible locations for permanent resting stops. Until a north-to-south railroad was built to take
immigrants into Montana Territory, this had good possibili-
ties as a trail—but only if the military decided to support it.

We reached the Big Horn basin—so wide it demanded
over a day's travel from one side of the valley to the other—
with no further incidents to either the expedition or to Lieutenant Grimshaw, although he did not ease up on regulations,
and it was not difficult to sense his leadership eroding day by
day.

We followed the Big Horn basin north, with the red-
brown, arid buttes of the Wind River Mountains miles to our
left, and the granite blue of snow-capped Bighorns miles to
our right. The route was easier here, and we stayed along the
Wind River, taking a narrow path along its banks where it cut
a narrow ten-mile gorge through the Owl Creek Mountains to
become the Big Horn River on the other side of the canyons.
There we found an old, crudely built, wooden boat sunken
and rotting in the shallows on the far side of the bank. Knife
carvings in the wood identified it as one that Jim Bridger's
crew had built ten years earlier to ferry wagons across.

We camped one night where the Grey Bull River met the
Bighorn, enjoying the good grass and sweet water. North,
however, we discovered why Bridger's Trail had never become popular.

Sun-bleached ox bones marked many locations where
livestock had faltered, for the next stretch of travel was mile
upon mile of barren country where nothing grew in the wind-
swept, sandy soil but sagebrush, greasewood, prickly pear,
and weeds. We found more bad water than good, with some
of the alkaline hole's stagnant pools the color and consistency
of cream.

Traveling light as we were, we suffered no serious hardship, but if the military wanted to establish this as a permanent road, outposts would definitely be needed in the area.

The trail's best point, of course, was its lack of hostile Sioux. We did once see a band of Shoshone moving through a valley, but as Mick Burns and I both insisted to a nervous Lieutenant Grimshaw, the Shoshone had never once gone on the warpath and were unlikely to begin now.

Our real worry would be the Sioux, especially as we progressed north of the confluence of the Bighorn River with the Stinking Water River, which some maps were already calling the Shoshone River. Soon we would be in the richer valleys which fed the Yellowstone River, the summer hunting grounds of the Sioux.

The worry was well justified one day south of the joining of the Bighorn and Yellowstone Rivers, one day south of our northernmost point of intended journey, one day south of my intended departure from the detachment.

For at dawn that morning, we woke up to discover one of the buffalo soldiers very dead at the picket lines, his cause of death obvious: a feather-decorated war spear in his back.

TWELVE

SIOUX," *MICK BURNS ANNOUNCED* as he examined the dead soldier. Burns knelt and touched the side of the soldier's neck. "Cold already. Maybe four, five hours ago."

Lieutenant Grimshaw and I stood to the side of the dead man. He was the big, square-shouldered soldier who blew the bugle. He'd fallen face forward—or been driven face forward into the ground by the force of the spear's impact. The spear had entered the left side of his back, just beneath the shoulder blade. Coagulated blood stained the blue of his uniform, clustered by dozens of flies.

"Sioux," Grimshaw repeated numbly.

"It's the feathers. Sioux markings," Burns explained, plucking one from the shaft of the spear. "See these three red circles. One for each enemy killed."

"Any horses missing?" I asked. To take my mind off the image of the dead man, and my stomach from its usual queasiness, I concentrated my sight on the willows along the streambed below us.

Grimshaw looked down the hillside at the other soldiers gathered in a knot of grim silence. He repeated my question loudly and directed it at Nathaniel Hawkthorne, who reluctantly headed in the direction of the picketed horses.

"This man was on sentry duty?" I said.

Grimshaw nodded.

"Alone?"

Grimshaw furrowed his eyebrows. "No. Regulations say—"

"Who with?"

"Private Scott." One of the whiskey-guzzling veterans.

"If this man's been dead that long," I said, "Scott should have alerted the camp."

"He's right," Burns interrupted. "All of us could have been killed in our sleep."

Grimshaw glanced at the soldiers. "I don't see him."

We had our answer soon enough. Nathaniel Hawkthorne was running and stumbling as he rushed toward us.

"Lieutenant!" he called. Hawkthorne's chest was heaving, not from the run, but from panic. He pointed back behind him. "No horses missing, but—"

He gulped more air. "Private Scott, he's . . . he's. . . ."

Hawkthorne turned away and managed to get behind a clump of willows before he retched. It was a horrible sound above the silence of the morning and the buzzing of flies on the dead man at our feet.

Hawkthorne had my full sympathy. He had my understanding too, when we discovered the body of Private Scott, still sitting against a tree, a bottle of whiskey at his side where it had fallen from his hand. From a distance, it looked like he was wearing a dull-red handkerchief around his neck. Close up, we saw it to be the spread of blood, blood which had flowed down his neck beneath his uniform, blood from the gaping smile of a throat neatly slashed from ear to ear.

****

Burns elected to attempt to track the Sioux killer or killers. I was given the task of scouting the surrounding countryside to find signs of any nearby camps. Grimshaw had decided to hole up, for all of us doubted the Sioux would openly attack a force of soldiers behind fortifications and armed with repeating rifles. Burns and I were to rendezvous with Grimshaw and his soldiers near sunset.

I felt I had two choices as I rode. One was to move with as much stealth as possible, keeping away from ridge tops, stopping frequently and avoiding open ground. The other was to move boldly, as if I had no concerns and nothing to hide.

I chose the latter, rigging a white cloth as a flag at the end of a stick. It would give me the freedom to cover much more territory, while also protecting me from ambush. With my white truce symbol, Sioux warriors would capture me before killing me, and my grasp of sign language would let me explain that I was here with Red Cloud's blessing. It would also give me the chance to speak of the peaceful intentions of the expedition. If they didn't immediately believe that I had Red Cloud's permission to travel through Sioux land, they would hold me until I was proved right or wrong. Proved wrong, I would be turned over to the Sioux women to be tortured. Proved right, by confirmation from someone within the Sioux, I would be given a feast.

I rode the valleys of the tributaries of the Big Horn, knowing I could expect to find a circle of tepees anywhere among grassy flats.

It was a glorious day to ride. Here the Bighorn River cut around the northern end of the Bighorn Mountains, and the land was gentler, greener—and higher up, dark with spruce. Rain had threatened earlier in the day, but winds had cleared the sky of clouds and now the hills were clearly cut against deep blue.

I rode with my eyes always searching the hills for movement, and my nose constantly sniffing for wood smoke. A camp might hold as many as thirty tepees and should not be difficult to detect from a mile or two away.

It took me until early afternoon to find a camp. From the

top of a hill, I knew it to be Sioux, not Crow. The tepees below me were arranged in a circle, a sacred symbol to the Sioux.

I rode down the hill slowly, not daring to hope that of all the camps in the summer hunting grounds, this one might hold Rebecca.

Barking dogs announced my presence long before I arrived at the camp. Two young warriors—barely more than boys—galloped toward me on horseback, screaming high-pitched taunts and swinging warclubs as they closed the gap between us.

I did not react. This was a test, and the worst I could do was show fear or attempt to fight back.

Three times the warriors swung past me, so close their bouncing braids seemed to whip at my face. On the fourth pass they slowed and wheeled their horses alongside mine, one on each side. At a walking pace, they accompanied me to the edge of the camp.

There, an old medicine man was waiting. He wore an antelope-horn medicine pendant around his neck, and white ermine skins dangled from a feather medallion on the side of his head. He held a lance in his right hand, its top curved in a sharp "u" like the top of a cane, the end trimmed with a scalp lock and eagle feathers.

I gave him the hand signal for "friend" by raising my right hand to shoulder level, with my index and middle fingers extended upward and held together, with the other fingers closed.

He slowly nodded agreement and invited me down from my horse. The boy warriors remained on their horses and stared down on me.

I held my left hand open, palm up, fingers together. I placed the edge of my right hand on my left palm, and with the fleshy part of my right hand, I rubbed my left palm in a circular manner, as if I were picking up bits of tobacco.

He grinned, showing dark gaps in his mouth.

I nodded gravely, turned to my saddle bag and dug out the promised tobacco.

He held both his hands at mouth level, the right one farther ahead of the left, cradling an imaginary tube. Then he pretended to puff on a pipe.

I nodded agreement again. He'd invited me to smoke a peace pipe.

Wordlessly, the old medicine man turned and began to walk toward the center of the camp. The boy warriors on their horses moved ahead with him.

With sharp, guttural words, he waved them away. They hesitated. The medicine man uttered one more abrupt word. Grudgingly, the boy warriors moved away from me, casting dark glances my way to show they were not fooled by the white man who carried gifts.

I held my horse's reins in my left hand and walked my horse forward, keeping a respectful distance from the medicine man. I also studied the camp carefully.

A few of the women were returning to their fires. Some were grinding grains and dried vegetables with stone-headed mauls on flat rocks. Others tended fires filled with stones. Nearby were the buffalo hide pouches, sagging with water and supported with four sticks. They would drop the hot stones into the pouches to boil their food. I saw skinned rabbit carcasses, but no deer or buffalo. Neither did I see any men. Out hunting, an easy guess, and unsuccessful thus far. The women and children would have snared the rabbits to supplement their pemmican as they waited for the hunting party to return.

I was watching hardest, however, for Rebecca. Surely if she were in this camp, she would have come forward by now. Unless she were thoroughly Sioux by this point, a thought which did not please me.

As we passed another fire, the old medicine man grunted again, this time to a girl in a buckskin dress. The girl rose quickly and darted away toward another tepee.

I remained following behind him, conscious that all eyes were upon me.

When we reached a tepee, well decorated by paintings on the buffalo-hide covering, the medicine man barked instructions again. This time, a young boy leaped forward and took the reins of my horse from my hand.

The medicine man gestured at the tepee flap. I lifted it slowly and stepped inside. The flaps at the top of the tepee were open and gave good light. Heavy buffalo robes lined the ground; near the opening was a rack made from bones and sticks wrapped with sinew.

I knew which tepee we had entered—a society tepee, not part of any family's. During my boyhood, after the deaths of my parents, I had spent time with mountain men and later, a tribe of Shoshone. I knew their customs were different from the Sioux, but not so different that I could not make sense of the societal equipment set out on this rack in precise order. Two pipes leaned at the southern end of the rack. Next hung two rattles, then drumsticks and finally, whips, used to discipline members of this particular society. Which society, I could not guess. A war society, perhaps. A police society. Definitely—as my nostrils informed me—a fraternal society. The Sioux had a way of preparing bear fat to stiffen their hair; animal and human urine were among the added solutions to the sticky salve which dried like iron, and this smell alone was often enough to tip downwind scouts of the warriors' presence. Here in the cloying, still air of the tepee, the smell was that much stronger.

The old medicine man sat cross-legged.

I did the same.

I did not speak. This was his parley.

He prepared the pipe. Once lit, he handed it to me. I inhaled and grunted. He took it from me and puffed slow and long. I could not refuse when he offered it back to me. I was becoming dizzy with smoke.

Still, he did not speak.

After a long, long silence, a tapping on the tepee walls alerted us to a visitor. The medicine man called out, and the flap opened again.

It took some time for my eyes to adjust to the darkness. The visitor was a slender young man, wearing the buckskin dress of a woman.

THIRTEEN

I 'D HEARD OF MEN like this among the Sioux, but had never met one. He was a *winkte*, escaping from the rigorous hunting and war system of Sioux society by adopting a female role.

Although I would have declined any offers to dance with him, he did not necessarily have my derision and scorn.

The Sioux society was built on warfare. Total aggression. In a warring society, the games the boys played were extremely rough and brutal, designed to steel them to the conditions of battle. A kinder person would call them sensitive, the boys who feared or abhorred violence. The less kind would call them sissies or mama's boys. These fighting games early separated the timid boys from the brave ones. The Sioux had no grays in terms of bravery—either you became a warring, hunting man, or you did not. That some of the more fearful boys eventually became winktes to escape from this pressure was understandable.

They dressed as women and followed the womanly pursuits of tanning and quilling, living in their own tepees at the edge of the camp circle—the area relegated to orphans and ancient widows. To their credit, it was generally conceded that the winktes excelled in their chosen tasks, and pieces of tanning and quilling produced by them were highly desirable, highly marketable, and frequently cherished as masterpieces.

This winkte immediately answered my unspoken question about the need for his presence in this society tepee.

"I have been called here to translate," he said in slow, careful English. "Our holy man wishes to extend his greetings."

"I am honored," I said. I did not expect to be introduced to them by name, for the Sioux consider it bad form and bad luck to speak their own names.

The medicine man spoke briefly in Sioux.

"He asks if you have met Red Cloud," the winkte said. I nodded yes.

More Sioux from the medicine man, which was then translated "Your face. You are the one known as Ghost Rider."

Again, I nodded yes to both the winkte and the medicine man. I had a long scar on my face, the result of a man slashing my cheek with his gunsight as he pistol-whipped me years ago. When Red Cloud put the word out among the Sioux, he would have naturally referred to the scar as an identifying mark.

"Red Cloud granted you permission to hunt buffalo on our sacred grounds," the winkte said.

"No," I said clearly. "He merely promised me I would not be harmed by any of the Sioux."

The winkte translated my words for the medicine man, who grinned and chuckled. By disagreeing with the offered falsehood, I had passed his test.

The medicine man drew heavily on the pipe, exhaled, and again spoke. After a pause, the winkte passed on the old man's words. "You seek the woman Morning Star?"

My face must have registered surprise, for the holy man chuckled and wheezed and slapped his thigh.

"How could he know?" I asked the winkte.

"We do not have the white man's newspaper," the winkte told me directly. "Yet during winter camps, we hear much of what is important, and more of what is not important. When a woman of Morning Star's beauty and renown pines for a white man, it becomes common knowledge among the tribes."

I tried to keep my face straight and somber. Inside, however, I felt like a boy on Christmas day. *When a woman of Morning Star's beauty and renown pines for a white man. . . .*

"She is in a camp two valleys to the south," the winkte was saying. "On the other side of the Bighorn. Perhaps a half-day ride." His voice was sad, almost wistful, as he perhaps thought of love reunited, and in that moment I understood how terrible his own isolation and loneliness must be.

The medicine man interrupted by firing a volley of words at the winkte. I can only assume the winkte relayed to him our brief conversation, for the medicine man nodded wisely.

He then looked directly at me and spoke Sioux. I waited for translation.

"Have you hunger?"

"My belly is full," I said. "However, there are other matters of which I must speak."

"Go on," the winkte said.

"I travel with blue-coats."

The winkte stiffened. I saw distrust fill his face. He spoke quickly to the medicine man, who also lost some of his relaxed peace.

"The soldiers mean no harm," I said. "They seek a road which will not encroach upon your hunting grounds."

The winkte passed that on. Both waited for me to say more, so I obliged.

"Last night, one of the soldiers was killed by a Sioux spear. Do you have men on the warpath? If so, I will instruct the soldiers to depart from your country."

I waited nearly five minutes for a reply. I dared not shift my position on the buffalo robes, nor wrinkle my nose at the strong smells of the cramped quarters.

Finally, the medicine man spoke.

"Our men are north of here, searching for buffalo," the winkte said for the medicine man. "Until they have secured a good supply of food, they will not seek warfare with blue-coats."

More rapid-fire Sioux.

"Do you ride for Long Hair The Woman Killer?" I was asked.

I shook my head no. George Armstrong Custer had led his Seventh Cavalry to a Cheyenne winter camp near the Washita River in November of '68. He'd led the charge which killed over a hundred Cheyenne, mostly women and children unable to defend themselves. His cowardice had not been forgotten.

"Custer is no friend of mine," I emphasized. "I will not travel with him."

The winkte spoke directly to me again. "You would be wise not to change your habit. I hear of the Cheyenne and Sioux warriors planning to gather in great numbers near the Yellowstone. This summer or the next, they will destroy Long Hair."

I politely said nothing. Custer routinely bragged to journalists that his Seventh could lick any force the Indians threw at him. I also knew the one great weakness the Sioux and Cheyenne faced was their inability to organize themselves into armies. But if they did indeed gather in great numbers. . . .

I shook myself away from idle speculation. In this brief conversation, I had discovered the two things I wanted. Morning Star's location. And that the Sioux were not on the warpath. Unless. . . .

"With all respect," I said quietly, "could it be some warriors attacked our camp and such news had not reached your holy man?"

The winkte passed on my question, and shortly after answered for the medicine man. "It is possible. Yet our braves traveled north, and you came from the south. More importantly, our braves would not risk this camp by fighting nearby and leaving it unguarded."

What should I think now about the dead soldiers?

"You have my deepest thanks," I said, looking directly at the medicine man. "Please let me show you my gratitude."

I made hand signals for sugar and flour, and the medicine man smiled. Both of them followed me from the tepee. I unloaded the supplies from my horse and handed them to the winkte. I could safely expect the flour and sugar to be shared with those who most needed it; the Sioux were well known for providing for their poor.

In the sunlight, I could see weary lines across the winkte's young face. Yes, there was something pathetic in seeing a slender-shouldered man in a bead-decorated dress, his hair braided like a woman's. Yet how could I mock him; he carried a tremendous burden from which he could never escape. I struggled for something to say in farewell, but came up with nothing. Our worlds were too far apart.

"May *Wakan Tanka* travel with you," the winkte said softly as I moved my horse away from them.

"May God be with you," I said equally softly.

It was in conflicting moods that I rode through the hours which took me back to the cavalry camp. On one hand, I could clutch at the fragment of joyful news I'd heard about Morning Star. And I knew where she was. Had I decided to check the valleys on the other side of the Bighorn River, I would have met her today, for from what the winkte had described, her camp was only a morning's ride from the cavalry camp. Tomorrow, after the long ache of winter, she would be in my arms.

On the other hand, our bugler had been savagely killed, and I now had reason to suspect the murderer was within the same cavalry camp to which I now returned. For if the medicine man had been correct, and no Sioux warriors had been nearby, then two other things made sense: The fact that the war spear had been left behind, and that no horses had been taken—both unusual in light of Sioux warriors' habits. Someone had wanted this to appear as Sioux handiwork.

It was dark when I rode to camp, and the movement of my approaching horse was challenged by a nervous voice which I recognized as that of Private Nathaniel Hawkthorne.

"Who goes there?" he called.

"Samuel Keaton," I replied. "Take your finger off the trigger."

"Yes, Sir," he said.

I dismounted. He approached from the trees where he'd been standing.

"I'm glad you've returned," he said. "We've all been worried."

"Why's that?" I asked. "Scouts are paid to roam the hills."

"Well, Sir," he said. "We lost another one today. Private Friedberg. He was getting water when Sioux arrows cut him down."

FOURTEEN

AFTER BREAKFAST THE NEXT MORNING, Private Nathaniel Hawkthorne approached me near my fire. His face was drawn, and in its exhaustion, hinted at how he might appear a decade from now without the boyish roundness.

"Please, Sir," he said, reaching into his jacket, "will you take this letter?"

He handed me a small packet wrapped in wax-skin paper. Unsure of his meaning, I nodded yes anyway and accepted the folded paper. I began to open it.

"No," he said quickly.

I lifted my head to glance at him.

"Only upon my death," he said. "I've been up all night writing it. Please make sure it reaches my parents if I don't return to Laramie."

I held the letter between my thumb and forefinger and waved it gently. "This raises a host of questions," I said. "One of them being your sudden expectation of death. The other, your certainty that I'll survive."

He blushed. "Injuns won't get you. I heard about Red Cloud and how he promised you would never be harmed.

Plus you're so fast with guns that—"

"Didn't I tell you to ignore such hogwash from the Red Rose Saloon?"

"Yes, Sir. This isn't from Suzanne. Some of the enlisted men have been saying you don't have anything to fear."

"And you expect to die soon?"

He gulped. "Private Friedberg, he wasn't away from camp but five minutes. Someone went looking, and there he was, dead in the creek, Sioux arrows in him like he was a pin cushion. If the injuns can strike like that. . . ." He shook his head in respectful admiration of the unseen enemy.

I had my own thoughts about the unseen enemy. Despite my suspicions, I wanted to believe no murderer was in this camp. I wanted to believe a solitary Sioux brave was hiding nearby, determined to stealthily pick off cavalry soldiers. I wanted to believe he'd been forced to leave his war spear behind in the bugler because something had startled him, or else he'd left the spear as a warning. I wanted to believe he hadn't taken any horses because keeping them nearby would make it impossible for him to remain hidden for any length of time. I wanted to believe the same Sioux had waited yesterday for the best moment to shoot the first soldier to stray from the confines of camp.

Yet. . . .

The Sioux, while wild and independent, were not solitary hunters. Their tactics were to attack and disappear, not fight and remain. The Sioux too, loved the glory of war. Any Sioux braves who had stolen into a blue-coat camp and killed the sentries would have been anxious to return to their own camp to brag and feast—taking with them cavalry-branded horses as proof of their conquest. Lastly, yesterday the medicine man had made a telling point—the Sioux would not engage in warfare and leave their family camp unprotected.

But I could think of no conceivable reason for someone within this detachment to murder three men. A bugler from the buffalo soldiers. A whiskey-guzzling veteran. A German unable to speak English. What could possibly link them? Without a link, their deaths were random. And if random, why kill them?

My own confusion was nothing compared to the young lieutenant's. My advice to him had been to head south. He had ample notes and information for the military to make a decision on reopening Bridger's Trail. I'd suggested he let Mick Burns and me scout ahead the remaining portion of the Trail. I'd also let him know I would be away most of this day, scouting the other side of the Bighorn for hostile Sioux, which privately I did not expect to find.

All these thoughts went through my head as I faced the young soldier in front of me.

"Nathaniel," I said, "if you make sure to stay within camp, and always be in sight of someone else, you'll be just fine."

I bent the letter in half, creased the new fold in the wax-skin and tucked and buttoned it inside my shirt pocket.

"If need be, I'll deliver this," I continued. "But you just set your fears aside. I highly doubt we'll be seeing action. Fact is, most of the surveying's done. I shouldn't be surprised if Lieutenant Grimshaw gives orders to turn back to Laramie."

"There's been grumblings, Sir. We can't just run away with our tails between our legs. Not a United States cavalry troop."

He was so earnest, I wanted to chuckle. I resisted the urge to pat him on the head. "Private Hawkthorne," I said, "worrying is like trying to saddle a cow. You work like the dickens, but there ain't no point."

He tried an uncertain smile on me. "Yes, Sir," he said. He opened his mouth to say something else, then shut it again.

"Nathaniel?"

He shook his head. "Nothing, Sir. It's just that some of the men are calling you an injun lover."

I should have listened more closely. Much more closely. Instead, I dismissed his comment with a wave. "There's good ones and bad ones," I said. "Same as with us. I never found it wise to tar an entire group with the same brush. Take each man and woman at their own worth."

My answer didn't seem to satisfy him, but I had other concerns. Like saddling up for a ride into the valley which held a woman named Rebecca Montcalm.

"If you don't mind, Nathaniel, I'll need some of the sunlight you're blocking." I gestured at my shaving kit and a small hand mirror. "I have some of my own duties to tend to."

Private Nathaniel Hawkthorne walked away in troubled silence.

Stupid as I was, I began to whistle as I worked the shaving soap into a lather.

FIFTEEN

I CRESTED A RIDGE AND SAW a dozen tepees in a circle far below me. Instead of urging my horse downward, however, I dismounted and held the reins in my hand to stand among the pine which dotted the ridge.

Doc had been right earlier in Laramie. My memories were of a powerful love. What if the memories were more than what truly existed? Would I be riding down to the Sioux camp to be disappointed? Or to disappoint her?

I delayed, trying to calm myself by becoming part of the land. I absorbed the sun, concentrated on the gentle brush of wind against my face, listened hard for the chickadees which bobbed and weaved from tree to tree. Because I had stilled myself, I noticed I was not alone on the hillside.

Halfway down, a dark-haired figure sat, pale buckskin dress, legs tucked beneath her, back resting against a large boulder, as she too surveyed the valley below her. I saw no weapons nearby, just a basket woven from willow branches.

I told myself my eyes were deceiving me, that I was straining too hard, imagining too much.

The dark-haired figure lifted a hand to brush long, loosened hair away from her face, and I saw clearly her profile.

Morning Star.

That glimpse of her face answered half of my questions. I would not be riding down to be disappointed. A warmth surged through me and I wanted to cry out in joy and rush down to embrace her.

But what about the other half of my question? Would she be equally glad to see me?

I tied my horse's reins to a sparsely branched pine tree and began to ease my way downward. And yes, I was afraid. Very afraid it would not be the same for her as it was for me.

So afraid I did not call out as I moved, step by slow step, toward her.

She was gazing across the valley, and she had no clue of my nearness until I was close enough for her to hear the whisper of long grass against my pant legs. Then she turned her head with the same graceful motion of a startled doe.

I could not speak. Nor breathe.

She smiled. My memories had treated me falsely, for even during my loneliest moments, I could not recall her to be this beautiful. Her hair was black satin, her eyes deeply dark, and her smile promised a wholeness to fill my winter's ache.

She rose. Her smile trembled, then broke.

Wordlessly, slowly, we moved toward each other.

I saw why her smile had broken. Tears welled at the corners of her eyes.

Still we said nothing. She stood in front of me, so close the breeze could not carry away the sweetness of her scent. She raised her eyes to mine, and I reached to her face, filled with wonder and awe at the tears which wet my fingertips.

We did not kiss. Simply embraced, her chin against my chest, my chin pressed against the side of her head. Our only movement was the rise and fall of her chest as she shuddered with the release of tears.

I breathed deep of her hair, taking in the entire valley, the mountain ridges against infinite blue, the winding streambed below, the swaying grass on the sides of the hills. I wanted forever to be able to close my eyes and summon this moment.

She lifted her hand from the small of my back to my shoulder, then ran her hand down my arm until she found my hand to intertwine our fingers. Only then did she move to step back from me.

She did not release my hand.

"You have returned," she said. Her lovely, soft, British accent had not disappeared. "Yesterday a messenger brought word of you. Today I have climbed this hill to watch for you."

"I have returned. Nothing except death would have kept me."

She took my other hand. Unaccountably, facing each other, holding hands, we both became shy. I thought of a dozen things to say next, thought of all the things I had planned to say, and discarded all of them as inadequate.

I wanted to kiss her, but also wanted to delay, like holding a nicely wrapped gift and savoring the anticipation.

"This is remarkable," she said to break our silence. "Five minutes together and we have yet to disagree on any matter."

"Which way south?" I asked.

She pointed north.

"Wrong," I said. "Happier now?"

She answered by kissing me with such exuberance it knocked my hat from my head. When we finally broke for air, I gasped out my next question.

"How many horses?" I asked.

She squinted puzzlement.

"As a gift," I explained. "How many horses must I offer your family in courtship?"

A devilish grin played across her face. "If you must know, Samuel, the latest offer was ten."

I sputtered. "Latest?"

"The first three braves obviously thought little of my

cooking talents. The best offer from them was five horses."

"What kind of winter did you have?" I exploded. "All I had for company was a crotchety old doctor and a deputy with one arm."

"Wasn't there a dance girl in Laramie? Remember, the one who visited your jail cell one night last summer."

"That doesn't count," I said. "You'll recall I declined her offer and that was before I knew you."

She burst out laughing. "If you could see your face, Sam. This is not a serious conversation."

"Maybe not to you," I grumbled. "I've been worrying all winter about this day and how you'd decide."

She picked up my hat and dusted it. Stood on her tiptoes to set it on my head. I tried stealing a kiss as she did so. She ducked away from me and laughed again.

"Promise you'll always worry about me, Samuel."

"That won't be difficult. I couldn't find anyone more contrary."

"Stop searching."

I grinned. "That mean the other fellow's ten horses weren't enough?"

She gestured at the willow branch basket. "Will you eat?"

I allowed as I would, though I was busting to have her confirm the decision she'd hinted at.

We shared some dried vegetables and a cold, dark meat.

"This is good," I said, for I hadn't realized I was this hungry. "But it hardly seems like buffalo."

"For you, the best in Sioux delicacies. Boiled young puppy."

"Wonderful," I said. I set the remainder of my meal aside. "I shouldn't be selfish with it then, should I."

"Don't be a sissy. It's goose."

My queasiness settled.

"I want to leave the Sioux," she said without further preamble. Her face was quiet. "Not necessarily in spirit, but I cannot live among them."

She drew a breath. "Samuel, I have seen too much of the world to be content as a Sioux woman. Even as Red Cloud's granddaughter, there are too many constraints. I find it difficult to accept that a brave may own several wives, yet if the wife is unfaithful, the tip of her nose is snipped off as punishment. I do not like it that the women eat last and dare not make eye contact with the braves as they eat. I do not like it that I cannot contribute to the tribe's well-being except through cooking and tanning and quilling."

"Woman's suffrage could use someone like you," I offered, and instantly regretted my lighthearted mocking.

"Lastly and most importantly," she said as if I hadn't spoken, "I do not like it that my life among the Sioux would mean life without you."

She stopped.

I was staring down at the stream and the movement among the faraway tepees.

"Samuel."

"Yes?"

"This would be an excellent time to tell me in return you could not imagine life in Laramie without me."

Again, I found myself struggling for words to explain the great force of love within me.

"I cannot imagine life in Laramie without you," I finally said. "And I have little more to add to that statement."

She shifted sharply, for my tone told her I was not joking.

"You are my one love," I answered to her look. "But I won't go on and on in flowery words about it. I was raised to believe what a man does, not what he says. But I can promise if you return with me to Laramie, my actions will say that there will never be a day you doubt how I feel for you."

"I accept your promise," she said without hesitation. "Will you help me defend the Sioux where it matters? Among government agencies and politicians?"

That was what she'd meant by remaining among her people in spirit.

"Yes," I told her. "You have that promise."

She leaned over to kiss me again. She kissed me slowly and deeply and nothing else mattered on that quiet hillside except for her.

SIXTEEN

LIEUTENANT GRIMSHAW SMELLED of the stale, long-dried sweat of fear. He seemed so gray his freckles were bleached of color, his eyebrows invisible wisps.

Three soldiers stood behind him. Two of the buffalo soldiers and one of the whiskey-guzzling veterans.

"You rode in late last night," he said. "Again." It came out as an accusation.

"Yup. Coffee?"

I held the pot out. I'd rarely tasted a breakfast so good, yet it had been nothing different than the usual yellowed bacon and biscuits. I felt the tonic of new life coursing through me at thoughts of Rebecca and was ready to whip a mountain lion with my bare hands. Murders or no murders, as soon as this detachment headed south, I was resigning from my duties to escort Rebecca back to Laramie.

Lieutenant Grimshaw refused the offered coffee.

"You might remember," I added, "last night I immediately reported the lack of hostile Sioux in the area."

"Explain, then, why Private Williams was found dead this morning at the latrine area."

I spat choice words with no regard to grammatical structure. Death is ugly at the best of times, senseless death that much worse.

I asked how Private Williams had been killed.

"Slit throat," Grimshaw said. "The Sioux didn't even have the decency to wait until he'd pulled up his pants."

More choice words on my part. How many more would die? And why? Did I have a responsibility to worry about a military problem?

"I find it strange that you haven't seen any hostile Sioux, yet four of my men are dead." Grimshaw was slapping his leg nervously with his quirt. "I also find it strange that you are able to ride at will in this country—night or day—and remain unharmed."

I set my coffee down and stared him in the face. "Before you ride into that canyon, Mister, you'd best know your way out."

He licked his lips and looked away, but still spoke.

"I'm no fool but—"

"Anyone says he's no fool has his suspicions. You want to accuse me of something, spit it out. Otherwise walk."

He drew himself up. "I am a lieutenant of the United States military. You are under my command. You will not talk to me in that manner."

I stared at him until he flushed.

"Lieutenant," I said, "my advice from yesterday stands. Head south. Burns and I will provide you with the final details for your expedition's report."

"Am I also to report I have left four men behind, dead to hostiles? And that I did not take action against it?"

"I do not believe there is any action which can be taken. If this indeed is the result of Sioux hostiles, they are like ghosts and trekking after them is futile."

"*If* this is Sioux?" Grimshaw asked. "Who else?"

"Decide for yourself," I answered. "There are no warriors in nearby camps. They're farther north, searching for spring buffalo. And Sioux don't fight like this. To them, war is a glorious game."

Grimshaw frowned—a nervous, tired frown. But he spoke with conviction. "Unprovoked, hostiles have attacked members of the United States militia. They must be punished. If we cannot find the warriors responsible, we will take hostages until the Sioux surrender those warriors."

It flashed through my mind, the domestic peace I had witnessed while the medicine man escorted me through the circle of tepees. "Taking innocent women and children is not the solution, Lieutenant."

"I'll repeat something you said earlier in the expedition," he replied. "Something about respect through intimidation. Quote, the tradition, structure, and force of the entire U.S. military stands behind me, end quote."

He paused. "I will not shame the tradition or structure or force at my command by idly standing by during this attack. Furthermore, if the Sioux see us run, it will reflect badly on all soldiers in the territories."

I moved closer and lowered my voice. "Lieutenant, I promise you this is not the way to earn respect. You'll anger the Sioux at a time we cannot afford to anger them. You may also face repercussions for acting without authority."

"Hardly." He grew more confident. "In '61, a second lieutenant named George Bascom forced Cochise and his Apaches to a standstill with the same tactics."

I was beginning to understand and didn't like it. Young Grimshaw, worn down by bewildering events, was anxious to redeem himself and the record of his short and uncertain command. By holding Bascom as an example, Grimshaw could resolutely follow a battle plan—one sanctioned in the military history books at West Point—and perhaps even become part of the history books himself.

I closed my eyes briefly and took a deep breath to give myself strength in the face of a looming bloodbath, one which would surely follow in the wake of this man's ignorance.

"Lieutenant, the Sioux don't surrender. You take hostages and they'll raid settled territory to the south to take hostages in return. It might not end for months."

"I will not permit a U.S. Cavalry force to run from hostiles. As lieutenant in command of this detachment, I order you to direct us toward the nearest Sioux camp."

"I will not. Furthermore, I resign."

I picked up my coffee cup, this time with my left hand. I tilted the cup and pretended to drink, carefully watching the lieutenant and his three men.

"Arrest him," Grimshaw ordered.

I had felt something like that was coming. The three soldiers began to step forward. I let go of the cup. The coffee cup was a useful distraction for my other hand, which I'd rested on the butt of my revolver. I had the Colt out, hammer cocked and barrel pointed directly into Grimshaw's face before the cup hit the ground.

"No one moves," I said. "I ride out. When you next see me in Laramie, we'll let a judge sort through this."

The three soldiers froze. Lieutenant Grimshaw gulped.

Four men dead in under two days, and jumpy, resentful soldiers as a result. Me branded as an "injun lover," even suspected in the murders for it. Two weeks' ride from any settlement. An edgy, inexperienced boy of a lieutenant determined to become a hero, one with the authority to court-martial me right here and hang me from the nearest tree. It did not seem healthy to allow myself to be put in handcuffs.

"Believe me, Lieutenant," I said. "There are no hostile Sioux in the area. Only peaceful camps of women and children. The Sioux would not attack you and put their families at risk. Look in this camp if you want the murderer. But look in my absence."

I was determined to get out of here. Not only to save my hide, but to warn Rebecca and the others at the Sioux camps. It would not be a traitorous act; the military would lose far more than it could gain by taking hostages.

"You will accompany me to my horse, Lieutenant," I said quietly. "Keep in mind I will not hesitate to shoot to escape."

Grimshaw's eyes widened.

Right then, I thought it was because of my harsh words. But the nudge of something narrow and hard in the small of my back convinced me how badly I was mistaken.

"Drop the pistol," Mick Burns said from behind me. "Me and my shotgun ain't gonna miss from this range."

I dropped the pistol.

"Thank you, Mr. Burns," Grimshaw said. "You are to be commended. Keaton reacted just as you predicted."

I heard Burns spit tobacco juice onto the ground. "Showed hisself to be a real injun lover, all right. But I tole you that from the git-go."

"Do we take him with us?" Grimshaw asked.

By his tone of voice, it wasn't hard to guess where Grimshaw had been seeking advice over the last days.

Another splat of tobacco juice. "Your choice, Lieutenant. I know the hills good enough to guide us there from what he described in his report. Trouble is, can you afford to leave any troops behind to guard him? And what if we take a different route back? We'd have to waste good time to rejoin the troops you leave with him."

Burns moved beside me, short, squat, and flat-nosed ugly, shotgun cradled in his arm. He spit again, tobacco juice splattering the toe of my boot. "You could always hang him, Lieutenant. Plenty witnesses seen him pull a gun on you."

Grimshaw slapped his leg a few times with the quirt as he thought. It didn't take him long.

"He'll go with us. On his own horse. Hands bound." Grimshaw slapped his leg a final time with his quirt. "We can always hang him later if he makes trouble."

SEVENTEEN

WE WERE WAITING among a small stand of pine trees two miles downstream of Rebecca's camp when Mick Burns returned. Most of the soldiers were dismounted; I wasn't. My hands were bound by rope in front of me, and dismounting from my saddle and mounting again was awkward and time-consuming.

It was a windless morning, and all of us in the shade of the trees clearly heard Burns as he growled out his report.

"Camp is quiet. No sign of warriors."

I found no consolation in his confirmation of my earlier report. Grimshaw had his mind set that Sioux had killed his men, and he was equally set in punishing the Sioux. I could only pray Rebecca was not in the camp when we arrived.

"You'll want to surprise them," Burns said. "Follow this here creek for about twenty minutes. You'll come to a bend marked by a tree busted by lightning. From there, you'll have maybe a quarter mile of open ground from a stand of willows. The less time it takes for you to cover that ground, the better."

"Where will you be?" Grimshaw asked, his voice suddenly plaintive. It raised my level of concern. A frightened, uncertain man with power is a dangerous creature.

"Well, Lieutenant, I'd appreciate a half-hour head start. Gives me time to circle around the camp. Back of it is some dense tree cover, and I'd like to be certain no danger comes from that direction."

"Good, good," Grimshaw answered. "Want a couple of men for protection?"

"Naw." Burns spit. Dribbles of dark tobacco juice clung to his chin. Having established his casual regard to Grimshaw's question, Burns continued. "I don't need 'em getting in my way, and you probably don't want to divide your troops."

I wondered if Grimshaw knew the impression he was giving to the soldiers around him. They'd certainly see him as I did. Afraid to proceed without Burns nurse-maiding him. How was it such an inexperienced man might receive promotion to lieutenant, let alone be allowed to take soldiers into the field?

"Sound advice," Grimshaw said. "Proceed when ready, Mr. Burns. We'll follow in a half hour."

****

I rode near the back of the line of horses, hands still thoroughly bound. One of the buffalo soldiers, on the horse ahead of me, held the reins of my horse. Under normal circumstances, as prisoner, my horse would be roped to another. With possible trouble ahead, however, no soldier wanted to be encumbered by my horse. Under fire, I would be left to fend for myself, difficult as that might be with no control over my horse and little control over my balance.

We stayed on flat ground and avoided the occasional thickets of willow near the stream. Travel was easy and Burns proved correct in his prediction. It took twenty minutes to cover the distance to the final bend before the Sioux camp, marked by that stand-alone tree recently torched by lightning.

And, as Burns had informed us, we were screened from the camp by a stand of willows. Grimshaw, wearing white doe-skin gauntlet gloves with large, flared cuffs, raised his saber with his right hand. At that signal, the line of soldiers brought their horses to a halt.

Silence, save for the gurgling of the stream, and slaps of leather as soldiers jerked on reins to keep their horses from reaching down to the tall grass.

I had my own distractions. Flies swarmed my face, and the only way to wave them away was to lift my bound wrists and sweep my forearms from side to side.

More importantly, I was straining to see past the willows. Would Rebecca be resting at her viewpoint halfway up the hill? If so, would she remain unseen by the soldiers?

If so, I already had my plan of action.

I would roll off my horse as the troops charged across the open ground. This far back among the soldiers, chances were good I could avoid being trampled by the few horses behind me, and I doubted any of the soldiers would halt their charge to attend to me.

Seeing my hands bound, Rebecca would know, then, something was wrong and, I hoped, stay hidden. Nor would I try to reach her. I did not want any attention drawn to her. It was a gamble—contrary as that woman was, she might respond instead by running to camp to futilely try to protect the other Sioux.

"Soldiers," Grimshaw said as he wheeled his horse to face us, saber still high, "you have your instructions. We surround the camp and contain all routes of escape. If any hostiles flee, do not shoot. Turn them back with your horses. When the perimeter is secure, we choose our hostages. Five shall suffice. Any questions?"

One of the veterans raised his voice. "Fire if fired upon?"

"Our scout has assured us this will not be a concern. Our task is to take hostages."

No other questions rose above the stream's gurgling.

Lieutenant Grimshaw turned his horse toward camp, dropped his saber, and charged past the edge of the willows. His soldiers thundered behind him, and we broke onto the grassy flats at full gallop.

I was holding the horn of my saddle with both hands, concentrating hard on balance, glad for the charge because I doubted any of the soldiers would be looking upward into the hills.

Hoofs drummed against the ground. I rocked with the rhythm of my horse. I took my eyes off the tepees ahead and scanned for Rebecca.

She was not on the hillside.

In that second, I knew one of the prices paid for love. Without love, a man never risked pain. With it, there always lurked the possibility of incomprehensible loss, and seeing the bare hillside, I was stabbed with blind, unreasoning, helpless fear.

The horses were now halfway across. Ahead, the first flurries of panic as women sprang from beside campfires and ran for children.

The cavalry charge spread as horses raced for the corners of the camp. The soldier ahead of me dropped the reins to my horse, and I clung to my saddle. My horse continued to gallop with the other horses, the herd instinct within it strong.

Another heart-pounding hundred yards.

We were drawing hard up to the camp. Above the pounding of the horses I heard screaming. The entire camp was in helter-skelter motion.

I managed to lean forward and lift my bound wrists to grab my horse's mane. I pulled back as hard as I could and it started to slow.

To my right, I caught a glimpse of two teenage girls running toward the trees. One of the buffalo soldiers circled wide around them and, slowing his horse to a canter, cut off their escape. He pulled his saber and with threatening waves of the bright metal, turned them back toward camp.

As quickly as it had begun, we were there. Horses at a standstill, mounted soldiers facing the tepees. The running of women and children among the tepees continued, loud cries of terror ringing through the air as families sought their own members.

I looked for Rebecca. Saw her standing proud and tall in the center of the tepee circle, two children gathered to her side. With less than twenty steps between us, the pain and bewilderment on her face was clear. And her stare was directed into my eyes.

I raised my bound hands and shook my head from side to side, hoping desperately she wouldn't call out to me. I wanted her to be invisible, wanted her to be left behind. Later, no matter what price it took, I'd find my way back to explain. I knew too, by sickness coiling inside me, how hellish it would be, moment by moment, the wait to try to exonerate this, knowing the entire time her own disbelief of this betrayal of her and her people.

"Soldiers!" Grimshaw cried out. "Dismount!"

No resistance, as Burns had promised. Some teenage boys stood near the tepees, clutching spears in clenched hands. Old women stood passively at campfires.

The soldiers began to dismount.

I did not.

"Privates Beck and Walters," Grimshaw shouted. "Advance."

Both soldiers stepped forward to join Grimshaw. They held their bayonet-tipped carbines at the ready.

An explosion roiled the air. Grimshaw fell sideways onto his knees. He looked down on himself, vague puzzlement on his face. He probably died before he toppled forward, before his eyes registered the spreading gush of red across the chest of his fine, blue uniform.

There was the frozen heartbeat you can expect as an aftermath, the frozen heartbeat as minds match the sound to the effect and search for the source of gunfire.

Then an another explosion, and the horse beside Private Nathaniel Hawkthorne screamed in agony and plunged backward in panic.

The frozen heartbeat ended as the soldiers charged camp in a single body.

I could only think of Rebecca.

I squeezed my horse's ribs with my thighs, and it surged forward, past two soldiers. A hornet brushed my ear, the boom of gunfire an instant behind.

My body seemed to be acting without me. Event by event, in a disconnected blur I found myself with a fistful of mane, pulling back so hard my horse reared, in the same motion diving off and outward, then breaking my fall by tucking in my arms, pushing to my feet, ramming my shoulder into Rebecca's waist, driving upward and grabbing at her flailing ankles so her head and shoulders fell over my back, clutching her legs with my bound hands and dashing ahead without pause, rolling us into a tepee as more screams and gunfire filled the air.

"I swear, I swear, I swear," I pleaded, frantic words tangling my thoughts, "this wasn't me."

She landed on a buffalo robe ahead of my face, stunned by the fall. I got to my knees. "Believe me," I cried, holding up my hands as proof.

She said nothing, only began to crawl toward the tepee flap. "The children."

"No!" My voice was far away, inhuman to me. Outside the keening of terror filled the gaps between gunfire. A body crashed into the buffalo hide of our tepee.

I fell forward to pin her to the earth. "Please. Please." I'd never felt such horror, such abject helplessness, such ripping fear.

She lay motionless.

"Rebecca?"

"I have no words for you."

"Rebecca!"

Her silence worsened the sounds of carnage outside.

Sunlight pierced the tepee as the flap opened. I rolled to my side to face the new threat, struggled to get to my feet. All I saw was blue uniform and bayonet as I stepped over Rebecca. I brought my forearms up to protect us what little I could.

"It's me," the soldier said in a ragged gasp.

Private Nathaniel Hawkthorne.

I was beyond pride. I dropped my arms, left myself exposed to his rifle. "Leave her," I begged. "That's all. Do to me what you need, but leave her."

He thrust the rifle at me. Sideways.

Disbelieving, I took it from him into my bound hands.

Hawkthorne sobbed as he spoke. "What do I do? What do I do? Dead out there . . . killing . . . what do I do?"

Rebecca had begun again to crawl toward her people. Toward soldiers crazed by bloodlust. I dropped the rifle and awkwardly scooped her up to her feet, holding her from behind.

"Let me go," she hissed. "They will not die without me." She half turned and raked the nails of one hand across my face.

I couldn't do it. I couldn't do it. I couldn't do it.

But I did. And learned at that moment to hate myself.

I brought my bound wrists up and clamped the palm of my right hand hard over her mouth and squeezed her nostrils shut with my thumb against the base of my forefinger. She squirmed and kicked and I felt like vomiting for how much I detested myself.

It took an eternity for her to settle and slump, dead weight in my arms. I released my hand from her face and held her, moving my face to the softness of her neck until I was sure she was still breathing. Then I set her down gently and covered her with buffalo robes, alive and hidden.

Nathaniel Hawkthorne stared at me, his eyes large and white.

"Pick up the rifle," I said. I felt so wooden I could not

even cry, could not even whisper good-bye to her, my love. How soft her neck had been against my cheeks, how precious to hold her in my arms.

He only stared, so I picked the rifle off the ground for him and put it in his hands.

"You owe me your life," I said. "The grizzly, remember? You pledged a debt to me." Each spoken word was a boulder, heavy and slow from my mouth. "You will remain here and protect her from soldiers. When it is quiet, you will leave her hidden and go with the rest of the detachment."

He nodded dumbly.

"Now hit me," I said.

"What?"

"Take your rifle butt and hit the back of my head."

"I . . . I can't."

"You came in here to take me prisoner. That's what they will see. Not her. You understand? Me on the ground. Not her."

He began to shake his head no.

All my rage exploded and I shoved my face in front of his and shouted for him to take the rifle and hit me and kept shouting insane fury until his fear of me outweighed his fear of the act.

Private Nathaniel Hawkthorne gripped the barrel of his carbine and swung the heavy stock toward my head.

I did not duck. I wanted the pain as badly as I didn't want to ever wake.

EIGHTEEN

THE LIGHT AROUND ME was softened amber, and it took some time to bring the tent roof above me into focus. I was lying inside one of the half-tent shelters, sunlight filtered by the canvas. I could not lift my head. To see past my feet, I rolled my head to one side, suddenly aware of cloth wrapped around my skull. What shadows I saw were long, and I guessed evening, instead of early morning, because the air was not frigid. The entrance to my shelter was open to the activities of camp—muted conversations, clanking of pots, and feet and legs occasionally shuffling across my line of vision.

That effort drained me, and I closed my eyes again. Slowly I rolled my head to bring my face upward, a movement which brought stabbing knives of pain.

The rest of my body ached, and thirst consumed me.

Much worse, however, were the slowly returning memories of my last conscious moments. I knew where I was, and could make assumptions as to how I got here, but did not know the answer to the only question that mattered.

I tried to shout. It came out as a croak.

I waited five minutes for nausea to pass. I sucked what

little moisture I could from my cheeks and swallowed. I was able to bring my voice to the volume barely above a whisper.

More nausea rolled through me at the effort. Blackness pressed upon me, but I forced it away. I took shallow, rapid breaths, trying again to work up power to shout for attention.

Before I could muster the strength, a blue uniform loomed at the entrance to my tent. The soldier dropped to his knees and pushed his way inside.

I focused my eyes on the figure swimming before me.

"Ah is glad to see you be awake," the buffalo soldier said, a thick southern drawl giving me as much a clue to his background as his dark skin and broad cheekbones. "Water?"

I opened my mouth to the tilted canteen. The act of swallowing sent pain throbbing through my skull.

"It's been nigh two days," the soldier said as he screwed the cap back on the canteen. "We was afraid you'd never come 'round. We be hoping—"

"Hawkthorne," I said. "Where's Hawkthorne?" I tried pushing myself onto my elbows but couldn't summon the strength.

"With the horses." He cleared his throat. "This here situation ain't looking so good and we be hoping—"

"Send him."

I should have been surprised he nodded and crawled backward out of the shelter at my command. I should have been surprised my hands were no longer bound. But I didn't care much about myself or my situation.

Hawkthorne arrived barely a minute later, puffing for breath as if he'd run. He dropped to his knees and moved forward into the half-tent. "Sir, I've been worried beyond despair. I didn't want to hit you but, you were yelling like a lunatic. I—"

"Is she alive?" I had made it to my elbows and was staring him down.

"I believe so. I—"

"You believe so. That's not good enough. Tell me she's

alive." With my growing anger it seemed I could feel my pounding pulse directly between my eyes.

"When we left, she was still hidden. The soldiers had not touched her."

I slumped back to the ground and closed my eyes.

"Sir."

I kept my eyes closed.

"Sir?"

"I wish to be left alone."

"Sir, the men need you."

"I resigned already. Good-bye, Private Hawkthorne."

"You don't understand. We've been traveling with no scout."

I didn't answer.

"Burns," Hawkthorne said. "He's gone. We figure dead. Like Lieutenant Grimshaw. Killed by rifle fire. We found the boy with the rifle hid in one of the tepees."

"I pray they both burn," I said. "They don't deserve anything but brimstone."

Nathaniel Hawkthorne answered with silence. Silence so long I finally opened my eyes. He was crying, his boyish face crumpled and tear-stained.

"Good-bye, Private Hawkthorne," I said.

"Till I die," he said, his voice strangled as holding back sobs, "I'll never get it out of my mind. How can men do such a thing? Little babies, killed right in their mothers' arms. Old women, shot. All of them. . . . "

"Good-bye, Private Hawkthorne."

He rubbed his eyes. Screwed up some dignity by finding his own anger. "Of anyone I thought you might understand."

"Good-bye, Private Hawkthorne. I'm not a priest. Nor your mother."

I closed my eyes again, but not before I saw his face crumple again.

"Oh, dear Lord. My mother. What would she think?" he said. "I never joined to be part of this. Mr. Keaton, say something to me. Like before when you gave me the friendly words I needed. It hurts so much to be away from home and thinking about what happened and who else is going to listen and—"

"Good-bye, Private Hawkthorne."

I knew it would be a slap across his face. I didn't care.

He backed away without another word.

As the shadows lengthened, and the amber light faded, I waited for sleep or unconsciousness or death to take me away from the thoughts I could not ignore. Instead, long after the black of night had fallen on my wakefulness of pain and regret, an intruder crept into my tent to accomplish the task which neither sleep nor unconsciousness nor death had been kind enough to do for me.

NINETEEN

BEAR FAT OIL, CAMPFIRE SMOKE and the peculiar rancidness of Sioux hair grease filled my nostrils. The intruder was as silent as his silhouette, the only sound, his shoulders brushing against the tent's canvas roof.

He pinned my arms to the ground by dropping to straddle my chest, slapped his palm across my mouth and nose, and leaned, stiff-wristed, against that hand.

I sucked for breath. Could not find any air.

Just as a roaring began to pound in my ears, he pulled his hand away. I heaved to fill my lungs. With his other hand, he rammed a chunk of cloth into my mouth. He'd timed it perfectly, gagging me with no chance for me to yell warning.

My straining ears heard a soft, quick sliding, and when I felt sharp pressure against the small of my throat, I understood he'd pulled a knife loose from a leather sheath at his breech cloth.

I remembered the dead private with a handkerchief of dried blood covering his neck. The thought of my own sliced throat did not fill me with fear or dread. To my surprise, I half welcomed the prospect of relief from my tortured thoughts.

The knife's touch, however, was merely warning of its

presence. The Sioux rolled me over onto my stomach, straddled me again, shifting so he faced my feet as he sat on my
shoulders. In good health I would have been helpless with his
full weight upon me—weak with a bandaged head, and half
suffocating from the gag in my mouth, I was totally subdued.

He lifted one of my wrists onto my back. Then the other.
With quick, sure movements he wrapped a cord around both
wrists and cinched it tight. Then he slid down to sit on my
calves, and with the same sureness, bound my feet. Finally,
he rolled me onto my back again.

He placed the knife against my throat.

I could not hope he would end my life so quickly. Not
after the effort to gag me and tie me. He pulled me upward
into a half-sitting position, knife still at my throat. He moved
behind me and began to push me toward the tent entrance.
Moments later, we were outside.

He grabbed my collar and lifted me to my feet, spun me to
face him, rammed his shoulder into my gut, and straightened.

This was a powerfully big Sioux warrior. He ran across
the grass and through the sparse tree cover as if I were a
sack of flour.

No sentry called to stop us. No warning shouts broke the
steady creaking of night insects.

Still carrying me, he ran without pause for several hundred yards to another stand of trees downstream of the camp.
Once there, he hoisted me across a horse's back, throwing
my head down one side of the ribs, my feet down the other.

He led the horse away. Far downstream we splashed
across the water, up the far bank. Moonlight broke through
cloud cover, throwing eerie blue across the open sagebrush
plains ahead of us.

Each step of the horse jolted me and threw excruciating
pain into my skull. I wondered if this were only the beginning, if he was taking me away to torture me at his leisure, or
worse, taking me away to provide entertainment for Sioux
squaws expert at prolonging a man's death.

I told myself instead Rebecca had arranged this, that she was waiting ahead and I'd be able to plead my case and the injustice my presence had brought upon her camp. Vain as I knew the hope to be, it was the only way to endure this strange procession.

The warrior led the horse until we reached a small rise. He continued upward until we were at the edge of the bluff, looking down on the plains we had just crossed. Unceremoniously, he dumped me onto sandy ground from the horse, pulled the gag from my mouth, and without uttering a word, rode back down to the sagebrush flats.

****

All night through I thought of the stream which ran alongside the cavalry camp. I thought of water streaming down my parched throat. I thought of water rinsing me of the ants which worked their way beneath my pants and shirt. I thought of water to soak my bonds until they loosened enough for me to pull free.

I accomplished nothing but frustration with those thoughts. I could not reach the river. My ankles were too tightly bound, my balance too precarious without free hands. I fell on each of my only two attempts to hop, landing heavily on my shoulders. Weakness sickened me with the effort, and both times it took several minutes to find the strength to roll onto my feet.

It left me nothing to do but wait, although I had no clue telling me for what I was waiting, or how long it would be.

I gave up speculating about why I had been taken from camp.

I moved as often as possible to shake away the ants, but in the end, gave in to fatigue, and laid back on a meager patch of grass to try to sleep. My closed eyes only shielded me from the moonlight, however, not from the remembered sights and sounds of the Sioux camp being torn apart by blue-coats on horseback, and I could not fall into restful oblivion. To haunt me further, Venus grew crystal bright as it rose into my sight.

Morning Star.

****

Dawn arrived with the slowness cursed upon those whose nights are filled with demons.

The new day was first vague grayness, then a narrow band of orange, ringed pale blue at the horizon's edge — growing deeper blue until the sun burst upon my sorrow. Shadows of the low sagebrush sharpened around me, and from my side of the small valley, I was able to look across the flat plains onto the tiny cavalry camp.

Without the guidance of Mick Burns, the soldiers had chosen poorly, backing into the valley's opposite bluffs, guarded by the meandering stream and sand banks in front. I saw the picketed horses near the willows at the stream, saw solitary figures, small and dark against the gray-green of the sage between us.

I looked at those horses again. If the Sioux intruder had been able to take me from camp, he certainly could have taken some, if not all of the horses. Nothing was more important to the Sioux than the status given by stolen horses. Why leave behind such wealth?

I saw the answer before the sun lifted itself completely clear of the horizon. And when I saw the answer, I tried to scream warning across the distance between us.

Wasted effort. My throat was too raw from lack of water to make sound. The approaching warriors were too close and moving too quickly for any warning, well-sounded or not, to help the soldiers.

They came from the downstream direction, maybe a dozen of them spread across the plains as they galloped. They came from the upstream direction, another dozen, closing in the pincer at full speed. And on top of the bluffs behind the soldiers, I saw the rising figures of more Sioux outlined against the sky.

Rifle shots from within the camp told me that finally someone had spotted the Sioux. But the detachment was trapped. Along with daylight, retaliation had arrived for the Sioux women and children slaughtered two days earlier. I expected all the soldiers would be dead within the hour.

I was wrong.

The Sioux on the flat plains rode back and forth just outside of rifle range, screaming and taunting, drawing unsuccessful rifle fire from the trapped soldiers. The warriors above the camp fired sporadic shots downward, each volley returned by a handful of shots from the soldiers.

It did not take long to understand the Sioux warriors' strategy. They intended to run the soldiers short of ammunition. The Sioux would not be content with simply shooting the soldiers dead, but wanted to ride in and savage them.

I wondered how many of the soldiers in the camp were experienced enough to recognize the situation and would pull a lace from one of their boots. In the growing viciousness traded by both sides of the Indian Wars, it had become the established veteran's way to the mercy of a quick, self-administered death—looping one end of the lace around the trigger of the rifle, another to his toe.

The sun rose.

One soldier made a dash to the stream. He was gunned down halfway there.

Noon arrived. I was frantic with thirst, agonized with cramps, half-crazed by the ache of my skull. But I was not facing Sioux warriors who wanted to kill me as horribly as a man can die.

It was mid-afternoon when the Sioux swarmed the camp. Lying on the ground, exhausted, I turned my head away. I knew, however, for as long as I was alive to fear my memories of Rebecca's camp, I too would be unable to escape this battle, for there was nothing I could do to close my ears to the screams and cries lashing out across the desert dryness.

Finally, far too much later, the only noise to reach me was the sighing wind.

I struggled to sit. My tongue was a blanket of wool sucking all moisture from the roof of my mouth. I began to buckle with agonizing muscle cramps.

Was this the way I would be punished? Abandoned to die over a period of days?

I wondered if I were hallucinating to see, out of the haze below, the approach of a single Sioux warrior on horseback, leading a horse. He came out of the shimmering heat and slowly up the bluff toward me. I fought to my feet and waited, weaving to keep my balance.

He was expressionless, his bronzed muscles coated with the gleam of sweat. Yellow paint ringed his eyes; a medicine bag hung by leather cord over his shoulders. I did not know if he was the one who had taken me here beneath the moon's light.

Behind him his war pony, painted with the red circles and black dots for fortune in battle. Beside his pony was the saddled horse I recognized as mine.

The Sioux warrior wordlessly hopped from his pony. He whipped loose a Bowie knife and advanced upon me. With his other hand, he pushed me. I tottered and thumped heavily onto my back.

He cut the rawhide cord from my feet first. Then he cut loose my hands.

Still wordless, he reached into his medicine bag. He pulled loose a folded piece of paper and dropped it onto my chest.

Moments later, he was riding away again, leaving me with my horse and a one-page letter.

TWENTY

I *STRIPPED TO MY SKIN* and dropped into a pool at the stream's bend. Late-afternoon sun still sweltered, and the water brought relief, but no comfort. I drank greedily, straining the water through my handkerchief, and found no joy to be alive. I moved to the stream's edge, sat in the shallow water, and rubbed circulation into my wrists and ankles. Instead of taking pleasure in the sensations, I pained myself with the memory of a sudden summer storm on the heat-crackled plains of Nebraska and how I had danced alongside Rebecca in the lashing rain.

If I believed the passage of time could alter the words of Rebecca's neatly curled handwriting on the letter in my shirt pocket, I would have waited forever to return to the clothes draped over my saddle.

Earlier, with the warrior's departure, I'd trembled to open the letter, afraid it was from Rebecca, afraid it was not. Parched, cramped, and ready to collapse in the open sun, I'd read the words now burned into my mind.

To Samuel Keaton. Red Cloud has decreed your death should you return to Sioux lands. Nor can I ever live with you.

Go, and do not return.
Rebecca Montcalm.

A cold note. Formal. Distant. Written from across a gulf of betrayal and death. She was gone as surely as if I had killed her instead of our love.

I remained in the water until the sun fell behind the bluffs. Shaking chills drove me from the stream, and I dressed, unsaddled my horse, and wrapped myself in a blanket. I sat with my back against a large, sandstone boulder.

Where was God?

Downstream were the mutilated bodies of soldiers I might have been able to save from death had I listened to the pleas of Private Nathaniel Hawkthorne. For even the most ignorant scout would have guessed the Sioux to be on our tracks and bent for revenge. When I'd dismissed Hawkthorne so coldly, there had still been enough daylight for me to leave the tent, inform them of the danger, and suggest a safer place to camp. By doing nothing, I'd sentenced them.

If I didn't care to regret their deaths as time crept slowly with the turning of the constellations above, I could always dwell on how the last time Rebecca was in my arms, I had suffocated her. If not that, I could listen in my mind to the cries of children slaughtered by soldiers led into their camp by my carelessness. Or I could relive every moment on the last afternoon with Rebecca on the quiet hillside and torture myself with thoughts of how much I had lost.

No fire and no sleep.

I sat so rigid for so long that an antelope was almost upon me before my scent startled it into leaping away from its path down to the water.

Hours more passed before I remembered the bottles which the whiskey-guzzling veterans had passed back and forth at their campfires. Could I find any remaining in the ruins of their camp?

I led my horse back among their bodies, numb to the

carnage of torn scalps and mutilated bodies I knew would be horrifyingly plain in daylight.

Where the moon did not cast enough light, I used a candle. I was patient and cunning in my search. Here was a purpose to take me away from my thoughts. I found ten bottles in the packsacks and collapsed tents, and I gloated over each one.

****

My pillow was a half-empty bottle of whiskey, and I woke furry-mouthed with the sun high and ants crawling across my face. Getting to my feet rocked me with such nausea that I lowered myself to my hands and knees and retched dry heaves into the base of a bush. There I remained, shivering like a whipped dog, until the whining of flies penetrated the buzz in my skull, and I remembered the bodies.

Burying those bodies took the rest of day. Although the soil was sandy, I was too weak from my injuries and abuse of whiskey to dig. The best I could do was drag the bodies to a hollow at the base of the bluffs and cover them with branches and sand, and the shadows were long by the time I finished.

I took stock.

I had my horse. Enough provisions were scattered in camp to easily provide me with the food I needed for two weeks of travel. I filled my canteen and a dozen others and knew I would be able to replenish my water at least every second day. In short, since the return trip would take me through vast, untraveled, arid basins well south of Sioux summer grounds, my chances of survival were excellent. I would retrace the route back to Fort Steel, the nearest military outpost. If I pushed hard, I figured it to take a week.

With most of the day gone, I forced myself to eat a supper of cold beans and stale hardtack. The food could have been mud for all I tasted of it. Once I had finished the mechanics of eating, I faced the evening and night, knowing an attempt to sleep would be futile.

I decided to begin my journey. Clear nights on the tree-less plains do give ample light, especially with a full moon. I could assume the chance of danger was remote, and rest confident my horse would give me ample warning where my own eyes and ears might not.

I led my horse across the stream, levered my aching body into the saddle, and headed south, knowing I could travel to the end of the earth and not be one step farther away from the grievous ghosts which clung to me. I could barely endure my thoughts, let alone the prospect of facing those thoughts step after plodding step, mile after barren mile, day after day.

I pulled a bottle of whiskey from my saddlebag.

In the days of mountain men, whiskey was often used to barter for furs from the Indians. Often, the alcohol would be cut with the water of the closest creek, and to disguise its lack of potency, would be seasoned with tobacco, red chiles, or even snake heads. The Indians, knowing this, would spit a mouthful of booze on a fire. If the booze proved itself as fire water by flaring the flames, the Indians would accept it.

I took a gulp of this whiskey and saluted those dead veterans for their discerning trading skills. Definitely fire water.

This time, however, I refrained from guzzling. I did not want to fall unconscious from my horse and again wake up to a high sun and ants on my face.

Instead, I took another few gulps and cradled the bottle for a couple of miles. A pleasing numbness pushed against my temples as I rode. I gave the numbness full concentration; when it threatened to subside an hour later, I swallowed another large mouthful of whiskey.

Over the next days, I took pride in refining my ability to judge exactly how much whiskey at exactly what intervals would maintain the wonderful core of numbness without severely blurring my vision or knocking me from the saddle.

I reached Fort Steele just before my whiskey supply gave out.

TWENTY-ONE

I LOOPED MY HORSE'S REINS over a post, and moved up to the shade of the veranda. An earnest, young private, barely more than a skinny boy, stepped in front of the doorway and blocked my entrance to the colonel's quarters. They all seemed earnest and young and skinny, parading about the grounds in full uniform.

"I wish to speak to your commanding officer."

"See the quartermaster for civilian matters." He wrinkled his nose and tightened his lips. "I recommend you clean up first."

He held his rifle crossways in both hands, as if it were a pole he'd use to push me away. I grabbed the rifle, twisted it upward, and walked toward him, forcing him backward through the doorway, keeping myself close enough that he couldn't do me any damage unless he let go of the rifle we shared.

"I recommend you take yourself less seriously," I said. If he had any brains, he would have stomped on my foot with his boot heel and thrown a punch into my face. It was what I wanted to do to him but didn't feel it worth any time in the stockade.

He strained to push me back out of the office. Still gripping the rifle with my left hand, I dropped my right hand and grabbed his belt. I lifted rifle and belt, not strong enough to take him off the ground, but able to bring him onto his toes.

I looked over his shoulder. Colonel Lawson was at his desk, squinting upward with an annoyed expression.

"North of here on the Bighorn you'll find the bodies of most of Detachment E, Fifth Cavalry," I told the man. "Sioux got them roughly a week back."

I let go of the skinny soldier.

"If you want to know more," I continued to the colonel, "you'll ask this buck private to quit waving his rifle."

"Dismissed," the colonel said wearily to the private, who straightened his uniform and saluted before marching out.

"Who are you?"

"Samuel Keaton."

On his shiny desk, an open diary. An ink bottle. Nothing else. The colonel set his quill down, stood, and surveyed me from head to foot.

"You stink of whiskey." He was solid in his uniform, bald, with a beak of a nose and cold, blue eyes.

I moved to a map above a chair at the opposite wall. With the point of my knife I scratched at the paper. "Here's where you'll find the bodies. I marked a trail any of your scouts can follow."

I turned to face him. "Now, if you don't mind, I have places to go."

"Not that fast," he said. "Sit down."

I remained standing.

He moved around his desk. "All right then, how did it happen?"

"The usual way," I said. "Arrows, lances, bullets."

"Spare me the insolence."

"Colonel, I am not a happy man. Don't give me a target."

"Watch your manners. You'll find me much more formidable than a private too young to shave."

"Flex those stripes. I may wet my pants with fear."

He stepped up to me and punched me full in the face. I fell backward into the chair behind me. He leaned on the arms of the chair and stuck his face in mine.

"Consider my stripes flexed. Lift a hand against me, and you'll spend a year in the stockade."

Blood dribbled onto my lips.

He stepped back. "I want a full report."

"Several men were killed on sentry duty. The commanding officer suspected Sioux warriors and led a raid on one of the Sioux camps up near the Yellowstone while the braves were out on a hunt." I recited the words in a bored monotone. "All the women and children were slaughtered. Sioux warriors tracked down the detachment and took revenge."

"How do you know this?"

"I was one of the detachment scouts. Until I resigned over the c.o.'s insistence on raiding the Sioux camp. By the time I got back to the detachment, it was far too late. The soldiers were dead."

The colonel watched my face for long minutes.

I finally closed my eyes. He could believe it or not. Although it wasn't the entire truth, who was there to disagree with me?

Something touched me on the shoulder. I opened my eyes to see him offering me a handkerchief.

"Sam Keaton," he mused. "Seems to me there was a marshal by the name of Keaton. Out of Laramie."

"Was," I said. I handed back the handkerchief unused, caked blood being the least of my worries.

I stood.

"There will be a formal inquest," the colonel said. "You'll be required to testify. I know there's more to it than you've explained."

I shrugged.

"Where will we find you?" Lawson asked.

I shrugged.

"Perhaps house arrest will ensure your presence," he said.

I snorted. "Nice bluff. You'd need charges."

"I'll come up with something."

I'd had hours upon hours in the saddle to anticipate all possible variances to this entire conversation. "Nothing close to legitimate," I said. "Survivor returns to report and gets jailed? The newspapers will love taking apart your career."

He studied me further.

I recalled how that pleasing numbness had served me throughout the days of travel and smiled inside at my craftiness.

"Arrange for my accommodations at the Grand Hotel in Rawlins," I said, referring to the next town down the Union Pacific line, some fifteen miles west of this outpost. "You'll have me nearby as long as you need."

He sighed and returned to his desk. "I'll see to it." He continued, more to himself than to me. "Disbursements will come out of Fort Sanders anyway. Colonel Crozier can worry about it—running that detachment out on a fool's errand without clearing it through Washington first."

TWENTY-TWO

MISTER, WHAT'S YOUR POISON?"
I was leaning on the saloon bar, the voice coming from beside my left shoulder. I turned to regard a tall, dark-haired man, dapper with bow tie, wearing a white shirt hardly creased or specked with dirt, rich purple vest, and black jacket with tails. He was smiling and showed strong, white teeth below a trimmed moustache.

"What I got now is fine," I told him and resumed staring at an angle into the mirror ahead of me. It gave me a fine view of the rest of the saloon, because I refused to look into my own face. The room held probably fifteen tables all told, a half dozen dance girls trying their luck at the tables, and a couple good-sized poker games, one from which this stranger had just stood.

Cigar smoke fogged the air, of course, and the back edge of the room was hazy to me. My view was getting hazier with each passing minute too, but blame for the added haze belonged to the tumbler glass in front of me.

"The way you been sucking it back," he said, "your drink won't be fine for long."

I slowly moved my gaze back to his handsome, unscarred

face. He watched me in return without the slightest sign of ill-ease.

"You're probably forced to move from town to town plenty often," I said. I hadn't gotten to the point where my tongue stumbled over words, but I knew I was verging on it.

He squinted at me.

"Your eyes," I said. "One brown and one blue. Not many men have such a distinctive attribute."

It felt so good to roll my tongue successfully over the phrase, I said it again. "Yes, Sir, a very distinctive attribute."

I swallowed back a burp and continued. "In your profession, you probably find that a disadvantage." The air in my stomach was persistent and found its way out through a hiccup.

"Hence," I said, "the need to move from town to town."

I drained my tumbler and motioned for the barkeep to refill it.

Mr. Handsome moved closer to me and grabbed my left elbow. "Why don't you explain yourself," he said in a quiet voice.

I smiled and reached around with my right hand and dug my fingers into his biceps and squeezed as hard as I could. "Why don't you move back some? I don't crowd easy. Especially in my present mood."

His face whitened, and he let go of my elbow.

I took another gulp of whiskey and leisurely turned to face him square. "Not much to explain," I said. "Changing the way you dress or the shave won't ever hide your eyes. And from what I've been watching in the mirror, you're too smart and too cautious to risk staying put long enough for those lambs to hazard any suspicions about the methods you use to fleece them."

"If you're accusing me of cheating in poker—"

"I'll accuse you louder if you care. And in the same loud voice I'll explain to those cowboys about the little rig you got stitched into your vest. Or maybe I'll suggest they ask for a close look at the matchbox you had resting beside you on the table. I reckon then you'll discover exactly how fighting mean those poor lambs get when they're riled."

His eyes narrowed. I watched his shoulders closely. Were he to make a move with the sleeve derringer I was certain he carried, the first move would come from there. I'd have to decide though, whether I cared enough to defend myself.

Instead of pulling a gun, he forced a smile back onto his face. "What is it you want? Half the winnings?"

I considered it briefly. Compared to letting those soldiers die, compared to the stupidity which had led to slaughter at Rebecca's camp, accepting tainted money had the significance of a mosquito on a buffalo's hind end.

"I just want peace," I finally said. He probably thought I simply meant for him to go away.

He poured a little more sunshine into his grin. "How'd you figure me from over here on your stool? Especially since I've hardly been here a half hour since sundown."

"Save your charm for a dance girl." I put my elbows back on the bar and stared into the mirror beyond me again.

He didn't move away. It would worry him to no end, how I'd seen through his game. Because someone else might too—unless he fixed the problem.

What this man couldn't know about were the years I'd spent in Denver with a woman named Clara, as sharp with cards as she was good-looking and smart.

The matchbox he'd left open on the table had to be what was called a *shiner.* Otherwise he'd have been quick to offer a light every time one of those cowpokes pulled out another cigarette or cigar. Matchbox shiners had a small mirror fit inside the open end at a forty-five degree angle. Placed properly, the mirror gave the owner a chance to see part of the underside of each card as he dealt. Sometimes shiners were rings worn facing inward on the pinky finger, the shiny part serving as a small mirror on the head of the ring. A smart cardsharp only used his mirror occasionally during a night, for the big hands.

As for the little rig attached to his vest, he'd given it away by shifting in his chair before raking in a big pot, casually bending and stretching his left leg a couple of times as if uncomfortable. His coat and vest machine was a fine example of mechanical genius. There'd be a hook at the end of a thin fishing line, the hook attached to the loop at the back of his boot. The fishing line would run up a small, flexible tube inside his trouser leg. At the top, the fishing line would be attached to a wide, retractable slide sewn inside the vest. With tension on the fishing line caused by a stretched leg, the slide would clamp the cards and disappear downward. With tension released by bending the leg, the cards would pop up again inside the vest, ready when needed for a switch.

"You're still here," I pointed out.

He ignored me and called for two more whiskeys. I was beginning to understand an old saying about whiskey. *One more's too much and a thousand more is never enough.* I grudgingly accepted the offered tumbler.

"You're obviously a sharp man," he said, toasting me.

"Obviously." I did not toast back. Sharp men do not head north to get married and return with the blood of innocents on their hands.

"Word's round you survived the massacre north of here. Aside from spotting my game, that makes a man sharp in my book."

"Mister, I got nothing to say to you."

"Saving it for the inquest?" he asked. "Word's out on that too."

Again, I found myself turning to face him squarely. His face wasn't as clear to me as it had been a few drinks earlier.

"You a journalist or a cardsharp?"

He laughed. "Just a man looking for conversation."

"Tell you what." More air pushed from inside, and I didn't care enough any more to squelch the burp. "I don't care to make murder a topic of conversation. You got that straight?"

"Murder?"

I took my gun out of my holster and set it on the bar.

"For someone as careful as you appear, you're taking your chances now," I said. "This peacemaker's on the bar because I'm getting ready to throw a fist at your face. You can set your own gun or guns on the bar beside it. Or you can walk away."

He did neither. He smiled and threw his own punch, one I could see coming from a mile away because it appeared he was trying to dust the ceiling with his fist as he got ready to drive his knuckles into my face. I saw it coming and I saw it hit. It left me flat on my back, the bar stool askew over my belly.

"It appears I don't crowd easy myself, now don't it," he said.

I tried to push up onto my elbows, but he kicked me in the ribs. I saw that one coming too but only watched.

I tried maybe five or six times to get up, but each time he'd calmly kick me down again. After I couldn't move any longer, he kicked me a half dozen times more.

Worse part was, my eyes were still open. I had to endure watching him drink what was left of my whiskey before he walked away.

TWENTY-THREE

IT WAS THE NEXT DAY SOMETIME — at a different saloon — when layers of petticoat crossed above as a woman moved between me and the large manure-stained boots belonging to a sheep rancher. From where I lay on the saloon floor with my head soaking up spilled beer, tobacco juice, and sawdust, I could see the black heels of her shoes below the bottom edge of her dress.

"I'll thank you kindly for ending this," the woman said to the rancher. I'd heard her voice before, knew I liked the way it laughed, suspected I'd helped bring the laughter on occasion.

"Ma'am, he threw a beer in my face. Called my mama names I'd rather not pass along in your presence." The rancher's voice came out in short gasps. A good fight will do that, take some of a man's wind. "What I'm saying is — I ain't finished with him."

"I'll finish for you," she said, "And by the end of the afternoon, I promise he'll wish you'd stayed and I'd left."

Poker players at nearby tables chuckled.

"Barkeep," she said, turning her voice toward the long, smoky mirror at the front of the saloon, "how about you stand some drinks for this man and his friends."

"Come on, Virgil," another voice called. "You done got your licks in. Pretty woman like that offers you whiskey, you c'aint refuse. 'Specially if it leaves *us* dry."

"All right, Ma'am," he finally grumbled. "But I see this snaky skunkhole when I turn around, I won't be held responsible for my actions."

Clunky steps told me the rancher and his companions had moved to the saloon bar. The dress bottom shifted and turned until I saw the pointy toes of her black shoes instead of her heels.

"Up," she commanded.

I struggled briefly, then quit and lay my head back down.

She leaned over to lift me. In other circumstances, I might have appreciated the perfume and the fine view of the pale flesh of her neck and upper chest. But my stomach was too queasy, and other parts of my battered body called for equal attention.

She flopped me back down.

"I need the help of a good man," she called.

Moments later, I felt myself pulled to my feet.

"Ripe one, ain't he?" the newcomer said to the woman.

I grinned. It brought the taste of blood from my split lips.

"He does need cleaning," she replied. "I'll pay you for your trouble if you assist us to his hotel room."

"Shucks, no trouble," the man said. "You just keep your purse shut, Ma'am."

By then, I understood why he was so willing to please her. It was Suzanne, from the Red Rose Saloon. I'd seen men wait in line just for the chance to get in a fistfight over her.

"Hey," I said, trying for friendliness. Whatever I said next came out fuzzy, and soon I gave up and lolled my head to wait for familiar and comforting darkness.

****

I woke in a tub of hot water.

"Hey," I said again.

"You shush." Suzanne was sitting on a stool at the side of the tub, lathering a brush in shaving soap. Beneath the window, in the shade cast by late-afternoon sun, my clothes were piled atop my boots.

I checked to make sure I was decent, and sure enough, she'd left me in my undershorts. So I shushed and closed my eyes again.

I was dimly aware of the next activities. Pushing and pulling at my face as she scraped away beard. Lifting one arm and then the other as she scrubbed at my upper body with a sponge. Lifting one leg, then the other. Turning me on my side to sponge my back.

My contribution to all this effort was unrestrained groaning whenever the sponge bumped hard against old and new bruises.

When I woke again, the water was cold, gray with soap.

"You'll stand," she said.

I obeyed, needing my arms to push off against the high edges of the tub. Water coursed down my body back into the tub, splashed against her calico dress. Suzanne ignored it and handed me a towel.

"You'll dry yourself. Bed's ready. When I step back in this room, I expect you to be in it and your dirty undershorts on the floor."

I took a deep breath and applied myself to the task of toweling my body. I managed without falling, remembered to drop my soggy undershorts on the floor, and crawled beneath the covers.

"Good," Suzanne said as she closed the door on her return. She moved a chair in front of the door and sat in it, crossing her arms and frowning at me. "You'll sleep now. Come morning, I want to know what's possessed you."

TWENTY-FOUR

I WOKE LONG BEFORE MORNING. Suzanne was shaking my shoulders.

"Sam," she said, "I heard you crying out."

The soft, yellow light of an oil lamp on a nearby bedstand showed concern on her face. She had a blanket wrapped like a shawl around her shoulders, clutching the corners of it to her neck with her free hand.

"Suzanne," I said. "I didn't know if I dreamed you earlier."

"Did you dream this?" She touched my split and swollen lips by brushing them with the back of her fingers.

I winced. "There should be a bottle of whiskey under my bed. It'd take away a goodly amount of sting."

"No," she said. "What you need is a hot bowl of soup. It's hardly past ten o'clock. Should be a nearby eatery open this time of night."

"Yes, Ma'am."

She fussed with me a bit more, pushing away hair from my forehead, clucking at how sweaty I'd become.

No man would have complained about such treatment. Suzanne was a dance hall girl, tawny hair, not quite red, not quite blond, and when she let her hair hang loose as it was now, it flowed like a honey river down both sides of her shoulders. She had a strong face, not quite symmetrical, and the unevenness gave it allure few men could see without stopping to stare. Invariably, their gaze would drop, for Suzanne made it a habit to dress in a way that showed as much chest as decently possible, which, given her figure, was indeed substantial. And when she spoke professionally, it was with a husky breathlessness that emptied their pockets of silver and gold as they kept paying the price for just one more drink in her presence.

Suzanne and I had really first met in Laramie's jail cell the previous summer; me inside waiting for the hangman's noose, Suzanne sent in during the middle of the night by a now-dead deputy marshal who took half of what prisoners might pay for her company. I was too distracted then to do anything more than talk, and later I was so moonstruck over Rebecca that the many conversations Suzanne and I shared throughout the winter during quiet mornings in the Red Rose Saloon had been just that—conversations, enjoyable and friendly.

Despite our comfortable acquaintance, I couldn't make any sense of her presence in my hotel room. In a croaky voice, I said as much.

"Well, Sam," she answered. "Shouldn't be a surprise to you. The marshal here in Rawlins knows you wear a star in Laramie. He wired a telegram to Jake, telling him you've spent the last seven nights in the Rawlins jail for drunk and disorderly conduct. It worried Jake considerably."

I thought of the whiskey bottle beneath my bed and how it would get rid of the sweat on my brow and the throbbing in my skull.

"Jake didn't feel it was proper for him to leave Laramie," Suzanne was saying. "He figured one of the two of you needed to be there to represent the law. Doc couldn't leave either, not with the McCullough boy laid up bad with pneumonia. So

Jake asked me, quiet-like, would I be able to take the next train west and—"

"Quiet-like?"

"Sure, Sam. You've got your badge waiting for you back in Laramie. Jake didn't want folks talking about you and how unusual it was—you hitting the bottle so hard."

Jake. Good old Jake.

"Sam," she said. "First thing I did getting here was look up the Rawlins marshal. He said I'd find you where I did. Said if today was no different, you'd be drunk by noon, and looking to pick fights you made sure to lose. It just don't sound like you, Sam."

I felt my first prickle of defensiveness. "No law says a man c'aint drink."

"But Sam, you look like a dead man. Skinny, gray. And I hardly recognized you, there on the floor, letting that runt kick you around. It just—"

"Hot soup sounds real good, Suzanne."

She bit her lower lip. Opened her mouth to say something, changed her mind, and rose with a rustle of soft clothing.

"You rest easy. I'll be back soon's I can."

She moved the chair from the front of the door where she'd been sitting with the blanket wrapped around her shoulders while I slept. With one backward look, she stepped outside and clicked the door shut behind her.

It left me alone with peeling wallpaper and spindly, worn furniture.

I let out a deep breath. It hurt just being alive. Seemed as good a time as any to reach under my bed for a few slugs of whiskey.

****

If Suzanne smelled anything on my breath, she let it pass. I accepted soup as she spoon-fed me from a steaming bowl.

"Anything you want to talk about?" she asked when I finished.

I was sitting up in bed by then, propped by a couple of pillows. I had the blankets pulled up as high as possible. Not from modesty, but because I couldn't seem to stop the shivers.

"Soup was good," I told her. "Much obliged."

She frowned at me. "Don't think me and Doc and Jake didn't hear about the soldiers losing their scalps on the Big-horn River. Fact is, until we heard you were alive, we were the sorriest creatures you could imagine."

"Much obliged for your concern."

Her frown deepened, casting a tiny shadow across her chin. "And still you have nothing to talk about."

"Not much to say. You die or you don't. I didn't."

She crossed her arms. "Your clothes were filthy beyond repair, Sam. I threw them out."

"That's one way to keep a man in bed."

"Wasn't my intent. You'll find new, store-bought clothes hanging up on the far wall."

I couldn't figure her new frown but let it pass.

She did not. "Sam, before I threw your clothes out, I went through the pockets. I found both letters."

Both letters? All I thought of was Rebecca's farewell letter. Then I remembered Nathanial Hawkthorne had given me one. I frowned back. "A man's business is his."

"I wrapped them in the waxskin paper and replaced them both in the pocket of your new shirt." She set the empty soup bowl on the floor. "There's plenty folks back in Laramie who think real high of you, Sam. And a few of us who care a great deal about you. I didn't feel no shame reading those letters, not when me and Jake and Doc found it so worrisome getting the telegram we did from the Rawlins marshal."

"A man's business is his."

"Sam, I understand you feeling busted up inside. All winter, you told me about Rebecca and—"

"Shut your mouth," I said. "Shut it now and shut it good. I didn't ask you to come here and nursemaid me."

I couldn't have slapped her in the face and widened her eyes any more than they did.

"I'm sorry, Sam."

I realized how I'd raised my voice so savage. "I am too."

She looked for something to keep her hands busy, and found a white handkerchief and wiped my sweaty forehead. I doubt either of us enjoyed the silence, broken only by drunken shouts of two men out on a nearby street.

"Sam," she said in a much more formal tone, "Jake asked me to pass along something he said you might find of interest."

"I'm listening," I said, trying to keep my voice light and polite.

"Recall that poor fellow got shot at your desk?"

I nodded.

"Jake said about a week after you left, a full-blooded Ute squaw rode into town with her brothers. Up from Colorado. She was looking for her husband, said he scouted for the army, promised to be back in the mountains come early spring. Jake didn't pay her much attention, but she insisted even though her husband was white, he'd gone native and always returned to her when he said he would. Jake pulled out the antler-bone knife you found in the dead man's pocket and she started wailing right there in the marshal's office."

"Clears that up, don't it." I knew there was half of the whiskey left, and I could feel the bottle pressing from where I'd tucked it beneath the lumpy mattress.

"There's more. Jake did some checking after she told him about the knife. It had been carved from elk antler by the man's friend, another scout by the name of Mick Burns. So Jake went over to Fort Buford and discovered Mick Burns got sent out with you and the other soldiers. Not only that, the dead scout was supposed to go on the expedition. When he showed up missing, you were picked as the replacement.

Jake remarked on the coincidence, and wanted me to pass it on."

"You tell Jake that Mick Burns is dead. Makes all of Jake's speculations useless and of little matter."

She waited for more explanation, but I stared ahead at the door in stony silence.

"Sam ... " Suzanne moved her chair closer to the bed and took one of my hands in hers.

The cheap defense for my shameful response is to blame the whiskey glowing inside me. But it wasn't the whiskey. I believe God instills such a deep hunger for love in each one of us, we too easily fool ourselves into accepting a substitute, and without love, will grasp at the actions of love, even if love is not behind those actions.

Her fingers were soft and warm in my hand, and I was so lost and lonely and afraid, I thought of Rebecca and pulled Suzanne's hand to my mouth and kissed her fingers.

"Spend the night beside me, Suzanne. It's cold beneath these covers."

She squeezed my fingers gently, then pulled her hand away.

"No, Sam."

It hurt. "No?" I asked. "All winter—"

"All winter I made it plain you only had to say the word, and I'd be your woman, even if I could only have one night." Tears brightened her eyes. "You made me stronger, you know. All your talk about living and dying and the importance of searching for what life means and how God must be behind everything. You didn't know it, but I was listening. Even started reading the Bible."

She put her hands in her lap and stared at them. "I can't do it, just one night with you, Sam. I ain't spent time like that with anyone for so long because I'm learning there ain't no shortcuts to the peace you showed was so important."

She laughed softly then raised her eyes to mine. "Imagine me, finding faith."

"You still work at the dance hall." I said it like a spoiled boy.

"I dance and serve drinks, but I don't let no one take me upstairs. Partly for you, Sam, cause I was hoping you'd notice. And mainly for me, cause I was tired of feeling cheap."

Suzanne blinked. A few tears escaped her eyes. "I'll still be your woman, Sam. But not like this. Not when I know exactly why you're hitting whiskey like it was water in the desert. I read her letter, remember? Tomorrow she'd be on your mind again. As much as it hurts now to not have your love, I c'aint imagine how bad it'd be after you used me up and threw me away."

I was still mostly sober and understood too well the truth in her words. That truth and her pain stabbed me, and I hated myself for both.

I swung my feet out the opposite side of the bed, taking care as I stood to wrap a blanket around me for modesty.

"Sam. . . ."

"Don't mind me," I said. The floor was rough and cold on my feet as I moved to the far wall and reached for my pants.

"I'm a sorry man," I told her. "You're right to stay clear of me. Best thing you could do right now is go on home to Laramie. I wish you well."

"Sam!"

I shook off her protests as I continued to dress. Down the hall, down the stairs, and somewhere down the street, there'd be a place a man could drink in peace.

TWENTY-FIVE

I *BELIEVE I WENT TWO DAYS* straight without sleep or returning to my hotel room. Sometime in the middle of what I guess was the third day, maybe the fourth day—with only the evidence of sunshine outside to tell me it wasn't night—I became aware of jail cell bars in front of me.

An old, tiny man sat on a bunk opposite me. Wisps of gray hair were greased back on his large skull, his cauliflowered nose a skewed monument worthy of any circus tent sideshow. He wore a plaid shirt framed by wide red suspenders.

"Durn it," he said, once he noticed my eyes upon him. "Weren't you so big, I'd lay a good whomping on you Mister."

"Don't let my size stop you," I told him.

He glared at me as if I were mocking him.

I, in turn, took an experimental taste of the inside of my mouth. And regretted it.

I looked beyond the cell bars. Like the marshal's office in Laramie, this one had a rifle rack on one wall, a nicked, old desk, a swivel chair, and potbellied stove. Like the marshal's office in Laramie, it had no marshal.

"Say, where's a fellow get water?" I asked the belligerent gnome.

"Bucket and dipper beneath your bed frame."

"Obliged."

He watched me drink. When I finished, I offered him the dipper. He shook his head to decline it.

I sat on the edge of my bed and rubbed my face. It came back to me, feeling the growth of hair against my palms, that Suzanne had once been in town and shaved me clean.

"A woman didn't come by for me, did she?"

The gnome cackled. "Blonde? Only about a half-dozen times last evening. Some kind of build she has too. You must be a crazy man to send her off like you did."

I thought of asking him what I'd said, but decided I didn't want to know. I grunted, and the gnome was welcome to take the sound as agreement with his judgment about my sanity.

"I'd like to whomp you good," he said to break our next silence.

I blew a heavy breath. He was going to tell me anyway, so I asked why.

"All that talk about injuns. First of all, you went the entire night through, arguing out loud like you was facing a judge and jury. No way in tarnation could I find a wink of shut-eye."

"Judge see it my way?"

The gnome had little sense of humor. He spit on the ground between us. "If he had any sense, he'd have strung you up for what you was saying. All that nonsense starting with Sand Creek and about butchery between two peoples and God turning his eye."

I rubbed my face again, this time to collect my thoughts without returning his beady-eyed scowl. Sand Creek, I understood.

Sand Creek, 1864. There had been 500 Cheyenne there in Colorado, led by their chief, Black Kettle, who believed in steadfast cooperation with the whites, and in fact had chosen that location for camp on specific instructions from the army, whose protection he thought he could trust. He trusted their protection long—far too long. At the bugle calls of approaching troops, he raised an American flag atop his tepee, with a white flag beneath it. Black Kettle counseled his people to remain calm with each new bugle call, then watched with disbelief as troops opened fire and charged through camp, shooting and slashing, even killing babies in their mother's arms. Final count, 123 dead, 98 of them women and children.

"Sand Creek," I said. "You know what happened there?"

He nodded. "What fool don't. Ask me, the army went soft, should have wiped them all out." He chuckled. " 'Course, then Custer did his best, didn't he. When was that, '67?"

Sixty-eight, but I didn't care to correct him. Chief Black Kettle survived Sand Creek and steadfastly refused to condone violence during the ensuing raids and retaliatory attacks which followed. He was camped peacefully on the Washita River in western Oklahoma in late November, when incredibly he woke to find his people under attack again. This time by Lieutenant Colonel George Armstrong Custer. Black Kettle died this time, along with his wife and a hundred women and children.

I began to recall some of my earlier rage.

"Mister," I said, "have any idea what it might be like to watch someone kill your wife and children?"

He was on his feet and shaking his right fist at me before I finished speaking. "Injuns took both my wives! First one in '68 in Arizona, second one a year later in Texas! Chiricahua Apache and let me tell you, injun lover, Apache make you wish you were dead."

At my long stare, he finally sat back down.

"You got my sympathy, Mister," I said so soft he asked me to repeat myself. "Not much sense in any of this."

"Oh, no," he said. "Don't you get started again. Last night you near to frothed at the mouth, beating your gums how life ain't fair to either side. Give me a rifle and set a injun in front of me, and I'll show you what's fair and what's not."

"Why you here?" I said abruptly. This was a discussion with no end, and my pounding head wasn't in shape for his quarrelsome voice.

"Same as you." His voice was suspicious. "Drunk and disorderly."

"I've been feeling something push hard against my ankle and. . . ." I coughed as I leaned forward and struggled to pull off my boot.

The boot finally pulled loose, and a flask tumbled onto the ground.

"Thought so," I said. "Tucked it away expecting a need like this. Care for some?"

He didn't sound none to happy about agreeing, but agreed nonetheless.

When he handed the flask back, I took a few eager swallows. Coughed again. Noted with little interest that when I hawked my spit onto the ground it contained the bright red of blood. My measured response was to take a few more swallows.

The office door outside the cells opened, bringing in a flood of sunshine painful to my eyes.

"Keaton," the marshal said from his silhouette against the sun. "You got a new visitor. Maybe this one will talk some sense into you."

I shoved the flask in my back pocket as I stood. A surge of bile threatened to punish me for the sudden movement. When my vision cleared, Jake was standing in front of me. Both his sleeves were rolled down to hide his arms, the way he always preferred around strangers.

"Tarnation, Jake," I said with the best grin I could muster, "if Suzanne couldn't bring me home, you don't expect me to follow an ugly ol' dog like you."

He dangled a pair of handcuffs in front of me. "If you make it difficult, partner, you won't have a choice."

TWENTY-SIX

FIRST THING JAKE DID when we stepped outside was to take the flask from my back pocket and dump its contents onto the dirt street.

He caught me licking my lips and staring at the rapidly soaking puddle.

"What is going on, Sam?" he said, face grim. "You trying to kill yourself?"

"Shoot, Jake. Wasn't it you once said sweat was a waste of good whiskey?"

"Only if whiskey ain't wasting a good man."

He took my elbow with his good hand, and marched me along the sidewalk. Rawlins didn't look much different from Laramie. False storefronts. Couple of banks. Saloons. Wide, dirt street, filled with horse and carriage traffic.

"Where we headed, Jake?"

"Your hotel room. Eastbound train arrives at five o'clock. Gives us a couple hours to grab your gear and get your horse."

"Mind easing up a bit?" The water in the jail cell hadn't slaked my thirst. My head felt like a split log. This walk was reacquainting me with dozens of aches and bruises.

Jake eased some, but I still panted as he hurried me along.

"You might want to loosen your grip on my elbow, Jake."

He did, just in time for us to part for a lady in a fine dress moving down the sidewalk between us. Jake lifted his hat in a gesture of respect. I reached for mine, but discovered I didn't have one.

"I c'aint believe the things I'm hearing," Jake said as we resumed walking. "Seems like you tried picking a fight with every man in Rawlins."

A ranchhand stepped out of the general store, carrying a sack of flour over his shoulder. His head snapped toward me. "You!" he said. He dropped the sack at his feet. "Injun lover! I've got a good mind to...."

Jake flashed his deputy badge. "He's mine, partner."

"Then string him up."

We continued past.

"As I was saying," Jake said.

I shrugged. "Probably is best I move on."

"Move on? Move on? I'll ask again. What is going through that thick, stubborn skull of yours? You walked out on Suzanne, sent her back to Laramie cryin'. Marshal here's got your gun locked up. I paid two week's wages to get you out of jail. That ain't the Sam Keaton I know."

"Jake, you don't want to know me."

He stopped. Spun me around with his good arm to face him. "What kind of nonsense is that?"

I just shrugged again. Shameful enough, being responsible for those dead soldiers. Shameful enough, how my stupidity had brought death to Rebecca's camp. Painful enough knowing she was gone from my life forever more. Painful enough, my cheap behavior with a good woman like Suzanne. No need to share any of it with Jake.

He took my elbow again and stepped me down onto the street. He led me across to the steps of the Grand Hotel. He paused there.

"Sam," he said, "I already promised Colonel Lawson over to Fort Steele I'd get you back for the inquest. What say we go up to your room, clear out, head back to Laramie, and pretend none of this ever happened."

"Sure, Jake," I said.

"Mean it?"

"Yup."

He tried a small smile across his broad face. "I'm glad to hear you say it, partner." He pulled out his pocket watch and consulted it. "Plenty of time. After we grab your gear, it might not be a bad idea to meander past a bathhouse before we meet the train."

"I smell that bad?"

"Naw," he lied. "I was thinking I could use a good soak myself."

"Sure, Jake."

****

The bathhouse was not a house, but a large, white canvas tent darkened by the constant swirling dust of the street beside it. Just down from the tent, vats of water cooked over fires, vats so large it took two Chinamen to move it inside the tent.

We left my horse at a railing, and Jake paid four bits to allow us each the luxury of a hot bath. The attendant shouted for water and took us behind the flaps of the tent.

A series of ropes crisscrossed beneath the roof of the tent. From these ropes hung walls of canvas which reached no higher than a man's head, giving each tub the privacy of an area roughly the size of the jail cell I'd so recently vacated.

The attendant pointed us to a corner of the tent and promised us the water would arrive soon. I took my stall, Jake the one beside mine.

My tub stood off the dirt on iron, claw feet; beside it was a single chair to hold my clothes. I groaned at the thought of how much effort it might take to undress.

I heard the splash of water being added to Jake's tub.

"Hey, Sam," he called as he settled in, "ain't this the life?"

"Sure, Jake," I said.

Two Chinamen pushed aside the canvas wall nearest me and struggled with their vat. I still hadn't undressed.

They finished pouring water, bowed, and departed.

I sat on my chair.

"Hey, Sam," Jake called, "riding out here on the train, I got to recollecting our times together. Remember the day you doctored that cowpoke's moustache?"

The memory hit me sudden, and I laughed, which turned into a painful cough.

"Yeah," I said as I hacked to get my breath. "Turned out better than a man could hope."

Jake laughed and slapped water on the other side of the canvas flap between us.

It had been a quiet, snowed-in, Saturday afternoon in late January. Jake and I were sitting in the Chinaman's restaurant when a barrel-chested, mustachioed cowpoke swaggered in, clutching a whiskey bottle, the contents of which he'd obviously imbibed with some abandon.

Jake and I watched silent as he settled at a table. We continued to watch silent as he hollered, none too kindly, for steak. The Chinaman liked keeping his eatery warm, and it wasn't five minutes later the cowpoke had passed out, chin on his chest, snoring gentle.

I'd been none too impressed with the cowpoke's bullying disregard for the Chinaman, and when a devilish thought hit me, I was unable to resist. On my toes, I went back and convinced the Chinaman to give me hunk of limburger cheese. I tiptoed to the sleeping cowboy. Stealth hadn't been necessary though, as he was solid asleep. Without pulling on his face, I managed to roll a liberal portion of limburger cheese on each side of the handlebar moustache, then returned to my chair alongside Jake.

The Chinaman finally brought the steak and had to shake the cowboy for nearly a minute to rouse him. The big man yawned, stretched, blinked, and looked around. Then he sniffed the air a few times. And a few times more. He lifted the steak and examined it and sniffed it with deliberation.

"Hey," he shouted. "This here steak is rotten!"

The Chinaman insisted it was fine.

"I'm telling you," the cowboy shouted. "It stinks!"

The Chinaman stood his ground. Unfortunately, he hadn't mastered English enough to explain the situation. He pointed at the man's face. "It is you who smelly," the Chinaman said with great politeness.

"Me!" The cowboy stood and roared. "The steak stinks! You stink! This eatery stinks!"

He picked up his chair and began to shake it at the Chinaman. I stood and without a single word, opened my vest to show the cowboy my marshal's badge.

He flung down some money and marched out into the snow to, as it turned out, the nearest saloon. Jake and I finished his steak for him, and in the evening we heard from Suzanne that the very same cowboy had complained so long and so loud and so persistently about the smell of the Red Rose Saloon, he was finally escorted to his horse and sent back to his ranch.

From his bathtub, Jake was now laughing at the memory, but to me it was a reminder of how sweet life had been before the Big Horn expedition. Jake, Suzanne, the settled-in comfort of a sense of belonging.

I stared at my hot bathwater for several seconds. Jake, chuckling and content on the other side of the canvas, maybe thought because I'd agreed to return with him to Laramie, I was also returning to my previous life. I could never pretend none of the last few weeks had happened. A dead weight of sorrow pressing upon me from something as simple as recollection of happier times was ample proof.

I pushed aside the flap and stood beside the chair which held Jake's clothes. The tub was long and deep and he was able to stretch, resting his head on the back and his arms along the top edges of the sides, one arm massive with muscle, the other horribly disfigured from a stallion's bite long ago. Water covered Jake most of the way up, his dark blanket of chest hair now white with soap bubbles.

"Sam, your water's getting cold."

I sat in his chair, leaning forward, rubbing my face with my eyes closed. "In a minute, Jake."

I wasn't quite ready to admit to myself what I was driven to do, needing to escape, wanting to run. Jake was relaxed, unashamed of his naked, shriveled arm in my presence, because we were friends. Trust slowly built. I'd open my eyes to see his easy grin. And be forced to watch it disappear.

"Word has it the Sioux up north are plenty riled, even after revenging themselves on those soldiers," he said. "Tribes from all over are pouring into the Yellowstone area. Some folks wonder if the territory's got enough army to fight them all in a bunch like that."

I kept my face buried in my hands.

"My feelin' is something was wrong with the expedition you led up there," Jake said. "Right from the git-go. That dead scout shotgunned in our office. I got to thinking. What if we was wrong? What if the murderer wasn't trying to shoot you, like we figured all along? What if he was trying to kill the scout? Then we got to ask ourselves why."

"Sure, Jake."

"You ain't listening to me."

"Sure, Jake."

"Sam, I don't like the way you say that."

I raised my head and opened my eyes. "The way I say what?"

"Sure, Jake." He imitated the deadness in my voice.

"I don't feel too good," I told him.

"Hey, hot bath oughta help."

"No, I don't feel good about this." I stood and pulled Jake's holster off the chair.

He half rose and water slid off him.

"No, Jake. Don't make this worse."

I couldn't bear it I had to pull his own gun on him.

He sagged back into the water. I'd predicted right on two counts. His easy grin disappeared. And it tore me up.

I gathered his clothes, knowing full well it would leave his disfigured arm open to the stares of strangers.

"Don't do this, Sam."

"I'll go through your pockets and leave your return ticket with the attendant out front."

I couldn't find the strength to look him in the eyes. Plus there was a lump in my throat, and I didn't want to see anything to make it worse. So I turned my back on him.

"Sam!"

I stopped without looking behind me.

"Sam, I ain't told you yet. You know how you said to Suzanne how Mick Burns was dead? That's part of why I'm here. It pulled me from both sides, half of me thinking you needed help, and half of me thinking you had so much pride I should let you sort this through yourself. But when Suzanne told me you figured Mick Burns was dead, I came here straightaway."

"I'm taking your clothes so you can't follow."

"Sam! Listen! I know what went sour with the expedition has something to do with him. The antler-bone knife, his scout friend murdered, you saying he's dead."

I took another step.

"Sam, I'm telling you, Mick Burns is alive."

At the flap, I finally turned to face Jake. "It don't matter to me Jake. Nothing does."

His arms were beneath the water. Hidden. "Please," he said. "This ain't right."

"Back in the marshal's office in Laramie," I told him, "you'll find a cigar box tucked in one of the desk drawers.

There ought to be enough money to cover what I find in your pockets."

"I ain't lending you any."

"All right," I said, forcing myself to be cold. "Then I guess I'm stealing it from you. Replace what I stole."

His voice got real small. "What I meant was you don't need to borrow. You're welcome to anything I got. Always."

I walked away to leave Jake naked, alone, and gunless in a strange town.

TWENTY-SEVEN

BECAUSE I FEARED JAKE might find me, I did not seek out a saloon in the evening.

I did hope Jake was already on the eastbound train to Laramie; I'd found a boy on the streets and paid him two bits to run Jake's clothes back to the bathhouse. Immediately after, I'd taken my horse to a stable and sold it.

I was hoping Jake would assume I had immediately departed from Rawlins, and give up on an attempt to track me down. However, as Jake was a stubborn cuss, he might have decided to stay and search for me. So I'd returned to the Grand Hotel to reclaim my room on the second floor, gambling that it would be the last place Jake might look.

As it did seem likely Jake would be prowling the saloons if he wasn't on the train back to Laramie, it seemed safer to remain in this small, sparsely furnished room and drink in salutation to the shadows which deepened and grew as night fell.

I knew why I had returned to whiskey. Without it, I grew irritated.

Furthermore, I preferred the weightlessness of time which arrived as the whiskey's warm glow expanded to blur the edges of focus and sensation and memory into a drifting contentment, strong enough to finally drive away all shreds of guilt.

Whatever the troubles I left behind with each new shot glass of whiskey slowly sipped, I did realize there was the troublesome aspect of my future. I had no place I wanted to go.

One third of the way down my whiskey bottle, I decided freedom is vastly overrated. I had freedom all right. Total freedom. No ties anywhere. No expectations I allowed to shackle me. No people to visit. No actions needed to accomplish. Totally without purpose.

Another two shot glasses later, I toasted my freedom. Without purpose, it was that much easier to enjoy these molten worms of whiskey.

I sat in darkness.

Voices suddenly loud in the hallway snatched me from my contemplations. I held my breath, half expecting a knock on the door. Maybe it was Jake and the hotelier. . . .

The voices passed by.

I realized how stupid I'd been. Any second Jake *could* arrive. Then I'd be facing complications again. I knew I didn't like complications. Much easier to worry about the amount of whiskey left in this bottle, and how much money I had left for the next ones.

I relaxed briefly at another thought. Surely Jake would knock on the door, and I'd be right smart and just sit quiet 'til he went away. I gloated at my brilliance. Then frowned. Say the hotelier was with him and they unlocked the door. . . .

It made me angry to think about them busting in and disturbing a man's privacy. I began to pace, muttering into my whiskey bottle until I finally remembered something about my room. It had a window!

It made me appreciative of my resourcefulness. I went over and studied the latch. While I did have to set my bottle down to give me both hands free, I was able to open the window with hardly any extra trouble. Best yet, just below my window was an overhang, amply wide enough for a man to sit and rest.

I pushed the window up and put a leg through. Fell backwards and giggled. I got up and tried the other leg. I probably teetered a couple of times, but I eventually managed to slide out and onto the overhang.

I leaned back into the hotel room to retrieve my bottle. Being as smart as I was, I also moved the curtains back together. *Now* let that sidewinding Jake try to disturb me.

I returned my careful attention to the whiskey, crooning softly to the bottle as I held it to my face.

I was a full story off the ground. Opposite me: the roof of a bank, black and deep with shadow. Directly below me: a single-horse carriage with a leather cover, the horse still in traces and placidly standing near a railing.

Night sounds rose to me—piano music from a saloon, clopping of horses' hoofs, quiet conversations of people occasionally passing below on the street and unaware of my fingertips waggling a mocking good-bye as they moved out of sight.

It was a fine night. The whiskey was no longer raw fire ripping my throat, but velvet sweetness. No reason a fellow couldn't sit here forever. Or at least until the sunrise reminded him his bottle was empty.

New voices broke through my serenity. At first, I believed the words came from angels invisibly floating nearby. I turned my head, and at last understood the voices came from behind my curtains, out from the dimness of my room.

"He's *got* to be here," the first voice said. "We was watching the lobby the whole time."

"Well, if he's in here, fool, you show me where."

"Then I will."

I didn't hear the scratch, but at the small glow, I understood one of the men had lit a match.

"See him anywhere?"

"Nope."

"Check under the bed."

This time I did hear the match.

"Nope. Here neither."

A new sound. My chair being kicked over.

"Keep it quiet!"

"Don't make no difference. This is the luckiest drunk in the territory. We should have kilt him right in jail instead of waiting two days."

"Sure. With the marshal liable to return any second? You best remember we was told to take no chances."

Some indistinguishable mumblings. I found all of this amusing. I was half tempted to stick my head in the window and sing out hello, just to see them jump. Only reason I didn't was my balance didn't seem too reliable.

"Now what?" the whiny voice said.

"You're asking me? You was the one who insisted we wait."

"And it was the right thing to do. I'm telling you. Wasn't nothing to follow him here after he left the guy with the bad arm."

"And where's it got us?"

"Don't give me that tone, you mule. We can't afford to be seen. Not by no one. Otherwise we don't get paid."

"Well, we don't get paid unless he's dead either, do we?"

"So we just set and wait."

"And how long might that be? He's probably so drunk he couldn't find a barn if it fell on him, let alone his room. Then he'll end up behind bars again, protected by the marshal."

"Got anything better in mind?"

"Tarnation, no! Which is why I was asking you!"

Them two was fighting like an old-time married couple. It amused me greatly.

"Hey!"

"Hey what?"

"Did you hear that?"

"Hear what?"

"Like the noise of someone laughing. Soft-like."

I listened with them. It sounded more like someone shushing someone else. I giggled again. I'd just figured the shushing came from me, telling myself not to laugh anymore.

"Curtain's open!" one of the voices said from inside.

I knew what that meant. They'd be peeking out real soon.

I snuck right below the window, then slowly did my own peeking. I raised my eyes above the window sill about the same time one of them did.

"Ey-yi-yi!" He jumped back.

It gave me the giggles again. I dropped low, hoping to try the same trick on the other fellow.

Bad thing was, I didn't quite drop the way I planned.

My foot slipped one way, then the other. My hands were flailing too. Scraping sounds reached me, the scrapings of my feet and legs on the wood shake shingles of the overhang.

My shoulder bounced off the edge. Then my ankles.

It shocked me some, to realize I was in the air. Things were coming up at me real quick, specifically the black leather roof of the carriage.

I didn't even have time to shout. I did however, have the sense to tighten my grip on my whiskey bottle. It surprised me greatly, how quick I lost count of everything else after that.

TWENTY-EIGHT

MY NEXT MOMENTS of consciousness came in my own bed in Laramie. I knew this only because in the light of an oil lamp, my eyes first focused upon a neatly tied Sioux medicine bundle on a nearby shelf.

I groaned. The sacred ancestral bundle of spiritual medicine objects, wrapped in ermine skin, had been a gift from Rebecca, her most precious possession passed on to me.

The groan brought movement to the corner of my eye. I turned my head.

Doc Harper had moved beside the bed. Standing above me, he held out his right hand. "Count the fingers," he said.

"Four. Four fuzzy ones."

He grunted. "Close enough."

He stared down on me for several more moments, his narrow, worn face expressionless. His eyes were lost in the shadows of his bony brow, and I could not guess what he was thinking.

Doc grunted again and ran his fingers through his thatched, white hair. "Concussion and two cracked ribs. Along with all the other damage you picked up over the last while. You been out over a full day's worth."

"How did I—"

"Jake. Found you in the middle of a crowd and a busted-up carriage. He says a couple of cowpokes were trying to drag you away. They dropped you quick when he hollered. He hired a coach to bring you into Laramie. He didn't trust you to the doctor there. Didn't dare wait for the next train out."

"Maybe I prefer it in Rawlins."

"You probably do at that," Doc said. "But you're stuck with me until you're healed. Then you can go right on back to Rawlins if that's what your heart's telling you to do."

I shut my eyes.

When I heard the movement of him leaving the room, I opened them again. I saw the chair he'd been using for his vigil, wrapped in blanket.

Doc returned almost immediately. "You can sit up, I expect."

I refused to groan at the pain in my right side as I moved to an upright position.

"Good," Doc said, "and don't think you're fooling me. I know that hurts. It'll be a couple weeks before those ribs stop reminding you to leave flying for angels and birds."

He thrust a bowl of soup toward me. "You'll be feeding yourself. My nursemaiding stops at applying bandages."

It took some doing to get a spoonful to my mouth. My hand shook so bad the spoon clattered against the rim of the bowl. When I finally did get the spoon moving toward my mouth, a good portion of the soup sloshed from the spoon onto my lap.

I was finally able to take one full swallow. I measured my body's reaction and let the spoon rest in the bowl.

"Go on," Doc said. He'd moved his chair while I was struggling with the soup and was now sitting beside the bed.

"It'll be all over these blankets, Doc. And I don't mean from spilling."

He grunted again. "Suppose you're needing whiskey to

settle your stomach."

"Something like that."

He reached under my bed, withdrew an amber bottle and pulled the cork for me. "Bought this for you yesterday," Doc said.

I reached for the bottle, surprised that he offered it so easily. Then, half fearing he'd take it away, I jabbed the bottle toward my mouth, mashing the top against my lips in my eagerness for a drink.

I took a deep, long swallow. The fire spread through my insides like the roots of a tree reaching for water.

I set the bottle against my stomach and cradled it.

"Don't worry, Sam. I won't be taking it from you."

"No?"

"Why bother?" he said. "If you want to drink, you'd find a way."

In defiance, I took another gulp.

"What happened on the Bighorn?" he asked.

"Nothing I care to discuss."

Doc shrugged. "You hold that bottle tight. I want to get something."

I held the bottle tight. Doc went no farther than the end of my bed. From the floor there, he picked up my shirt and opened one of the chest pockets. While I plainly watched, he dug out some folded waxskin paper, and began to open it.

I remembered what it held. "That's not your business, Doc."

He ignored me. Two letters fell into his hands. The thicker letter he set aside on the shelf near Rebecca's medicine bundle. The smaller letter he opened and began to read aloud.

"To Samuel Keaton. Red Cloud has decreed your death should you return to Sioux lands. Nor can I ever live with you. Go, and do not return. Rebecca Montcalm." Doc raised his eyes to mine. "Sounds like you lost her, Sam."

"You dirty rotten—" A coughing spell took me and I

spent several minutes hacking. When I caught my breath, Doc was beside me again. He'd taken the bottle from my lap, poured some whiskey into a tumbler, and was offering it to me. I drank with gratitude.

"I'm going to say a few things to you," Doc said. "You might believe I'm saying it to turn you away from the bottle. Not so. Because if you want to feel sorry for yourself, take whatever poison you want and good riddance. I won't spoonfeed you soup, and I don't want a friend who needs his hand held every day."

"That's just fine with me, Doc. I don't need a friend who tramps through my business and—"

He slapped me backhanded. Dispassionately.

"Shut up and listen."

Doc took advantage of my shocked silence by pouring more whiskey into my glass.

"Folks who get wrapped up in how life treats them bad are forgetting one thing," he said. "Life is about loss. Life is pain. Life is grief. Because to have life means death awaits. To have joy means sorrow awaits. But Sam, some folks complain there's thorns among the roses. And others thank God He put roses among the thorns."

Doc Harper put up his hand to silence any of my objections. "I'm not making light of whatever happened up on the Bighorn. Far from that. It breaks my heart when I see some of the terrible things happening to people. Little boys or girls taken away by tumors eating their insides. A mother of five children gone to pneumonia. It tries a man's faith, trying to look beyond to understand how God might let these things happen when they do."

I drank more whiskey.

"Funny thing is, Sam. Wherever I've seen suffering, I've seen folks learn from it and—as long as they've been keeping their eyes on God—they've moved closer toward Him."

I snorted disgust.

"Sam, what I see about you is arrogance."

"That's me, Doc."

He shook his head sadly. "You don't have the arrogance most folks hold to be arrogance. It bothers you greatly when someone weaker is bullied, you always go out of your way to be kindly, and whether you admit it or not, you care deeply about people."

"Make up your mind, Doc. And while you're at it, pour some more whiskey."

He obliged, and I took another gulp. The molten worms were finally beginning to crawl through my veins again.

"Sam, your arrogance is between you and God. See, He built you strong and smart. Of anyone He put in these territories, you'd be the one to survive, you'd be the one to help those who need it, and you do that gladly."

Doc grabbed my wrist before I could take another gulp. "Not so fast. You listen."

I struggled briefly against his wiry strength, then laid my hand back down.

"Most other folks, why, life drives them down to their knees every day. They can't look in the mirror without seeing how needy they are. They're the one's praying, 'God help me out. Life's hurting and I can't see no way through it without You.' And there's others, when times are good, they ignore God, but remember to pray in a hurry when bad times hit."

Doc stopped to draw breath, real anger on his face. "Sam, when you pray, it's more like, 'Tell You what, God, I can live just fine without You, but being the accommodating man I am, why, I'm going to put my faith in You anyway, and God, You and me can be pretty good friends if You want.' "

Still clutching my wrist, Doc put his face in mine and yelled, "And to me, Samuel Keaton, that's what I call arrogance!"

He stopped for more breath, but lowered his voice. "So now the first real bad thing has come along and showed you you can't stand tall and proud, and you can't control everything in your life around you, and what do you do? You stop looking to God to be your friend, because if in your mind you and Him can't be equals and if you actually *need* Him, then you'd just rather be on your own again."

"Let go my wrist," I said.

"And it's exactly what you're saying to your friends too, Sam. You'll be with us when the times are good on your end, but heaven help us if you get to the point where you need us."

"That's enough, Doc. You just take your whip and go on home."

"Almost," he said.

"Almost?"

Doc stood from the chair, crossed the room, and stooped to reach into his dark leather doctor's satchel. When he straightened, he had a Colt .45 in his hand.

He cocked the trigger.

"Not enough to read through my letters?" I asked, stumbling through the words. "Not enough to call me down when I can't move out of this bed? Now you want to shoot me?"

In short time, I'd already drunk a third of the whiskey in the bottle. I knew I was verging on drunk. Not content, drifting drunk, but angry, confused, self-sorrow drunk.

Doc stepped back across the room to me. He lifted my left hand and placed the butt of the cocked .45 in my palm.

"Go on," he said. "Close your fingers."

Was it the whiskey? Or had he just put the gun into my hand?

"Close your fingers," he repeated.

Doc was the man I thought of as a father, replacement for the Pa I'd lost in boyhood. Doc couldn't be doing this.

"Take the gun. Or let it fall in your lap."

Finger by finger, I curled my hand around the butt of the gun.

"Look at yourself," he said. "Whiskey in one hand, a gun in the other. Which one do you choose?"

I'd lived a couple of decades without my father. I could live without Doc as a friend. I tilted my head back and drained the half glass of whiskey. "There's your answer, you crotchety, self-righteous, pox-eaten bag of horse manure."

"No different than what I figured," he said. "Not even man enough to kill yourself the fast way. No, you want the entire world to watch you suffer. You want all your friends to gather round and try to pull you loose, so you can slide right back into your sorrow each time and be all noble about what you lost up there on the Bighorn."

"That's what you want, Doc? You want me to pull the trigger?"

He sneered at me. "Better than watching you crawl."

All my pain and rage and loss seemed compressed into a single moment. I heard myself roaring in my drunken anger and without knowing I'd done it, I felt the cold barrel of the .45 against my temple.

"Here it is, Doc," I shouted. "Don't tell me who I need."

I watched his face. His sneer didn't change.

"Fine," I said. I pulled the trigger.

The hammer clicked dry against an empty cylinder.

The gravity of my act hit me with the cold force of death itself. I found myself lowering the gun and staring at it in my lap. Only I couldn't see much of it because of the tears filling my eyes and nose and mouth.

"Doc," I said. "Maybe this would be a good time to leave me alone for a bit."

TWENTY-NINE

HOW DOES A BODY KNOW — truly know — God listens to prayer? There are some who might dismiss its healing power as merely the body's own response to peaceful contemplation. Or healing brought on simply by firm conviction the healing will arrive.

I cannot, of course, answer their lack of faith. I can say, however, after Doc departed, I spent much time in thought which grew more sober with each passing minute. Whatever faith I had was useless unless I were willing to surrender myself. The same with love, is it not? It's probably no coincidence, for faith and love to be so closely linked in purpose and function, especially with God the source of both.

Thus, I found myself sleepless into the early morning hours.

My craving for the remaining whiskey did not diminish. Instinct told me only a few more drinks would bring back the molten worms which had turned cold in the aftermath of the pistol hammer clicking down dry against my temple. A cowardly edginess roamed the nerves of my body, seeking those very same worms. Bile seemed to fill the back of my throat, and repeated swallowing only served notice of a stomach queasy and desperate for the whiskey which previous mornings had shown would relieve the overwhelming, sinking sensation deep inside.

Yet I did not pick up the bottle. Doc had said some hard things. Much as I wanted to deny the truth of his statements, I could not escape one realization. I had pulled a trigger on myself.

I sat and trembled and thought. And continued to resist the bottle I knew was patiently waiting on the floor in the darkness of my room. I could not take pride in my strength at resisting it, for I was also keenly aware that I had not risen from my bed to hurl it out the window.

Finally, I bowed my head. My tears were for me and my weakness, for Rebecca, for the lives lost on both sides of the massacres, for my distance from God.

No person can convince me He did not listen. True, He did not provide a miracle; when I opened my eyes, Rebecca was not beside my bed, and my tormenting urge for whiskey had not subsided. Yet another hunger had been answered, one I hardly realized had existed until filled. I had a sense of the comfort of belonging, that my existence was right and proper, even if—or perhaps especially because—I existed simply to continue to attempt to look beyond myself to the source of all love. To be sure, I was not looking forward to the morrow. Nor to more nights alone with memories. Nor to fighting the seductive call of whiskey. Yet I did not feel the helplessness I'd carried over the last weeks.

To those who scoff at the notion of a soul, and at the notion of God as the keeper of our souls, I *can* say He also provided some direct and timely aid. Had I not been silent and awake in prayerful thought, I would not have heard the hurried, low muttering of words carried through my bedroom window by the night breeze.

Rusty and ill-used as I was, my body tingled at immediate recognition of danger. My best guess was four o'clock; at that hour of the morning, a man can expect visitors to be armed with bad intentions—and the hardware to back those intentions.

All I wore were undershorts, but I did not tarry to dress. Not even to slip on my boots.

My rented, woodframe house was tiny. This bedroom at the end, and on the other side of my bedroom door, a kitchen open to a front parlor. It took only seconds to slip out of my bedroom to reach the shotgun I always kept in a tall closet in the corner of my kitchen.

I had only one choice in leaving the house. It wasn't big enough to justify a second door, and the windows were too small and too high off the ground to risk getting caught halfway out.

I cracked open the front door and listened carefully. All I heard was the plaintive cry of a night bird and the yipping of coyotes who prowled the edges of town for garbage.

I debated the best method of stepping out. Doing so slowly gave the least chance of being noticed, and the best chance of getting shot if noticed, whereas a sprint or dive would do the opposite on both counts. What decided me was the unwilling state of my body. I hurt so bad it felt like even my tongue had the shakes.

So I knelt and eased the door open. At least on my knees, my head wasn't where a shooter might expect, and I wanted to increase my odds of survival as much as possible.

Slowly, I poked my head out.

My eyes were accustomed to the darkness from my hours of wakefulness in the bedroom, and with the starlight and moonlight, there was enough contrast for me to see with reasonable clarity.

No figures lurked on the flat grounds at the front of my house. I rose, and moved outside onto the boards of the veranda. I continued my slow movement, hugging the wall of my house as I slid toward the southeast corner, hoping my visitors weren't about to round the corner behind me.

Another snatch of muttered conversation reached me. If

my guess was correct, at least two men were at the back side of the house, close to my bedroom window.

I stepped onto the ground. Cold and unyielding, it hurt my bare feet. I held my shotgun at the ready and advanced. It took far too little time to reach the next corner of the house, the corner I'd turn to face my visitors.

I paused, and drew a breath, straining for any more sounds to give me a clue to their position and actions.

I heard none, save a scratching. The memory of a similar sound tugged at me, but I gave it no spare thought. Not with the cool night air bringing goosebumps on my almost bare body.

I gave myself the count of three.

At three, I stepped out and leveled my shotgun.

It was wasted effort.

They were already running in full flight. Two of them. Dashing away from the back of my house, toward a gap between two houses on nearby lots.

How had they known I was nearby?

A sputtering hiss broke through my puzzled thoughts. I looked to the noise and saw a small sparkle of light on the ground racing toward the house.

In roughly the same heartbeat, I realized two things. The scratch had been a match, the sparkle a lit fuse.

I understood why the two men had been running.

Dynamite.

Another heartbeat to realize the sparkle would reach the house before I could reach the sparkle. I spun on my heels and sprinted from the house, heedless of the pain of my bare feet against the hard ground and prickles of weeds. I hadn't even reached the street when a flash-clap of white light and thunder tumbled me onto my chest and belly.

I lay there, hands over my head, as kindling clattered around me from the starlit sky.

THIRTY

J AKE JUMPED, LANDED six inches back with his feet braced wide, probably the first time I'd seen him startled.

"Morning, Jake," I said. I'd been waiting with a blanket around my shoulders.

It was morning, but just barely. Jake had cracked open one of the main carriage doors to walk inside, and the gray, shadowless light of a cloudy dawn filled the stable.

It took him a ten-count to find a reply. " 'Morning' is all you can say to me?" he finally croaked.

"I'll get around to asking you for clothes right quick," I told him. "A friendly greeting seemed the best way to ease into it."

Not only did I need clothes, but a bath. I'd wrapped myself against the cold with the saddle blanket I found hung over a horse stall, and my skin itched from straw and horse sweat.

"Maybe I should run a pitchfork through you," Jake said. "If you're a ghost, it won't matter. If you ain't no ghost, I'll take satisfaction in puncturing your cussed hide."

"Good," I said. "I was hoping you'd figure I was dead."

"Hoping?" he exploded. "For the last two hours, me and Doc have been standing in the dark at the side of your tumbled-down house, calling out and praying you'd answer from beneath. What kind of torment is that to wish upon us?"

I grinned at him, although my body did not feel like supporting a grin. "Jake, a man couldn't ask for better friends. Someday I'll repay you for your concern."

It softened him some. "Don't get sentimental," he grumbled. "I'd prefer an explanation."

"It'd be real convenient if everybody figured I was dead," I told him. "For starts, whoever's trying to murder me will naturally lay off."

I told him how I'd heard mutterings and how I'd seen two men running from my house just before I noticed the dynamite. I also told him, best as I could remember, the conversation I'd heard in my Rawlins hotel room just before falling onto the carriage below.

Jake snapped his fingers. "Maybe it was the same two cowboys trying to haul you away when I showed up. They did seem particular jumpy for men claiming to be good samaritans."

"Probably. Seems like they'd been missing chances at me all of the week before."

Jake noticed I was hopping from bare foot to bare foot in the dirt and straw of the stable floor. "Let me find you some old boots," he said. "I probably got some overalls lying around too. Finding you alive's got me so distracted, I forgot what you said about asking for clothes."

I took in the comforting mixed smell of sweet hay, horse, and straw-covered manure. A horse somewhere back in the stable snorted. A few others swished their tails, sounds which reached me as clearly as the cooing of pigeons in the shadows of the rafters. It struck me that I should be grateful for the sensations of life, and then it surprised me that I *was* grateful, despite the tremors which came and went like cold wind, despite the ache of mourning for Rebecca.

Jake returned with the promised boots and overalls. He'd found a shirt too. I brushed myself off before getting dressed.

He watched me in silence.

When I was ready for more conversation, he began.

"Soon's the day is started," he said, "folks will be digging into what's left of your house, trying to find you. Shoot, Doc and I wanted to get going last night, but it was too dark and folks were afraid what was left might cave in on them."

"Dynamite did a good job, didn't it? Even the roof was in pieces."

He nodded. "If there ain't no body found, it won't take long for the murderers to hear you ain't dead. What say I fill a blanket with a lot of dirt, have Doc and I carry it out like it was you?"

"Unless you help me sneak back in. Then you and Doc can carry me out in that blanket."

"Then what?"

I backed up and found a bale of straw as a seat. It hurt, just bending.

"Then what? I don't know, Jake. Let me think out loud, see where you find fault with my thoughts."

He nodded.

I rubbed my face, hearing the beginning of a beard rasp against my palms. The action didn't revive me near as much as I knew a good belt of whiskey might. I forced my mind away from the tempting contemplation of that dark chasm.

"A man in our office died to a shotgun," I began. "In Rawlins, you did try to explain *he* was the target. Not me, like the way we'd first figured."

I caught the look on Jake's face. "You can't believe I remember that conversation, can you?" I asked.

He grinned his sheepish reply, and I waved him away with mock weariness.

"I'm going to assume you're right," I continued. "In the street, we only found one set of footprints, one set of horse prints. Whereas there's definitely two men gunning for me now."

"Sure," Jake said. "There's sense in figuring it that way."

"I'm also going to assume the death of the scout in our office had something to do with the expedition. Didn't you tell me he was one of the scouts first hired to work the expedition? Didn't you tell me he and Mick Burns were friends? There's the antler-boned knives they both had, carved from the same antler. And Mick Burns, of course, was part of the expedition."

Jake's grin stretched even wider. "Guess you also did some listening in Rawlins with what I passed along for Suzanne to tell. Lots other men in her presence would have done less listening and tried a little more—"

"I heard you and Suzanne in Rawlins, but didn't listen," I said. "Mick Burns rode a horse which left tracks just like the ones outside our office that night. His bootprints matched the ones in the street too. So all along as we traveled, I kept wondering why Mick Burns would try to kill me in my office, but not on the trail. Say he wanted the scout dead—not me—then it still fits it was Burns outside my office that night. Of course, he saw no need to kill *me* on the trail, because I wasn't the target."

"Before you get ready to congratulate yourself," Jake said, "you'll have to decide why Burns would want a scout dead, and those other two want you dead."

I rubbed my face again. My thoughts seemed disjointed. All it might take was a sip or two of whiskey and. . . .

I stood and paced in cramped circles.

"It's back to the expedition. Burns—if it was him—killed a scout *before* the expedition. Someone wants me dead *after* the expedition. Either the link is the expedition, or neither event has anything in common with the other."

"Go with the expedition," Jake said. "Aside from the soldiers dying to Sioux, anything at all strange about it?"

"Anything strange?" I laughed, and couldn't tell in my pain whether it was crying.

Jake waited until I finished the painful laughter.

I began to list it for him. An inexperienced lieutenant, leading the expedition when he'd had his stripes less than a month. A mix of unfit soldiers. Murders set up to look like the actions of Sioux. The fact that Mick Burns is reported to be alive after it appeared he had died at Rebecca's camp.

I stopped there. "You did say that, didn't you. Mick Burns alive? You told me back at the bathhouse. . . ."

I let my voice trail. The memory of our time there returned. I felt the heat of flushed guilt in my cheeks.

"Sam," Jake said, "don't you worry about it. I have a feeling when all this settles, I can understand what you did a lot easier. And even if I don't understand, I forgave you when it happened."

I really wanted whiskey.

Jake didn't let the silence build. "You're right. I told you back in the bathhouse that Mick Burns was still alive. He was seen in a Cheyenne camp on the grasslands north of old Fort Caspar."

I sighed. "Then add that to the list of what was strange about the expedition."

I snapped my fingers. "That, and what the colonel at Fort Steele said."

"What's that?"

"Understand whiskey might have been clogging my ears."

"I'll understand."

"He said disbursements for inquest expenses should come out of Fort Sanders, as Colonel Crozier had run the detachment out on a fool's errand without clearing it through Washington first."

I saw by Jake's widening eyes he understood.

"You asked me what next," I said. "Since I'm dead, how about you find out what you can about the expedition? Either from Crozier at Fort Sanders, or from someone willing to talk about it."

"Do I get double pay? After all, dead as you are, you

won't be drawing none."

"Sure," I said, "long as you pay back all the wages you collected from the town while playing poker at the Red Rose."

Jake decided it was a good moment to turn our attention to the details of sneaking me into the wreckage of my rented house. He also promised to drag the blanket gentle as he pulled me out.

He eventually noticed I was frowning as he spoke.

"I didn't play *that* much poker on town time," he said.

"It's Mick Burns," I said. "After you talk to Colonel Crozier, I should find out what I can from Burns."

"But he's up north of Fort Caspar. That's dangerous close to Sioux territory," Jake said. "The way they're riled, only a fool would go up there."

"Well, I know a fool we can send," I told Jake. "It's the same fool who could really use a drink of whiskey right now."

He tensed.

"But if you were to bring some coffee by instead," I finished, "I'd be more than grateful."

THIRTY-ONE

FAKING MY DEATH proved simple. Jake hid me in a carriage and parked it near the remains of the collapsed house. Daylight showed that bundles of dynamite had been planted not only at the back near my bedroom window, but at each side of the house. There was no way I would have survived the blasts.

While I waited in the carriage, Jake and Doc pretended to search among the beams and broken plaster, clearing their way close to where my bedroom had been. By then—an hour into the day—a small number of curiosity seekers had gathered to watch, while others attempted to move rubble near where the parlor had been.

Jake and I had debated which diversion might be best, shooting or a fire. The wind decided it for us. It blew away from Laramie and toward the river—ideal conditions for a grass fire which would not pose any danger to the town.

Suzanne lit it for us, and while the few dozen people around the ruined house stampeded toward the fire, I pulled a coat high around my face and stepped outside. Jake and Doc had created a small tunnel for me, and I crawled toward my broken bed. Once I was past any obvious sight lines, I rolled onto my back and pulled some boards across my belly.

For much of my wait, I fought nausea.

Doc had warned me it would be tough, pulling back from the whiskey so abruptly. He'd also glared and told me to be grateful I had only done weeks of damage to my body instead of years or decades; the withdrawal would have been that much worse. Gratitude was difficult to muster, however, when eggs and ham and coffee swelled my belly and fought to rise into my throat. Chills came and went, and the slightest noise made me quiver.

Worse were thoughts of Rebecca which I could not escape. Where was she now? What did she think of me? Why had I been banished so thoroughly without a chance to defend myself? Happy memories sprang upon me unasked. I would close my eyes and catch a glimpse of her smile, feel breeze against my face and remember her warmth on the hillside. I could not shut out her soft voice, the light touch of her fingers, the smell of her skin, and how I'd ached with joy to be kissing the small hollows of her neck. If I tried to hold the bitter sweetness of those memories, however, I would see her trying to crawl from the tepee and again remember how she had squirmed and kicked while I'd pinched her mouth and nostrils against life-giving breath. From there, the rest would flood me, for the screams of the dying children would echo in my head, followed by the savage butchery of soldiers which I'd witnessed, helpless, from afar.

I've heard optimists blithely say the darkest hour only holds sixty minutes. These simpletons have never been strangled by their own memories, never felt the imprisonment of soul within body. During the darkest hours, time is not measured by minutes, minutes are not measured by seconds. Instead, time is measured by the slow, dripping blackness of despair.

I did not even have action to distract me. I could only lie there in the shattered house, listening to my heart thud strongly, telling me with mocking certainty that my escape from the prison of despair would not be easily granted.

Dark, raging desires for my own destruction began to overwhelm me, began to screech along with my nerves for the soothing warmth of a tumbler of whiskey. Only when in my memory I felt again the terrible, jarring click of hammer against revolver against the bone of my temple, did I stop licking my lips in the hope of the taste of whiskey.

By the time Doc and Jake returned with the babble of the crowd, my sweat had absorbed the dust of plaster around me and clumped itself into tiny balls of dough on my forehead and neck.

Jake reached me first. He shouted over his shoulder for Doc to bring a blanket.

I lay still while they dragged me loose, and I tried to pretend I was a rag doll, far away from the clamor of this world. Jake called for two bystanders to help. I was rolled into the middle of the blanket, and the men each held an end and carried me, unconcerned about how I swung between them. Jake arranged for the blanket to fall open and show part of my face, knowing how quickly it would pass through town, talk of the discovery of my body and of that final glimpse of the unfortunate marshal.

Away from the house, Doc gave instructions for me to be set down on open ground. He lifted the blanket away and placed his fingers against my neck. They were warm fingers, solid and reassuring, even as he pronounced my death above me.

"It doesn't look good, Jake," he said grimly for the benefit of those nearby. "No pulse."

I heard the murmurs. Jake told me later all the men removed their hats at Doc's verdict.

Doc had the men carry me to the carriage which I'd so recently vacated. It didn't help my mood when one of them banged my head against the carriage door.

The carriage door closed upon me, and Doc flicked the reins for the horse to carry us away to my upcoming funeral.

****

Suzanne, a swirl of dress and lace and perfume, shut the door quickly behind her.

"How are you resting?" she whispered.

I was resting fine and quietly told her so. My hideout was her room above the Red Rose Saloon. She'd taken pains to hide the roughness of the cheap plank walls by hanging large sheets of cloth gaily decorated with flowers. Near her chair, she turned an empty apple crate upside down, and covered the top of it with a large doily. It served as a low table to hold a lamp. Her four-poster bed was covered with layers and layers of blankets and pillows stacked three high. I'd been able to sleep a few hours, grateful for the regular morning silence of the saloon below.

"Jake's gone over to Fort Sanders?"

She nodded but didn't look me long in the face.

"It's kind of you to let me rest here," I said to break the awkward silence.

She nodded again.

I noticed one of her hands was behind her back. She caught my glance and slowly brought the hand into my sight. She stepped forward and set in on the end of the bed.

"Jake found it in your house," she explained. "He gave it to me while you were in the carriage with Doc. I thought you'd be asleep, and I was just going to leave it on the bed."

Rebecca's medicine bundle. I smiled, but it felt sour.

"You miss her bad, don't you, Sam?"

"Yes, I do."

"I can see it in your face. After Rawlins, I—"

"I'm sorry for whatever I said and did there," I said. "You didn't deserve it, not when you were trying to help."

"No need for apology. I was doing it for myself, hoping maybe you'd look at me the way I imagined you looked at Rebecca." She smiled sadly. "In Rawlins, though, I learned you can't force love. What you did there helped, actually.

Cleared the way for me to move on."

"You're leaving Laramie?"

Her smile widened. "A young preacher's been by the saloon a few times, speaking out against the evils of gambling and drink. It appears he's taken a personal interest in my salvation, and I've decided it won't hurt to let him stop by more often. Give him a chance. Whereas before. . . ."

She waited for me to say something. I couldn't think of anything.

"Well," she said finally, "I'm going to find you some food. Jake told me you might stay the rest of today and part of tomorrow."

"I appreciate this," I told her.

"You just find a cure for what ails you." With that, she opened the door wide enough to let her out sideways, and slipped into the hallway, careful to close and lock the door behind her.

I lifted the medicine bundle and stared at it. A cure for what ailed me. I could think of no cure. All I had left was a determination to find out what was behind the ill-fated expedition, and that in itself was a meager crutch.

As I leaned out of the bed to set the bundle on the floor, I noticed a corner of waxskin paper sticking out from the fold of the leather pouch. The bundle had been on a shelf in my bedroom. Beside it, I'd left the letters wrapped in waxskin paper. When the shelf fell during the blast, both must have tumbled down together. Jake, with his usual thoroughness, would have taken the letters too.

I had no need to open the waxskin. Every word of Rebecca's letter was well etched in my mind. I remembered the other letter inside the waxskin—Nathaniel's—and remembered how I'd promised to mail it to his parents in the event of his death, a promise which would take very little effort to fulfill.

I did not want to read the letter, however, not with my memories of how Nathaniel and the rest of the soldiers had died. Yet I had to unfold it, simply to find out how to address the envelope.

Dear Mother and Father, it began, *we are camped near the Bighorn, and I am writing in fear that I may never return. Indeed, would that you might never read these words, for if you are, then you know I have left this world. Please do not grieve for me. I cannot say I am happy to die, yet I am grateful for what life has given me thus far.*

I could hear Nathaniel's earnest voice speaking these sentences aloud in the rounded vowels of his Boston accent, and I could not stop myself from reading more.

Life has given me your love, love I know will not end with my death. Perhaps, had I stayed in Boston and entered the family enterprises, I would have been given dozens of years more of your love. Still, with the prospect of death around me, I wish for you to know I do not regret my decision to leave.

I never intended to be gone for more than a couple of years. I only wanted to experience much more of life than I would have in the security of our family fortune. The sparrow would have returned to his gilded cage, but only after learning to fly. Will you forgive me for that desire?

Samuel Keaton, the person who delivers or sends you this letter can tell you more about the circumstances around me. I commend him to you. He saved my life once from a terrible grizzly, and has proved to be steady and courageous since. He is a man on whom you can depend.

I slammed my open palm against my thigh in anger. Nathaniel's trust too, I had broken in my determination to wallow in self-pity. Was there any way I could redeem myself?

Please pass on my abiding love to brother Theodore. Tell him I am appreciative of his efforts at Fort Sanders. We spent many wonderful hours there together, despite my determination to resist his suggestions to return to Boston. I also learned much from him; no matter what you think of him, I believe he is well suited to take the place I would have inherited at the head of our family enterprises.

In closing, please let me declare my love for you. My love for you, and the awareness of your love for me is much stronger than any fear I feel tonight as I wonder about my own possible death. Think of me kindly. Your loving son, Nathaniel.

The remainder of his neat handwriting gave a Boston address.

When Jake returned, I would ask him to find me an envelope so that I could send the letter on to his folks. I had badly failed Nathaniel on the Bighorn. At the least, I could perform this final and sad task for him.

THIRTY-TWO

SMELLS PURTY IN HERE," Jake said with a lopsided grin as he glanced around the room with obvious delight. "And you look mighty comfortable, lying in a dance girl's bed. Were I you, I wouldn't be in an all-fired rush to depart."

"You'll notice I'm lying here alone," I said. "And it's been that way all day. Beside, I done lost my chance. Suzanne's decided to let a preacher court her."

He whistled. "You don't say."

"I do say. Seems he's been at the saloon more than a few times. Know anything about the fellow?"

"Aside from the fact he's kept a couple pigeons from my card table with his preaching, I like him," Jake said. "He's only been in town a couple of weeks. Appears the type not afraid to get his hands dirty. I also get the feeling he don't back down from a fight."

"He won't know what hit him when Suzanne's finished."

"True enough," Jake chuckled. "True enough."

He moved to the chair beside the upside-down apple crate. "I had an interesting day," he volunteered as he sat.

"I didn't."

He ignored me. "Firstly, me and Doc had to get a coffin and fill it with enough dirt so it seemed like your body was inside. Then I had to offer words at the cemetery. I didn't know whether to laugh or cry."

I felt myself begin to stumble over my words. "About what happened in Rawlins," I said. "What I do remember is fuzzy or happenings I'd rather not remember. I can't say enough how terrible it was for me to—"

Jake stopped me. "You start bringing up forgotten bygones again, I'll lay a whupping on you. I know how much you was hurting, and what you did was something I'd have done to you in the same situation. Only I probably wouldn't have sent someone back with clothes and money. I'd have left you bare and broke, scaring women and children in the streets. Now can we move along with my story?"

Trust Jake to find a way to make it feel right between us.

"All right, then," I said. "What'd you learn out at Fort Sanders?"

"The colonel? Quite the dandy. I had to wait while a barber trimmed his hair. His aide told me the barber arrives three times a week. The colonel gets his fingernails buffed and polished too. Can you believe it?"

"That is high living," I said.

Jake snorted. "When I finally got invited in, he was standing like a pose for a photograph. Kept stroking his goatee the entire time we spoke."

Jake stroked his own chin and arched his eyebrows to imitate the colonel, lowered his voice to make it sound pompous. "Yes, Deputy, what brings you here to presume upon my time?"

I shook my head side to side in sympathetic disgust for Jake's benefit.

"I told him exactly what you and me agreed," Jake said. "I was investigating the dynamite explosion that murdered a U.S. marshal. Then I asked him straight out why he'd gone ahead without approval from Washington and sent an expedition up the Bighorn River into Sioux territory."

"Rattle him?" I asked. We'd decided there was no way to force the colonel to speak, that maybe we'd learn something by stopping just short of accusing him of criminal involvement.

"He started pulling at his goatee, like he was plucking a chicken," Jake answered. "Real show of nerves. Give me an hour at a poker table with a man that easy to read. . . ."

"What did he answer?"

"Well, he went into a long-winded explanation of how he'd decided—" Jake lowered his voice to pompousness again "—preventative advance action might prove to be an effective way to disengage the enemy."

"I find that peculiar."

"Him so willing to talk?"

I nodded.

"Me too," Jake said. "A man in his position has no cause to justify what he did. Not to someone like me. Unless he's got reason to be anxious about stopping more questions."

"Did you hit him with the Grimshaw question?"

"Yup. He started pacing then," Jake told me. "Said Grimshaw showed promise, needed seasoning, no better way to do it than let him lead a peaceful expedition like this."

"When instead he should have looked down his nose and told you it wasn't any of your business."

Jake grinned. "Makes you wonder, don't it?"

"Also makes me wonder about motive, Jake. Hard as it is to believe a U.S. colonel might be behind all this, I can't for the life of me figure out what he'd gain from it."

"I gave that my own thought," Jake said. "Trouble is, even with all the money I spent on beer at the saloon, I couldn't find even a whisper of a woman."

I scratched my head. "You're making less sense than usual."

"While you were napping here in a dance girl's bed," he said, "I was buying beer for some of the young buck privates here in town at the saloons. Best way, I figured, to learn a little more about the colonel."

"I'm still not with you, Jake."

"King David," he said. "Don't you recollect the Bible stories your ma and pa read aloud when you were a boy?"

"I have a headache."

"Poor excuse, Sam. What was her name? Bathsheba?"

I finally understood. I was incredulous. "You're suggesting the colonel wanted one of those soldiers dead so he could have his wife?"

"Easy way to murder a man and not have it appear like murder, wouldn't you say? Make sure he dies in battle."

"Too hard to believe, Jake."

He sighed. "Especially when every man in the expedition was unmarried. I got that straight from the quartermaster."

I relaxed some.

"The colonel does have one weakness," Jake added. "Gambling."

"Tell me more."

"He loves card games. The higher the stakes the better. And I hear he's not too good."

"So maybe he owed substantial money to one of the soldiers in the expedition." Now that Jake had planted the seed, I couldn't shake the suspicion that the colonel had indeed found the perfect way to murder someone.

"Unfortunately, no." Jake ran the fingers of his left hand through his hair. "Word has it the colonel sets up private card parties. None of the enlisted men would ever make it to his table."

"Shoot, Jake. This is like finding an orange beneath an apple tree. Something ain't right."

"I had a bad feeling you'd say that."

"Why?" I asked him.

"I'm glad to see you back, Sam. You're a mite shaky, but there's life in your eyes and a stubborn grit to your teeth. Don't get me wrong; I'm happy for it. Only I got a feeling it means you were serious about going north to find Mick Burns."

"Unless you got a better idea."

"I don't. But remember I read Rebecca's letter. You're a dead man if them Sioux get ahold of you."

"Well, I ain't much use just pining away either. It would rest my soul a lot easier to see if what happened was more than bad luck. Maybe then I could stop blaming myself."

And maybe then I could get Rebecca back. It was a hope I was barely ready to admit to myself, let alone Jake.

He sighed again. "You'll find three horses and provisions ready for you at my stable."

He thrust out his left hand and waited until I accepted a handshake.

"Just make sure you get back," he said. "I ain't in a hurry to preside over another one of your funerals."

THIRTY-THREE

FOLKS OUT EAST express amazement at the apparent miraculous ability to locate another man on the prairies. After all, in thousands of square miles of desolate, horizon-edged land, the wanderings of a handful of two-legged creatures would surely be impossible to track.

Yet I would argue the task is easier on the vast, open lands than it is in a city as big as New York or Boston. Here at least, there is not the confusion of hundreds of twisting and winding streets leading in all directions. Here at least, one man can rarely disappear in the anonymity granted among teeming tens of thousands.

As well, because travel on the prairies is slow; a man learns it well as he moves through it. Survival is also great incentive to study landmarks and memorize the names of creeks. The recent production of many fine maps added to my familiarity with the land, and I felt much more confident of my whereabouts here than I would have in the center of Boston.

As for the anonymity a body might find in the cities, the very fact that word had reached Jake of Mick's presence among the Cheyenne in these grasslands proved how difficult it was to travel unnoticed. One of the Cheyenne might have mentioned or described Mick during the gossip at a trading post. Someone traveling by wagon might have taken it with him and made mention of the fact in the next town. Out here, with so few folks, any and all gossip and rumor was traded and spread in a great web. This situation made it difficult for wanted men to avoid bounty hunters over more than a few months. If a man didn't stay on the move, eventually a pursuer would catch up, even if he fled a couple of territories away from the site of the crime.

I was confident that when I reached the grasslands north of old Fort Caspar — and if I stayed along rivers — I would find signs of Cheyenne or Arapahoe. I would follow the sign to their camp, and at the camp inquire about the half-breed scout who wore a red handkerchief. Sooner or later, and probably sooner, I would find the camp which held Mick Burns.

The same gossip and rumor which would lead me to Burns, however, was a two-edged sword. I had no doubt that I too was in danger. Red Cloud had decreed my death, and I was perilously close to the southern boundary of Sioux lands. If politics had shifted and a Pawnee or Cheyenne tribal chief wanted or needed to earn favor with Red Cloud, I might be taken captive or simply killed as I rode into their camp. This possible danger was not going to stop me, however. It still felt like losing my life was not really losing anything at all.

****

Three horses and provisions made travel relatively quick and easy. For miles in the saddle, I could alternate my horse between a walk and an easy lope, confident the other two behind would still have have plenty of wind and muscle when the first horse tired. Instead of failing horseflesh, my greatest impediment to fast travel was the treachery of my own body, for riding a horse is work, plain and simple. Cowpokes who spend a few months unemployed always face a vexing break-in once returned to the range. I suffered because my body had softened over the past weeks.

To compound my woes, my ribs and head hurt bad but, like a loud continuing sound you could eventually ignore, the pain became a dull ache settling in the back of my mind. The trembling weakness of my legs and arms, however, reflected too well the abuses which had softened me.

The urge for whiskey came and went. Since I was traveling through vast, unpeopled valleys and plateaus, however, it was an urge easier to dismiss here than in Laramie or Rawlins. Jake had not packed any whiskey bottles among the provisions with me.

Whenever thoughts of Rebecca crossed my mind—which seemed to happen with each breath I took—I would concentrate on the puzzle of the expedition.

It did seem Colonel Crozier must have had some hand in ensuring the expedition was a failure. On his own authority—not Washington's—he'd chosen to organize the expedition and send it northward. On short notice he'd promoted a green officer to lieutenant and put this unsuitable candidate in charge. Furthermore, the mix of soldiers given to Lieutenant Grimshaw had been a disastrous choice. Crozier had reached or retained the high rank of colonel when the glut of officers from the just-ended Civil War had produced fierce competition for a dwindling amount of positions. Custer himself had been a brigadier general at age 23 during that terrible war; now he rode as a lieutenant colonel. In the face of such competition, Crozier could not be such a poor military man that he accidentally picked such a bad combination of soldiers for the expedition. Neither could I ignore that Crozier had chosen to defend his actions to Jake, when any self-respecting and innocent army colonel would have had a meddling deputy forcefully escorted from the fort.

As I had explained to Jake, however, without motive, none of it made sense. If Fort Sanders' Colonel Crozier truly had planned for the expedition to be a failure, why?

Other questions bothered me too. Crozier had not been one of the expedition members. Yet soldiers had been murdered within the camp. Had Crozier orchestrated that before the expedition left? If so, why? And who had done the killings for him?

The obvious answer in my mind was Mick Burns as murderer, wily and fully capable of it, disappearing strangely, and strangely the only other survivor. I was also suspicious of Burns because of his apparent involvement in the shotgun death of the man found in my office.

Again, however, I faced the frustrating question of why? Hadn't Burns and the dead scout been friends, close enough to share knives carved from the same antler bone? As if I didn't have enough to fret over.

Lastly, and most puzzling, were the questions of my own role in all of this. Was it coincidence that I had been chosen to scout for the expedition? If not, what had been planned for me to unwittingly carry out? Were the attempts on my life related to the expedition? If so, why? And why hadn't I been murdered then during the expedition when the opportunity was easily there? Why wait until now to hire two men to ensure I died? Who had hired those men?

Mile after mile of plains, I struggled with those questions. To no avail, of course. My only accomplishment was the gradual toughening of my body. Each day, sunrise to sunset, became a repeated blur in my memory as I progressed through the emptiness of the territory. Each morning I woke with more strength and less trembling, each night I fell asleep more quickly, slept with fewer dark dreams.

It got to the point where, I only craved the forgetfulness of whiskey every hour, instead of every minute. I could almost enjoy food again, and my hand stopped shaking when I brought a mug of coffee to my mouth.

Sooner than I would have believed possible—given how the passage of time had seemed such torture—I reached the

North Platte River. I followed it downstream with little caution for another day, until I reached the distinctive sandstone ridges of the Red Buttes. Here the river squeezed into a canyon called the Bessemer Narrows, about ten miles short of where Fort Caspar had been situated until it had been abandoned in '67. Barely two years before that, a young lieutenant named Caspar Collins had paid with his life here for the privilege of a fort named later in his honor; he had led a detail of 25 men in an unsuccessful attempt to rescue a wagon train under siege by what was reported to be 3,000 hostiles. All told that day, 40 whites had died, something I preferred not to dwell upon as I rode.

Midway through the long bend, I reached the mouth of Poison Spider Creek as it joined the North Platte River. Deep grooves led from the sage grass flats down the banks into the water, these the grooves left by the thousands of Oregon Trail wagons which had used the river crossing at this location twenty years earlier when travel westward was at its peak.

I eased my horses to the water, and let them drink. This would be my crossing too, and I would follow the North Platte eastward and downstream. Ahead of me, where the North Platte widened and slowed again, I would find the grasslands which held the Cheyenne where Mick Burns was camped for the summer. And, roaming through those grasslands, I stood a better-than-even chance of meeting the Sioux who had sworn to kill me upon my return.

THIRTY-FOUR

A T A TRADING POST along the river, I discovered most of the Cheyenne had moved north to a rendezvous with a gathering of Sioux tribes; reportedly the great camp of tepees was located at the joining of the north and south forks of the Powder River. This was ominous, and seemed to confirm the rumors of a mass uprising. While the Sioux and Cheyenne were not traditional enemies, they did not customarily share hunting grounds.

Not only was this ominous for the territory; it did not bode well for me. I could either turn back and not speak to Mick Burns, or I could continue my journey and be certain of meeting Sioux.

What drove me ahead? Despair, anger. Mostly, however, I could not live without speaking to Rebecca again. I wanted desperately to have the chance to explain myself; I wanted desperately to try to win her back, despite the clarity of her final words to me. If I turned back, I knew I would forever be haunted by my cowardice.

So I did not turn back.

My journey from the North Platte took me across thirty miles of relatively flat and extremely dry grasslands, broken only by dry wash gullies and the occasional bobbing, white rumps of pronghorn antelope. I had no fear of losing my bearings; my beacon was the south edge of the Big Horn mountain range, swelling the horizon like the humps of craggy, gigantic buffalo moving with majesty in a long line.

At the far side of the grasslands, where the land rose from the flats, where the mountains ahead began to dominate the sky, I found the south fork of the Powder River and followed the riverbed northward along the base of the mountains.

Two more days riding brought me close to the north fork, and it was there that a hunting party of Cheyenne moved down from the hills to escort me to the great gathering of Sioux tepees.

****

"Despite my promise of safe passage within Sioux lands, you are foolish to arrive here," Red Cloud said, arms crossed, face impassive. "My protection may fail you among the Cheyenne and Arapaho. Indeed, some of the younger Sioux braves will thirst for your blood, simply because it flows beneath white skin."

I puzzled over his first words to me. Rebecca's letter had informed me this man wanted me dead—this man who'd led his warriors against Captain William J. Fettermen in '66, joining hundreds of Sioux and Cheyenne as they slaughtered 160 soldiers almost within sight of the walls of Fort Phil Kearney, some sixty miles north of this camp.

I had been waiting for his arrival for almost an hour, surrounded by glaring, posturing braves who had first taken my guns, and since then occasionally poked me with the end of their spears to see if I would be stupid enough to lash out. All that had saved me to this point was my insistence— through sign language—on speaking with the great chief Red Cloud.

Red Cloud spoke English; he had engineered the treaty which gave this land to the Sioux. I knew he was a man of honor, and it would weigh in my favor that I had not only openly returned to his land, but had sought him out. I'd intended to inform him of all the strange events of the expedition, hoping once he understood I too sought revenge for the deaths of innocent Sioux, he would forestall his death sentence upon me.

Yet could I believe my ears? The death sentence did not exist? For a moment, I considered trying to find out through indirect questions. I immediately dismissed the idea as stupid. He either wanted me dead, or he did not. Guarded conversation would not change the outcome.

"It is my understanding you, yourself, wanted me dead."

His wrinkles shifted in surprise. "It is not so." He thought for a moment. "If you believed it was, why return to ride among us?"

I took a breath. His answer filled me with questions, most of them pertaining to his granddaughter, Rebecca. But this was not the place, not with a couple dozen braves so closely knotted in a group around me that I could not see through or beyond them.

"I have returned to find one who can explain much of what led to the deaths of innocent Sioux women and children."

Red Cloud frowned at the reminder, an intimidating sight. He appeared to have changed little since our first meeting the previous summer. He was wiry, with an unmistakable strength of fierceness, his intensity reflected by the fire of his eyes, the power of his voice. His braids were bound with wraps of red cloth. The summer before, he'd been wearing a dark soldiers' shirt beneath a formal dinner jacket aged by dust and abuse. Now he wore a vest and breechcloth. Easily in his fifties, his belly was still flat, the skin still tight on the muscles of his arms and legs.

A brave behind him spoke quickly and urgently in the

guttural sounds of Sioux. Red Cloud put up an imperious hand without looking back; the movement brought instant silence.

"You speak of the blue-coats who attacked north beyond the Bighorns?" he asked me.

I nodded.

"What do you know of it?" he demanded.

Again, I fought any show of surprise. Wasn't Red Cloud aware of my role in the cavalry expedition?

"I know it was not as it appeared," I told him.

Red Cloud spit. I was glad he spit his disgust to the side, not at my feet. "Forty of our women and children dead," he said. "Appearance matters little with such results."

Before I could answer, another Sioux strode among the braves and marched to stand beside Red Cloud. He moved with dignity despite an obvious limp. What I didn't like was that I recognized this man. What I didn't like were the reasons I recognized this man, reasons beyond his extraordinary size and the distinctive limp, caused, as was well known, long ago by a Crow bullet in his foot. Reasons such as his hatred for whites and his capacity for killing those he hated.

The man staring me down was Sitting Bull of the Hunkpapa Sioux.

Probably a decade younger and fully a head taller than Red Cloud, Sitting Bull was broad-shouldered and lithe, a combination of physical attributes which spoke clearly of his renowned warrior skills. Thick, black hair wreathed his broad face. Thin lips. Steely eyes. No other Sioux—not even Red Cloud—neared Sitting Bull's accomplishments in war, politics, and religion. His name, as I'd once heard a white scout say, was a tepee word for all that was generous and great, and his influence extended far beyond his own tribe, indeed far beyond the Sioux, to the Cheyennes and Arapahos.

"Why has this white vermin not been gutted like a dog prepared for roast?"

"He rode here in peace, seeking word with me," Red

Cloud answered, showing respect for me by keeping the conversation in English.

"On which matter?"

"The blue-coat slaughter."

"Why did he ask for you?"

"He has my promise of safe passage through Sioux lands."

Sitting Bull grunted. "He does not have mine. We have sworn to revenge the blue-coat slaughter. My wish is to see him dead before the sun is down."

I saw Red Cloud's shoulders stiffen. His choices were limited. Agree immediately. Or challenge Sitting Bull with the certainty of loss, for the angered mutterings of the gathered braves were good indication of sentiment against me. And for Red Cloud, losing the challenge meant tremendous loss of face and status.

For my part, I had two choices as well. Speak out or remain silent. Silence meant sure death, while speaking out only meant a good chance of death. I made the easy decision.

"With much respect," I said to Sitting Bull, "I propose a wager."

During my teens, when I'd been among the mountain men, I'd seen a similar wager at one of the rendezvous they loved so much. It had worked then, yet despite the Sioux's great joy in gambling, I knew it could fail badly here. I had to word my wager carefully; I had to depend on the Sioux's love and admiration of trickery.

I pointed at Sitting Bull. "You are the mightiest warrior among the Sioux. My wager is simple. I will cast a war spear so far you cannot reach it with two casts."

He snorted. "Your wager?"

"If I win, I am given the opportunity to speak to the man I seek."

"If you lose?"

"I forfeit my life." Saying this seemed chilling.

"Your life is forfeit anyway," Sitting Bull said. "It is a

poor wager. I do not accept."

"Then I die satisfied that you will always live with whispers. The mighty Sitting Bull, fearful my single throw might outdistance two casts of his spear."

Red Cloud—and I wanted to hug him for it—was shaking his head sadly, as if the whispers had already begun.

"Bah," Sitting Bull said, "you are a bothersome mosquito."

Sitting Bull barked out orders in Sioux. A brave stepped forward to hand him a war spear. Another handed one to me.

Yes, the Sioux did love and admire trickery. I knew that from their fables, where the coyote enjoyed a favorable reputation. However, I needed to ensure more than Sitting Bull and Red Cloud understood what I was doing. For should Sitting Bull not find this humorous, I wanted others to be more enlightened.

"Red Cloud," I said, "perhaps some of the braves would care to wager as well. I have three horses. Put them up against their horses."

Red Cloud nodded, and translated my proposed wager. A dozen shouts greeted us. Then babble—as others joined in to place their bets, ample demonstration of their love of gambling. I wondered what odds it took for someone to bet in my favor.

"It is done," Red Cloud said. "As well, I have wagered some of my own horses."

I did not dare ask if he had wagered for or against me.

"Don't fail." Red Cloud said to my unspoken question. Then he flashed me a tight grin. "My horses are precious to me."

We could not throw within the confines of the camp. Beyond the braves who circled me, tepees stood in all directions. There was the usual busyness of cooking fires, playing children, and trotting dogs. Sitting Bull would not risk hitting a bystander with his spear.

We marched ahead of a surging crowd of Sioux braves.

Teenage boys began to follow, as word passed quickly of the contest. By the time we reached open grassland, the original dozen braves had become a crowd of close to a hundred spectators.

Red Cloud stayed at my side as we walked, almost pushed along by the growing group behind us. Once safely away from camp, we stopped.

I hefted my spear, pointing it at a distant hill. The line of my spear's flight would parallel the edge of the boundary of the tepees.

Sitting Bull nodded.

The spectators formed a horseshoe behind us and to our sides, leaving an open space ahead to cast the war spears.

"Will you tell them again my challenge?" I asked Red Cloud. "I will throw a war spear so far the mighty Sitting Bull cannot reach it with two casts."

Red Cloud obliged. Much hooting and hollering greeted his words.

"Good," I said, "Let us begin."

I directed my next words to Sitting Bull. "I ask that you throw first. It will let me judge how far I must throw."

He shrugged. His face showed disdain and boredom at my futile challenge. His war spear was the length of his body. He balanced it on his palm and pumped it back and forth several times to loosen the muscles of an arm smoothly rippled with the power suggested by a horse's leg.

He shuffle-hopped once, twice, then with a deep grunt of effort, flung the feathered spear skyward toward the distant hill. It carried for the length of time it takes a man to draw three breaths. Finally, and so far away it disappeared in the waving grass, the spear chunked into the ground. The crowd around us roared approval.

I kept my face expressionless, and studied the area where it had landed. For this to work, I needed to create as much suspense as possible.

"Red Cloud," I said, "can you have someone go forth and

stand near the spear?"

Red Cloud dispatched a teenage boy, who scampered ahead. When the boy reached the spear, he stopped, turned, and shouted back at all of us. The warriors joined together in gales of laughter.

"What did he say?" I asked Red Cloud.

"That he is tired from having run so far."

I nodded understanding.

Sitting Bull had no humor on his face. "Now throw. Delay your death no longer."

I picked up my spear, this one too as tall as a man's head.

"This spear," I said grandly, "Sitting Bull will not reach with his second cast."

Red Cloud repeated it in Sioux for the benefit of the crowd. They stilled themselves and watched me intently.

I balanced the spear in my palm in exact imitation of Sitting Bull's preparation to throw. I pumped it back and forth several times, aiming at the boy ahead of us in the grass. The movement strained my battered ribs. I did not look forward to the wrenching pain which would accompany the actual throw.

When I had dragged out the suspense as long as I dared, I pivoted away from the boy and Sitting Bull's spear, and threw my own war spear as far as I could, over the back of the horseshoe of spectators, far above their heads, and in the opposite direction of Sitting Bull's first throw.

Then I invited Sitting Bull to reach my spear with his next cast.

THIRTY-FIVE

IT TOOK A HUSH of maybe five seconds before anyone understood what had happened. Then the silence broke in an explosion of laughter mixed with angry shouts.

Sitting Bull slapped his hands against his face and forehead, and left them there as he shook his head from side to side. Red Cloud sat on the ground, and slapped the inside of his thighs as he chortled without control.

I simply lifted my own hands, palms up, in a classic, shrugging gesture which needed no translation. The last thing I wanted at this point was to appear arrogant in victory.

Laughter grew and soon drowned out any remaining angry shouts.

Sitting Bull finally brought his hands down. I felt much relief to see a grin wide across his large face. He clapped me on the shoulder with a massive hand. "Could I slit your throat, I cheerfully would," he said, grin still white against his sun-darkened skin. "However, I must appear gracious in defeat. Who is it you seek?"

"A half-breed, rumored to be among the Cheyenne gathered here." I described Mick Burns.

Sitting Bull frowned before calling for several men. When

they reached his side, he spoke Sioux. I assumed he was relaying to them my quest. There were probably a thousand in this great inter-tribal gathering of tepees; Sitting Bull could not be expected to know all that happened within the camp.

One of the warriors nodded several times, then spoke to Sitting Bull.

I waited until Sitting Bull translated.

"It is as I believed," Sitting Bull said. "This man lives with much honor, for he is the one who led a Sioux war party to the camp of the blue-coats, where we revenged ourselves for their slaughter of our women and children."

For a moment, I thought I hadn't heard right. *Mick Burns had led a Sioux war party from Rebecca's camp back to Grimshaw's expedition?*

I asked Sitting Bull to repeat himself. It came out the same the second time.

Anger drove the words from my mouth, when, without anger I might have been more cautious. "Then get ready for a showdown," I said. "Mick Burns is the same scout who first led those same blue-coats to your women and children."

****

Sitting Bull's response to my accusation was to have me taken to the center of camp. Three braves pushed me forward, taking me to a white tepee, painted with dozens of war scenes. I saw little of it, or any of the other hundreds of details of such a busy camp. I was keeping my eyes wide for a simple glimpse of Rebecca.

Red Cloud stayed with me. When one of the braves pulled open the tepee flap to send me through, Red Cloud spoke low and calm. The brave paused and stepped back to make room for Red Cloud.

"Sitting Bull has sent runners to call for the Wicasa Yatapicka," Red Cloud told me. "This is important, what you say. They will listen to your story to see if it holds truth.

They will also listen to the scout Mick Burns."

Red Cloud stared into my eyes. "I too will be here to listen. You seem to know much for a man who was not there."

He left me standing afraid and confused. Contrary to Rebecca's note, Red Cloud had not declared a death sentence on me. Now it appeared he had no realization of my involvement with the expedition. *How could this be?*

At Red Cloud's departure, one of my guards motioned for me to enter the tepee. Inside, with the sunlight filtered tawny, I was given ample time to consider that question, along with questions about Mick Burns.

My thoughts eventually shifted to what lay ahead. If I could not state my case as clearly here as if I were in a court of law in Laramie or Cheyenne, I would probably pay for it with my life.

Not many white folks understand the Sioux to be a nation, governing itself with structures as well-defined as those of the democracy the rest of us so proudly hail. A Seven Councils Fire like this, with the multitudes of people in a camp circle, was an annual event which drew all seven tribes of the Sioux, a symbol of unity of the people who dominated the heartland of the northern plains. They gathered in this manner to decide matters of national importance and to give a Sun Dance. This gathering, unfortunately, had more urgency because of the angry calls for all-out warfare against the whites because, from all reports, this year's Sun Dance was one dedicated to revenge.

At a Seven Councils Fire, the Wicasa Yatapicka, the four great leaders of the nation, traditionally met for deliberation. These four held positions of unparalleled honor, as deserved by their selection from among the outstanding headsmen of the Sioux divisions. The Wicasa Yatapicka had unsurpassed prestige, unimpeachable reputations, and their opinions were given paramount importance. This was the yearly occasion for these four great leaders to draw national policy and to formally approve or disapprove actions taken by the headmen of the divisions over the previous year. The Wicasa Yatapicka approved or rejected plans proposed by the other headsmen; they judged offenses against national unity and security. In Washington, D.C., they would be the equivalent of an exclusive Senate with Supreme Court authority.

I studied the interior of this tepee. I noticed no peace pipes, no ceremonial staffs, no medicine bundles, no war bonnets. This was a spartan shelter, with little more than a pile of buffalo blankets to the side of the cold, white ashes of a long dead fire.

I realized if the council meeting were to be held in this tepee, it meant I should not expect any formal ceremony. The elegance of centuries-old tradition would not soften our discussions. This was not meant to be campfire talk shared or passed on to those outside. Was this meant, then, to make it easier to execute the man they judged to be lying?

I sat for perhaps an hour. Brooded upon my doubts. Stretched against stiffening muscles. Thought of Rebecca. Craved whiskey.

Every breath brought my nostrils the pungent aroma of deer fat grease and smoky leather. A fat bumblebee dipped and rose as it explored the interior of the tepee, background to the muted buzzing of pain which throbbed in my skull.

Life had definitely held finer hours.

****

They arrived in silence.

Sitting Bull, the first of the Wicasa Yatapicka, stooped to walk through the entrance. He now wore a bone breastplate, a popular adornment among the Sioux—ironically manufactured in the East.

Red Cloud followed, a single eagle feather in his hair, and a hair-fringed shirt to show his high status.

Then the other three Wicasa Yatapicka. Older men, heavy with dignity. I did not know them by sight or by name. Nor would I discover their names, for I would not commit a serious breech of etiquette by asking.

The one following Red Cloud into the tepee was small and slim, wore three coup feathers, and a hair-fringed shirt nearly as decorated as Red Cloud's. The next also wore three coup feathers in his hair; he was distinguished by his fur-braid wraps and shell earrings. The final of the Wicasa Yatapicka was dressed in a white man's vest and shirt, a Washington peace medal heavy on a leather cord hanging around his neck.

They all moved to sit cross-legged across from me, the customary position in a tepee. I shifted to become as comfortable as possible, but I knew the strain of sitting in this manner would become more painful each passing minute.

Sitting Bull wasted no time. "Repeat what you told me earlier about the scout Mick Burns." His deep voice resonated within the tepee.

I had rehearsed my answer during the long wait for their arrival. "With all respect due to the great chiefs here, I have nothing to say."

Sitting Bull's eyebrows furrowed, only slightly. The other three looked toward him. Without turning his head, Sitting Bull spoke Sioux. They in turn stared at me.

"Do not make light of this," Sitting Bull said, his voice tight with anger.

I was well aware of the precariousness of my position. Alone in the center of a camp which held hundreds of warriors, all muttering war against white intruders, I had accused one of their heroes of the ultimate in treachery. It was such a serious offense, the Wicasa Yatapicka themselves had gathered not at a council fire, but on short notice in an unnoted tepee. I was on trial as much as Mick Burns might be.

I was also well aware that somewhere, among all these tepees, among these hundreds of warriors and hundreds more women and children, was Rebecca.

"I have nothing to say on this matter." I wanted to

squirm. My legs were not accustomed to the cross-legged stance, and it seemed to stretch at all the soreness in my lower body. "I ask for my three horses and for you to honor the gambling debt which gives me my life."

From boyhood, the Sioux learn to remain stoic in all public situations. Cheers, hoorays, or applause were unheard of in Sioux gatherings; the sternest disapproval would never reach more than whispered mutterings. So I placed no stock in their lack of reaction.

"Nothing more," Sitting Bull repeated. "You withdraw the accusation against the scout Mick Burns?"

I stared back at him. My silence would tell him I neither withdrew nor pressed it further.

"For what reason do you risk angering the mightiest and bravest among the Sioux?"

My answer was continued silence.

The chief with the peace medal spoke low and clear in Sioux, not taking his eyes off me.

"He says you should be given to the squaws," Sitting Bull said.

"I won from you the right to live," I answered. Sioux women were notorious for their ability to prolong a man's death for days. "I simply wish to depart from this camp."

Four of them—Red Cloud remaining silent and regarding me with a thoughtful expression—discussed the situation in Sioux, their voices slow, measured, and low. I waited with my arms crossed.

Red Cloud gave them five minutes before he interrupted. He stood, brushed his leggings clear of dirt, and spoke briefly before leaving the tepee.

In his absence, the discussion continued. My knowledge of the Sioux tongue was extremely limited, and save for hearing an occasional word I recognized, I had no notion of the direction of their arguments.

My strained legs ached so badly, I almost stood to stretch. Instead I pressed on my knees with my palms, hoping the

Instead I pressed on my knees with my palms, hoping the slight rocking movement would ease the pain.

Very shortly after, I lost all attention to the grievances of my body. For the tepee flap was pulled back again as Red Cloud rejoined us.

Following him was Rebecca.

THIRTY-SIX

SHE KEPT HER HEAD bowed and eyes lowered as she moved to sit to the left of the Wicasa Yatapicka, the deference and seating position both required of women by Sioux custom.

It broke me, seeing her so unexpectedly, and seeing the woman I loved—so proud and free—in the role of a subservient Sioux woman.

Her deference was even more painful because of her extraordinary beauty. In a tan leather dress, decorated with rows of elk teeth, and with a single, beaded necklace to emphasize the dusky smoothness of her skin, Red Cloud's granddaughter was truly a princess among the Sioux. To be so close, I could hardly breathe, and it took all my self-control to not rise or even speak out.

Red Cloud moved around them and sat beside me—an obvious move of support. I could not understand this, for to this point he had been neutral. It was one thing to guarantee me safe passage, another to openly take my side in a dispute of this magnitude.

"We will speak English," Red Cloud said, directing his words to Sitting Bull. "Let what is said remain private from the elders here."

"I will be the judge of that," Sitting Bull said. He radiated strength, anger, power. I understood why he was already a legend among not only his people but across the entire plains.

"So be it," Red Cloud said. "I trust your judgment."

To me, Red Cloud said, "My granddaughter Morning Star will not be punished for concealing your part in all of this. I presume that is the reason for your sudden silence."

Red Cloud, then, had guessed what I had guessed. Unless he was bluffing.

"Rebecca," I said, "what did you tell Red Cloud?" My throat felt strangled, for I wanted to blurt out words of love and apology and desperation, not a quiet question.

She did not lift her head, and her answer was a whisper. "I told him you were bound as a prisoner when the soldiers first arrived at our camp. I told him I saw no reason to condemn you with the other soldiers, and I arranged for you to be spared. I told him of the note I had passed on to you."

"He did not know of this until my arrival here?"

Rebecca shook her head no, her eyes still on the ground. "Not until now, when he found me at the campfire and asked for the truth."

Sitting Bull rolled from his cross-legged position forward onto his knees, pulling a dagger loose from his breechcloth in a fluid motion. He raised it high in a threat against me, and his voice exploded in a harsh shout. "This man rode with the blue-coats!"

"Hold!" Red Cloud commanded. Were Red Cloud a decade younger, and still the man he'd been when he faced down Fetterman and forced the U.S. military into stalemate, a battle between he and Sitting Bull would have been like a great roaring clash between bull elk. Even now, obviously wizened in comparison to Sitting Bull, Red Cloud's single word held raw power.

Sitting Bull checked his forward movement, then slowly rocked back onto his haunches. He did not, however, sheath the dagger. The other three elders watched all this closely, yet did not ask questions. They were patient men. When the time was right—they knew—they would be told.

"This white man shows bravery, fortitude, and wisdom," Red Cloud said. "He risked death to pursue the scout Mick Burns among us. Then he risked further death by choosing silence to protect this woman and her secrets. Were he Sioux, you would respect him highly."

"He accuses a man of treachery, yet fails to tell us he himself rode with the blue-coats." Sitting Bull glared, stabbed his dagger into the earth. "And your granddaughter betrayed our people by letting him live. What secrets are these?"

"Merely secrets. Not crimes."

"Not crimes? Our women and children dead and you absolve these two of crime?"

"We are here to listen to what this white man will say. If his accusations are true, the crime is not theirs. And if his accusations are true, it shall remain a secret that Morning Star protected him. My granddaughter shall not be victim to undeserved condemnation."

"And if the accusation proves false," Sitting Bull thundered, "they both die by my hand. Is that agreed?"

Red Cloud closed his eyes and drew a deep breath. Without opening his eyes, he answered. "It is agreed."

He opened his eyes again and bored them into Sitting Bull. "Now ask this man what brings him here."

I drew my own deep breath to plead a case which would save not only my life, but Rebecca's.

THIRTY-SEVEN

I BEGAN BY PAINTING a word picture of Laramie, describing its quiet streets on a spring night, and explaining the general peacefulness of the duties of a small-town marshal. I told them how one evening I had been returning to my office, armed with a cup of coffee, when that small-town silence had been shattered by the blast of a shotgun.

"Right then," I said, "I knew it was trouble. A single gunshot without return fire usually means there was no need for another shot. In other words, murder."

I paused to let Red Cloud translate to the other Wicasa Yatapickas. It gave me time to choose my next words carefully. I hoped to use these pauses wisely as I hunted for the most exciting and favorable way to present all my actions which had followed the discovery of a dead man in the marshal's office.

There was good reason I had begun the story as early as the shotgun murder, and equally good reason I would try to make this tale as riveting as possible in both words and gestures. Ironically, while any audience reaction was considered foolish and gauche, an orator at Sioux council was expected to speak as if he were attempting to bring the audience to the point of astonishment or tears. At best, I could hope for stolid assents of *how,* and occasional nods of reserved approval, yet the longer and more impassioned my speech, the better chance I stood, and I needed to use weapons of logic, drama, authority, accuracy, and most importantly, persuasiveness.

"I ran as fast as I could toward the blast," I said when Red Cloud finished translating. "Suddenly a man on horseback swung onto the street in front of me. I drew my Colt and yelled at him to stop, but he reached for a shotgun."

I paused there, figuring it wouldn't hurt to try raising the suspense a bit. After all, Red Cloud would get through translating this part, and then they'd have to wait while I went on with more English.

When Red Cloud was finished again, I forced my mind away from Rebecca's presence here in the tepee and told them how to save my life I'd fired two shots at the rider—I did catch a nod of approval from the elder with the peace medal at that—and how shortly after, I'd been obligated to serve as scout on the expedition. I was hoping they'd appreciate the honor of a man paying his debts.

I told them it turned out I was replacing the man who'd been shot at my desk, and how I wished I knew it then, for I would have realized much earlier that this would be no ordinary expedition.

I continued my narration, pausing at the spots I hoped would most hold their interest. I gestured freely as I told them about the grizzly bear attack and did not downplay my role in facing the grizzly—honest bragging was characteristic of the Sioux, and humility an indication of stupidity and a sign of deficient personal conviction.

I recounted the horsebucking incident—exaggerating it to the point of humor—and all the rest of Lieutenant Grimshaw's shortcomings as officer. I detailed the murders which had plagued the expedition and explained why I did not believe them to be caused by the Sioux. I told them of meeting

Rebecca on the hillside.

An hour had passed by then, yet I was only halfway through. Not once had any of the Wicasa Yatapickas so much as shifted; I was glad to be standing and moving as I spoke to them.

The next part of my narration became more difficult for me: How I'd been taken prisoner and forced along to the Sioux camp; how Mick Burns had gone ahead and around the camp as the soldiers approached from the near side. I did not skip any details of my role in saving Rebecca, and I made it very clear the ropes binding my wrist kept me from preventing any of the slaughter—stressing how I had hid Rebecca beneath the buffalo hides and then allowed myself to be recaptured by the bluecoats. I used another pause to choose my next words. I wasn't sure how much Rebecca had told Red Cloud, and I still did not understand why a Sioux brave had later rescued me at her request. So I passed over that part, explaining that after the blue-coats had been killed by Sioux warriors, I abandoned them and returned alone to Fort Steele.

I did not tell them how I'd shamed myself by abandoning my grief to whiskey. They did not need to know my weakness, and if Rebecca returned to me, I did not want it to be from sympathy. Instead, I detailed all the attempts on my life, the information I had learned about the dead scout and his friendship with Mick Burns, and my suspicions about Colonel Crozier.

"That is why I have traveled to your camp," I finished. "I seek Mick Burns. I believe he knows much of the riddle behind this. His horse's tracks match the ones outside my office the night the other scout was killed. He is the one among the expedition capable of making murders appear committed by Sioux warriors. He is the one who departed from the blue-coats and circled behind the women and children. He is the one now alive, who did not return to the blue-coats as would be expected, but instead led your warriors to find them. Surely this must appear strange to men of your wisdom."

I half bowed, then respectfully took a seat opposite them and waited. A long silence began, punctuated only by the laughter and delighted screams of playing children outside the tepee.

In the silence, I stole another glance at Rebecca. Her eyes were still cast upon the ground.

Did she know my words and defense had been directed as much to her as the Sioux elders? Did she now believe I should not be blamed for the events which had driven us apart? If the Wicasa Yatapickas absolved us both, would she then return with me to Laramie?

Cross-legged as I was, with folded arms against my chest, I felt small tremors of weakness fill me at the thought of hope for her love again. I tried to squeeze away the hope by pressing my folded arms against my ribs; I could not afford to let any expression cross my face as the Sioux elders deliberated.

I dry swallowed several times to force my throat from giving voice to my questions. I prayed there would be time and reason later to ask her.

Finally, the one with shell earrings grunted a few short words.

I raised my eyes to Red Cloud.

"It is time," Red Cloud said, "to let Mick Burns speak against your charges."

****

Mick Burns hid his surprise well, aided by the shadow which had begun to fill the tepee with the approaching evening, and aided by the heavy, dark beard which made his face a mask. I was watching for his reaction to see me alive, and the only response I could see was a slight flinch of the muscles around his eyes.

Wisely, he said nothing but sat and waited for one of the Sioux elders to explain the reason he had been summoned to the tepee.

I stared at him during the entire lengthy stream of Sioux which followed. His wide shoulders and short, compact body gave him the appearance of a square boulder rising from the earth. He was wearing his trademark red bandana wrapped over his skull, the corner knots lost in the thick, black curls of his hair. His buckskin jacket, pants, and boots were smudged smoky gray with accumulated dirt—much dirtier than when I'd seen him last—the buckskin fringes curled like greasy hair. His Bowie knife was a silent threat, so long that, sitting as he was with it tucked at his side in his waistband, the tip actually touched the ground.

He shook his head emphatically from side to side every few seconds as he listened to my accusations. He spit once in disgust and the strands of it hung in his beard like narrow, white yarn.

I was glad for Red Cloud's presence. Sitting Bull had dismissed Rebecca only minutes before Mick's arrival; had Red Cloud not been alongside to ensure the translation was accurate and fair, I would have feared the outcome of this tribunal.

Instead, confidence bouyed me. The aches and pains of my body had become nothing more than minor distractions, easily endured in light of the hopes I was allowing myself. There was nothing Burns could say to help him, not with Rebecca and me as two witnesses against his single testimony.

The middle elder finished speaking.

Mick Burns shouted in anger and jerked the Bowie knife from his belt. He spun and thrust it hilt-deep into the ground, narrowly missing my thigh.

"Give me the pleasure of slitting this man's throat," he said in clear, hard English. " 'Tis my name he disreputes, and my knife should spill his yeller blood."

"You deny his story then?" Sitting Bull asked it mildly, as if the answer had little consequence. I felt my first chill of fear.

"I aim to speak directly to him," Mick Burns said, his tone still harsh. "Maybe then you can pass along what we say."

Sitting Bull nodded.

"Understand this first," Burns told me. "I'm half-blood Cheyenne. My squaw is full-blood Cheyenne. We got our share of squallers, and I ain't fool enough to risk her nor the little ones by breaking the treaty betwixt the Cheyenne and Sioux. So you think the elders are gonna believe a white like you against me?"

"You scouted for the U.S. military."

He waved that away. "I ain't the only one. Thing is, I only ever scouted for the army against Pawnee and the odd Kiowas. It's almost like counting coup, leading the blue-coats to enemies of the Sioux and Cheyenne."

"You led Grimshaw's detachment into the Yellowstone valleys. No Pawnee or Kiowas that far north."

"Exactly," he said. "Only because it was to be a quick run to see the lay of the land, maybe find a way to move folks and miss the Bozemen. We was a peaceable bunch, and that's the only reason I agreed, knowing it would keep the Sioux hunting grounds clear of whites."

I shook my head. "Then why did you lead Grimshaw to the Sioux camp, knowing he wanted hostages?"

He threw his head back and laughed, cruel and long. When he stopped, he hacked a few times and wiped his mouth clear with the back of his hand.

"That's the whole reason I want to slit your throat, boy. An outright lie like that, you knowing full well it was your idea, being as you'd been there the day before and knew exactly where they was and that the warriors were scouting for buffalo."

Burns turned to Sitting Bull. "You should have seed him, laying it all out for the blue-coat lieutenant. Giving him the particulars of the camp and the best approach to attack. It about made me sick."

I began to protest. Sitting Bull held up his hand to silence me. He spent the next few minutes translating for the other Wicasa Yatapickas.

Low mutterings answered him.

Surely this was not going against me.

I struggled to keep myself calm. To act rashly now would cost me all credibility with the Sioux elders.

Mick Burns, who understood Sioux and knew when Sitting Bull had completely finished translating, got the next licks in before I could speak.

Burns pointed a grimy index finger at me. "Not only did this man lead the blue-coats, he fired the first shot."

I drew a breath, desperate to keep myself from lunging for his throat with my bare hands. "Your lies will not protect you," I said. "I have a witness."

He laughed again, longer and crueler. "The beloved Morning Star." He hacked more, this time not bothering to wipe away the flecks of saliva in his beard at the corners of his mouth. "Ain't her white name Rebecca something?"

"She knows I was prisoner," I said. "The elders know it from her too."

"The elders know a pile more. That she was plumb crazy with love for you. And that she was the only one who survived that day. Look at it in a different light, and it might seem like you marched in and found a way to save her, and she's looking for a way to save you now."

I looked over to Red Cloud, appealing for help. He remained impassive.

"See what it is," Burns continued, leering with triumph, "is out of anyone who was there, only you and me and her lived to tell the story. No one will believe her nor you. What I c'aint understand is why you were so stupid to believe you could fool anyone, and what it is you expected to get from me by trying to make my life miserable."

"What I expect is justice," I said, lips tight. "Your neck stretching against a loop of rope and your toes kicking nothing but air."

"You got any idea how this works?" Burns said, his teeth bared and yellow in a wolf's grin. "You cain't back your words. And because of it, I get the honor of skinning you alive."

Sitting Bull interrupted with another dignified lifting of his right hand. He conferred with the other Wicasa Yatapicka.

I didn't have time to begin to feel any more apprehensive than I already was, for their conversation was short. Too short. And that brought waves of new apprehension.

"Go," Sitting Bull said to Mick Burns. "We will deal with this man in our own way."

I raised my hands and half rose in protest as Burns moved to his feet. Quicker than I could believe, Sitting Bull had leaned and reached forward and pulled the Bowie knife from the ground. He slashed it through the air at my hands, nicking the heel of my right hand as I pulled it back.

"It has been decided," he thundered.

Drops of blood fell from my hand and soaked into the earth. Then I remembered.

"No," I said. I said it strong, freezing Burns.

It was my turn to point at Burns. "Ask him for one more thing," I said.

"Enough," Sitting Bull commanded. "Silence."

Red Cloud finally intervened. "Grant him his wish. This is a serious matter."

Sitting Bull waited. Two, three, four seconds. Then he nodded.

I closed my eyes briefly, trying to recapture the image of what Jake and I had found in the dirt that night. If I was wrong now. . . .

"When I walk the streets of Laramie as marshal," I said, "my pistol is loaded with buckshot. Not bullets."

Mick Burns stiffened. Only slightly. Not enough, perhaps for the others to notice, but enough to give me the first stirrings of relief. It meant there was a reason his buckskin seemed so much dirtier now than it did before during the expedition.

"How many other men you think load their pistol with buckshot?" I asked Sitting Bull.

He shrugged.

"Not many," I answered for him. "And you'll recall how I told you how stupid I was to be shooting at a grizzly bear with buckshot pellets?"

Again, a noncommittal shrug. Sitting Bull detested the whites. He did not want to see me proved right.

"What I ask is for Mick Burns to remove his jacket and shirt," I said. "When I shot at the man who murdered a scout in my office in Laramie, I drew blood. You won't see a bullet hole in this man's skin, but you'll see enough tiny holes punched into him, you'll know he's the one who was there."

I didn't add it was also the reason his buckskin was so much darker now than before. He'd had to replace the gun-shot one before the expedition began. Light colored then, it had since accumulated the dirt and filth to give it its more usual coloring. But that in itself was no proof. The buckshot marks were there on his skin and I was right. Or they weren't there, and Rebecca and I were dead.

Red Cloud translated all what I'd said.

The elder with the peace medal hanging from his neck gestured impatiently at Burns. Although I didn't understand the Sioux, the meaning was plenty clear.

Burns made a move to bolt to the tepee door.

Sitting Bull pushed off with his incredible quickness and pulled Burns down by the heels. He swarmed over Burns, flipped him onto his back and straddled his belly, his knees pinning down the scout's arms.

Red Cloud reached down and ripped open the buckskin jacket, then took the Bowie knife where Sitting Bull had dropped it before diving for Burns. Red Cloud moved back to Burns and cut away his shirt.

I didn't breathe.

The scars would be there, I was sure. Otherwise Burns wouldn't have bolted. But until I saw them, I would not relax.

There were two on the skin of his belly, tiny puckered pink circles against the paleness of his untanned skin. Three more on his right shoulder. Marks of life for me. Marks of death for him.

THIRTY-EIGHT

SITTING BULL, STILL STRADDLING the helpless
Mick Burns, leaned forward and yanked the red bandana, took a handful of the scout's thick, black hair and
asked Red Cloud for the Bowie knife.

Red Cloud complied.

The other elders did nothing.

Sitting Bull pulled the scout's hair high, and with his
other hand placed the blade of the knife where hair met
forehead.

Burns screamed. Probably not as much from pain as from
the knowledge Sitting Bull intended to scalp him alive.

"No!" I shouted over the hideous noise.

Sitting Bull hesitated, and Burns stopped screaming.

I spoke clearly. "With his death, you will never punish
the man responsible for the Sioux women and children who
died."

Sitting Bull's back was to me. He looked downward on
Burns and spit into the scout's face. "This is the man who led
the expedition to the camp."

"Another sent him," I said. I did not know this for certain, but it had to be truth. Burns wasn't the one who'd sent

two men to kill me in Rawlins.

"Yes, yes," Burns pleaded.

Sitting Bull levered himself off Mick Burns and stood.

It gave me a clear look at the scout's face. The sliding blood had formed a mask of red around his eyes.

"You will tell me who sent you," Sitting Bull commanded.

I had to admire Burns' courage. He shook his head no. "I ain't saying a word until you make oath I ain't killed."

Sitting Bull regarded him for several minutes, then, strangely, smiled.

"You have my oath," Sitting Bull said. "Neither will your wife and children be harmed."

I was as surprised as Burns. He pushed himself into a half-sitting position. The slash across his forehead was wide enought that blood kept pouring down over his eyes and into the beard high on his cheeks. I didn't feel squeamish though, not when the blood belonged to this man.

"You all heard him," Burns said. "He made oath."

No reaction from the elders.

"Say it again," Burns said, "in Sioux so they understand."

Sitting Bull spoke briefly in Sioux as Burns listened intently. The other Wicasa Yatapicka nodded gravely. Burns cackled in triumph.

"All right," he said, "I'll tell."

He got to his knees and searched the ground for his red bandana. He wrapped it around his forehead to staunch the bleeding. The cut would hurt far less than it appeared. Blood flow is rich to the forehead, and any cuts there tend to bleed as if a man is dying, when really the worst danger is infection later.

For my part, I could scarcely believe Sitting Bull had spared the scout's life. Yet I welcomed the unexpected gift. I desperately wanted to know what Burns had to say.

Sitting Bull took a seat beside me, so close our elbows almost touched, and Burns spoke more to us than the others.

"What it was," he said, mopping the blood away from his

face with the backs of his wrists, "was one night some feller approached me and Two Hats outside a saloon in Laramie."

"Two Hats?"

"My scouting partner. The one that got kilt in your office the very same night."

"Got killed?" I interrupted. "The partner *you* killed."

"Ain't so," he said, "and I'll get to that part soon enough."

"Go on," Sitting Bull growled.

"This feller offered us ten thousand dollars iffen we'd make sure a certain man died. Two Hats, he said him and I were a lot of things and not many of those things particularly nice, but no sir we weren't murderers. This man laughed some and said that was the beauty of it. We didn't have to necessarily kill the man, just make sure he got killed—maybe in battle or something—and it had to look like an accident. So I told Two Hats to listen. Ten thousand dollars? Iffen it didn't go to us, sure as shooting this feller would find someone else. I figured the other feller was going to die anyway, me and Two Hats might as well have the money."

"Who?" I demanded. Ten thousand was a substantial amount, especially when a top ranch hand might only earn $25 a month. "Who was offering the money? Who'd he want dead?"

"Second one's easier to answer than the first," Burns said. He blinked at blood growing sticky on his eyelids. "The feller called himself John Smith, but any fool could tell that weren't his real name, not with what he was asking. As to your second question, he did tell us he wanted dead a young pup named Nathaniel Hawkthorne. Course this John Smith didn't tell me right then. He was cagey, that one. Told us iffen we agreed, he'd wait on giving us the name until just before some military expedition left. I asked him what expedition, being as I hadn't heard of one yet, and Smith assured us it would happen. He grinned kinda funny too, when he said it."

I opened my mouth and snapped it shut. I'd do my best to wait until Burns finished before asking more questions.

"Two Hats, he didn't take a shine to the idea, said he wouldn't be no part of it." Burns shook his head. "That might have been the end of it too, except Two Hats got it into his head to get all righteous and report this to the marshal. That, of course, being you."

Burns paused. He licked the tips of his fingers, and dabbed them against his eyelids, trying to clean away some of the sticky blood.

"I had a bad feeling right then," Burns said when he continued. "It weren't too much skin off my nose Two Hats going to the marshal, only he shouldn't have announced it so grand with the feller staring us down right there. Two Hats spun on his boot heels and marched in the direction of the marshal's office. This feller and I watched for a bit. No sooner had Two Hats rounded the corner, there was a sleeve pistol stuck in my ear and Smith demanding my horse. I obliged of course, and once we reached my horse, he took my shotgun and pointed it at my back. Told me to git on the horse, which I did. He swung on behind, and the two of us on my horse headed to cut Two Hats off at the pass. By the time we reached the marshal's office, Two Hats was inside. Directly from my horse, Smith jumped onto the sidewalk, and without so much as a howdy-do, plugged Two Hats through the window."

So far it seemed to fit. If Burns was lying, he was remarkable at it, or he'd rehearsed it—and somehow he didn't seem the rehearsing type.

"What happened next," Burns said, "was I get down and see what he done. He broke open the barrel of my shotgun, emptied it of the shells, stuck 'em in his pocket, and handed the shotgun back to me. Then he told me how easy it would be for him to claim witness I'd murdered Two Hats, and said iffen I had any intention of going to the law, chances were I'd hang, not him. He ran down the sidewalk one way; I got on my horse and rode the other way and ran smack into you. I was hoping when I reached for my empty shotgun, it'd bluff you into backing down, but instead, you plugged me with the pepper-shot."

I hear the shot as Two Hats is murdered. I run maybe thirty, forty-five seconds, the same thirty-odd seconds they stand there talking. They finish. Mick Burns finally gets on his horse. He rounds the corner just as I'm reaching the side street to my office. . . .

The tracks Jake and I had seen seemed to fit his story too. Burns' bootprints where he got down from his horse to look at Two Hats; the other man staying on the sidewalk. How cold could this man be, seeing a friend murdered and showing more concern for the bounty money placed on Nathaniel Hawkthorne.

Burns was still talking. "So Smith finds me the night before the expedition is to leave, almost as if he'd been following me. Gives me five thousand dollars, tells me the other half is mine when I get the job done right, and that getting the job done right means however this Hawkthorne dies, it looks like an accident."

"The grizzly," I said, remembering the evening Hawkthorne had stopped by my fire to thank me for saving my life when Burns had seemed so paralyzed. "You held off shooting it, hoping it would kill Hawkthorne."

"Yup. Iffen you hadn't done what you did to save the boy's life, my own life woulda been plenty easy after that. Course, once the grizzly turned on you, I fired real quick. Last thing I wanted was you dead, knowing how you had safe passage through Sioux lands."

Was he saying the rest might not have happened if Nathaniel had died there? I didn't want to think about it, didn't want to regret doing what seemed best at the time, didn't want to begin on the what-ifs. I concentrated on listening to Burns.

"Seems from there," Burns said, "nothing went right. I wanted to get it out of the way quick. From the git-go, I'd brought along some Sioux souvenirs. I dressed up a spear with Sioux war feathers, only in the dark, I done kilt the wrong person. And the other soldier, he seen me walking away, and I knew come morning he'd be asking one question too many, so I had to slit his throat. Worked good, though, Grimshaw thinking it was Sioux. Then that German feller, he'd seen a couple arrows in my saddle bag when I was getting some whiskey, so on the sly he told me just that and said unless I gave him a passle of greenbacks, he'd report it to the lieutenant, and I had to ram a couple of those same arrows in his back. I didn't like it much, but five thousand was more than a feller like me could spend in a lifetime, and I also figured by the time I got Hawkthorne, no one would ever know it'd been him who was the target. Except after that, Hawkthorne always ended up near someone else. Fact is, the one time I snuck up on him, another soldier seen me, and I worried he might say something, so I had to wait to get him at the latrine."

Four soldiers dead as Burns fumbled his way from one murder to another, just smart enough to keep Grimshaw thinking it was Sioux. Had Hawkthorne died to the grizzly, of course, none of this. . . .

"Was taking Sioux hostages your idea, or Grimshaw's?"

"The lieutenant's." Burns said it loud, pleading, almost hysterical, not daring to look at Sitting Bull. "I swear it wasn't me. In fact, I was working on a way to make sure he didn't get no hostages. Honest. I swear."

"You shot Grimshaw," I said. "You circled the camp, waited until we rode up on the other side, and shot from the backside of camp."

"My thinking was with him dead, the soldiers would ride away. None of them were good soldiers. None of them fighters. I didn't want no Sioux hurt."

He finally raised his head again. The blood on his forehead was beginning to darken as it dried, and he appeared to be a pathetic monster, once proud but now gnawing at his leg to escape from a trap.

"I cain't say it enough," Burns begged his words for Sitting Bull's benefit. "I didn't intend for no Sioux to get hurt."

I wondered if it was true, if Burns truly had calculated the other soldiers would turn tail, or if he was making this part up, knowing it would sound believable. I also knew there was no way to prove his words false. All that did matter was the deaths of those women and children.

"You shot at Hawkthorne next," I said.

"I did. And missed. Then the soldiers charged the camp, and he ducked into a tepee, and I had no chance at all again."

Ducked into a tepee. He said it so simple, so plain, with no understanding of how the events in that tepee had so thoroughly seared change into my life. I felt the nausea I always did at the reminder of the cruelty of death when it took a loved one. I searched for, and found, rage to replace the nausea.

"You put the rifle into a dead boy's hands so it looked like he's done the shooting. And then you led Sioux warriors to our camp," I said between gritted teeth.

He shrugged. This was safer ground, reporting in front of Sitting Bull the deaths of blue-coats. "They'd have found you anyway."

"Just like someone else would have taken money to arrange Hawkthorne's death?" I said.

He shrugged again.

With a gun in my holster, I doubted I would have been able to resist the urge to blow a hot chunk of lead through his skull. As it was, I had to remind myself that someone else was behind this, and that if I didn't ask questions now, I'd probably never had the chance later. So I didn't hurl myself across the tepee and begin to batter his face with my bare hands.

"Who hired you?" I asked.

"I done told you," he said. "I don't know. Unless you believe his name's John Smith."

"What'd he look like?"

"Hard to say. The only times I seen him was a night, and he made sure the brim of his hat kept his face in shadow."

"He paid you half up-front?" I asked.

"Yup. The night before the expedition left Laramie. Same night he told me who he wanted dead."

"The other half. You haven't collected it."

"Nope," Burns said. "After we caught up to the blue-coats, I rode straight to the Cheyenne. Had a squaw waiting for me. Seemed best to lay low 'til it was safe to spend the money in my saddlebag."

It gave me sudden hope. "Were you supposed to meet him to collect the other half?"

Maybe I could go in Burns' stead, especially if it was to be a nighttime meeting.

"Marshal, I was supposed to meet him at least a week back."

"What?"

"I ain't no fool. Firstly, I didn't want no questions about the expedition, when it seemed like I was the only survivor. And then I got to thinking, like as not this man would have kilt me. Saves him five thousand, maybe he gets his first five thousand back, and for sure gets rid of anyone who might be able to pin Hawkthorne's death on him." Burns shook his head. "No sir, I had my hide, and I was far from Laramie and any trouble I'd find there. Thinking it that way, I decided five thousand was enough for me."

Nearly fifty people dead, and he was happy with five thousand dollars for it. If Sitting Bull was prepared to let him live, I'd be able to seriously consider some vigilante justice and worry later about the damage it might do my soul to cold-bloodedly kill another man.

"Can't you tell me anything about this man? Where were you supposed to meet him?"

"I was to leave a message at the stagecoach office in Laramie, telling him where he could find me."

The stagecoach office. Dozens of strangers passed through there a week. Dozens of John Smiths. That gave me little to work with on my return to Laramie.

"Was he big?" I asked. "Little? How'd he dress?"

Burns shrugged. "Weren't big. Weren't small. Wore a long coat that hid his clothes. I hardly ever saw his face either."

I waited.

"I already told you, he always kept the brim of his hat low, eyes always in the shadow. I wouldn't recognize him if he walked into this tepee."

"That's it? Nothing else you can tell me about John Smith." If he heard impatience in my voice, he heard right.

"Nope."

I couldn't think of another question, and Burns lapsed into nervous silence.

Sitting Bull stood.

"Enough," he said. "It is time for punishment."

"Hey! You made oath that—" Burns tried pushing his way up, but Sitting Bull kicked him in the chest and knocked him down.

"Fool," Sitting Bull said, "there are much worse things than a man losing his life."

Sitting Bull barked out harsh words in Sioux. The other elders nodded approval. Sitting Bull strode to the tepee flap and called for the braves who stood outside. They walked in and took Burns by the arms.

Burns fought and struggled and cried as they dragged him out. Sitting Bull and the other Wicasa Yatapickas followed and left me alone in the tepee with Red Cloud. All of this happened so quickly, I was still sitting cross-legged when Red Cloud patted my shoulder.

"Where can I find Morning Star?" I asked. "I must speak with her."

He chuckled dryly. "Your first question is not the fate of the scout?"

"Will I be able to walk freely through camp as I search for her?"

"You will not be harmed," he said. "However, it would be best for her if you were not seen. I shall send her back to this tepee."

"Best for her? What does—"

He shook his head no. "That is for her to tell you."

Before I could ask another question, screaming ripped the air, screaming which halted the sounds of camp which had been filtering into the tepee. The screaming stopped, and unnatural silence surrounded us. Until the screaming began again, screeching cries like that of a pig at slaughter.

Red Cloud stared at the tepee flap. "His nose first. Ears next. Tongue. If he faints, they will wake him. At last they will send him out of camp. And word will go out that he is never to be slain. Sitting Bull wishes for him to live many years."

THIRTY-NINE

GLAD TO SEE YOU BACK," Jake said to where I sat in his livery.

"Glad to see you back with coffee," I replied.

"Shoot, ain't nothing. Coffee's the least I could do. After all, this is a far cry from the dance girl's bed where I last woke you."

A far cry it was. I'd rode into Laramie sometime before dawn, brushed my horse down in Jake's livery, grabbed what sleep I could wrapped in the same blanket I'd used here before, greeted Jake upon his arrival, and begged him to run to the Chinaman's for the pot of coffee he was now offering me.

I was sitting on a bale of hay. He moved to one nearby. I poured the coffee into a tin mug and set the pot on the dirt floor of the livery. White vapors rose from the pot; the Chinaman did do coffee hot if nothing else.

"I don't smell sausage, do I, Jake?"

"Sure do." He grinned and reached into his vest for a cloth-wrapped parcel. "Hope you don't mind me stowing it here, but it was easier than trying to juggle coffee, sausage, and biscuits with my good hand."

He didn't get a reply, because my mouth was otherwise

occupied. *Sausage and biscuits after my campfire cooking over the last few days. . . .*

"If only the Chinaman could see you eating now," Jake said, "it would bring tears to his eyes. A day don't go by without him saying how much he'd like to see you walk in his restaurant again. And a day don't go by I nearly tell him you ain't dead."

I washed down biscuit with coffee, and paused long enough to tell Jake it wouldn't be too long maybe I could come back to life again.

"Good," he said as I lit into the next biscuit. "My poker winnings have dropped considerable since you departed from the tables."

He caught my eyes narrowing.

"I say something wrong?"

I swallowed and thought through his question. "Nothing wrong at all. Just that hearing you mention poker sets something to stir in my mind. Like it should mean something to me."

"Someone owe you money?"

I shook my head no. "Don't worry about it. Important enough, it'll come back."

He watched me finish my food and waited until I was started on my second cup of coffee.

"Doc will be happy to see you too. He's so desperate for conversation, he started talking books to me. Like maybe he figured I was you or something. I set him straight in a hurry and invited him to play some cards. Which he was desperate enough to accept." Jake laughed. "He cost me five dollars, that fox. Pretended he needed me to write down the order of the hands so he could keep them straight in his poor head."

I smiled, but it was a smile with mixed feelings. I wanted to spend time with Doc too, but we hadn't talked since the night he gave me the empty pistol. Not even during the carriage ride away from my dynamited house. I had some questions for him and some things I'd learned which I wanted to share for his comment.

Those concerns aside, coffee felt good going down my gullet. Sunlight worked its way through the crack between the main doors to the livery. Jake had taken the precaution of latching those doors on the inside to keep us from being surprised by an early customer. Sweet hay and horse sweat filled the air. I took comfort in the familiar noises of nearby horses. Swishing of tails. Occasional stamping of hooves. The rasp of hide against wood rail as one rubbed an itch.

"It is good to be back, Jake." My body ached considerably less than it had upon my departure from Laramie. I could twist and turn without stabbing myself with pain in my ribs. My head didn't throb with every heartbeat. My mouth wasn't constantly dry. And, although the craving hit bad when it did, I didn't feel it more than a couple of minutes every once in a while, the need to soak in whiskey.

"I imagine it is good to be back, Sam. You find Mick Burns?"

I nodded.

"Rebecca?"

I hesitated. Finally nodded again.

"Maybe ask about her some other time, huh?"

"Something like that."

He studied the broad fingernails of his good hand. "Say, you probably didn't hear. Old Lady Bertha left her porch door open the other day. Walked in to find all her goats inside. You can imagine the mess."

"I like that story, Jake."

"Thought you might."

I could see him struggling to find something else to say to fill the silence.

"It was Burns," I told him. "He killed the soldiers during the expedition. He'd been paid to make sure Nathaniel Hawkthorne died."

"Ain't that the young fellow whose parents you sent a letter?"

"Same one." I told Jake all I'd learned from Mick Burns. It took another cup-and-a-half of coffee for me to finish.

"This John Smith fellow, the one who hired Burns, he kept himself pretty well hid, didn't he," Jake commented when I'd told him the last of it.

I slurped more coffee. "I had plenty time to study on this as I rode back to Laramie, Jake. I truly believe Colonel Crozier had a hand in this. But I can't see why he'd want Hawkthorne dead."

Jake opened his mouth to tell me something, but I wasn't done.

"Maybe it'd pay to ride out to the fort and visit Crozier again," I continued. "Maybe run a bluff on him like we already know plenty about this John Smith. See what works loose."

"Yes, but—"

"I want to stay dead a while longer. And I can't think anyone better at running a bluff than you."

"Yes, but—"

"So, any chance you can go out there again?" I asked.

"No."

"Why not? He didn't run you off last time you paid him a call."

"Well, if you'd let a man get a couple words in, you'd have heard me say Crozier is dead. Happened just after you left."

"Dead?" In all my studying on this, I'd never thought of that possibility.

"Murdered dead. You know McKinnis, has a spread out southwest?"

I nodded. Knew the man. Quiet, except once every six months came into town and went on a bender, then meekly turned himself in at the marshal's office to save me or Jake the effort of arresting him.

"McKinnis found him in the hills. Shot. It wasn't pretty, Sam."

"You saw it?"

"Nope. The way McKinnis tells it, he found the dead horse first. Like the horse had been shot out from under Crozier."

"What was he doing out in the hills alone anyway?"

Jake shrugged. "You can ask him, but he likely won't hear, not with six feet of dirt piled above him."

I gave Jake a sour smile.

"As I was saying," Jake said, "McKinnis saw the horse first. Dead long enough for the blowflies to lay eggs. It hadn't rained in a while though, and McKinnis followed the boot-prints away from the horse. He said they were running boot-prints. A hundred yards later two sets of horse tracks joined up alongside the bootprints, like two men on horses chased him down. Crozier's body weren't far ahead. Shot in the back, four, maybe five times."

My coffee settled like bile in my stomach. *The last ten or twenty yards of panic running, knowing why your horse had been shot out from under you, hearing the horses behind, waiting for the bullets to strike. . . .*

"It don't stop there," Jake said. "Yesterday, another rancher rode into Laramie. He took me a couple miles down-stream of Laramie, showed me two men washed up against a fallen log. One man's wrist was tied to the other's. Both were cut up pretty good. What killed them, though, was lead poi-soning. A couple bullets each. In the back." He took a breath. "Sam, it was the same two cowpokes from Rawlins. The ones who tried to kill you. Am I wrong to think those two might have also kilt the colonel?"

I thought upon the implications for some time. Two pi-geons fluttered in through an opening high in the livery walls, throwing dust and small feathers which drifted in the sun-light.

"Maybe we should look at it this way, Jake. John Smith manages to arrange the expedition through Crozier—after all, he knew it was coming before Burns did. John Smith wants

Hawkthorne dead. Then he covers his tracks real good. Sends those two out to kill me, 'cause I'm the only survivor and might say something at the inquest. He gets them to kill Crozier, then kills the killers. Probably a good guess Burns would have been dead if he returned to collect the other half of the promised money."

Jake was nodding agreement.

"Does it appear to you like this John Smith went to extraordinary lengths to remove himself from Hawkthorne's death?"

"Cautious fellow, all right. Thing is, why not just lie about his name to Burns or the other two? No need to kill them if they don't know who he is."

"Maybe they would know," I said. "Maybe he can't hide his face. Maybe a false name don't help him."

"A judge? Politician?" Jake asked.

"Sure. High profile. Worried the killers can blackmail him later."

I grinned at Jake. "Of course, we should ask ourselves the obvious question. One I been puzzling one ever since Mick Burns told me his story."

"Go ahead," he said.

"Jake, the obvious question is *why*," I said. "Why would anyone want Nathaniel Hawkthorne dead?"

"Not a bad place to start."

"Being as I'm supposed to be dead, will you do me a favor?"

"Besides tote you coffee?"

"I'd appreciate it," I said, "if you could head down to the Union Pacific and send a telegram."

FORTY

MY CLOTHES AND THREE-DAY BEARD reeked of whiskey. I sat on a rickety bar stool, with my back to the poker tables, my elbows leaning on the bar, my hat on the stool beside mine. I'd been sitting there nearly an hour of the afternoon, waiting for him to make his move, a whiskey bottle in front of me, a shot glass just to the side of it. I'd been draining the contents with regularity, and less than a quarter of the bottle remained.

My mind and senses, however, were as sharp as they'd been all day, for the amber liquid in the whiskey bottle was sweetened tea, the reek of alcohol a result of pouring much of the bottle's original contents on me just before stepping inside from the sun's heat.

It had not been easy, holding the bottle upside down and watching the remainder of it soak into the soil behind the saloon. I still got the shakes occasionally, and smelling and feeling the whiskey had reminded me anew of its capacity to soothe my nerves. It had called so strongly, I'd almost licked the last few drops of whiskey from the bottle's rim, telling myself a simple taste couldn't hurt. Then I'd done what I always did when the craving was upon me. I'd closed my eyes and listened for the hammer's click on the empty cylinder of a gun pressed against my temple by my own hand. So I'd wiped the rim with the cuff of my sleeve instead and poured the cold, sweetened tea from my canteen into the bottle. From there, I'd led my horse onto the street and reined it to a post before stepping into the saloon. When the bartender had complained about me taking my own bottle into his establishment, I'd quietly given him the cash to pay for two bottles, not a small amount at the mining camp prices charged here in Rock Springs, a coal town down the tracks from Rawlins.

Then I'd begun my wait, more a test of willpower than patience, because the whiskey smell of my clothing kept urging me to try a shot glass of the real thing.

I knew he'd noticed me earlier, for I'd made a point of dropping my gun, something sure to get attention anywhere. Maybe he'd delayed because he couldn't or didn't want to leave the game. Maybe he'd delayed for me to drink as much whiskey as possible. But he took his time.

It wasn't until I was down to the final two fingers of amber liquid in my bottle that he made his move, leaving the card table without hurry and moving to stand beside me at my left elbow.

"I've seen you before," he said.

I turned my face to the cardsharp with one blue eye and one brown eye. Although my eyes were looking into his face, I tried to focus my vision on a point three feet behind him.

"You must be mistaken," I told him. I spoke very slowly and very clearly, the way a person would speak if he knew he were drunk but didn't want anyone else to realize it.

I looked back at my bottle.

"Rawlins," he said. "We met in Rawlins. Maybe a month back. You're the marshal who survived that massacre north of the Platte River."

I lifted my bottle and drained the last of my sweetened tea in four great gulps. Last thing I wanted was this man pouring some for himself.

I clunked the bottle down on the bar and swiveled my shoulders to give him my attention again. Still the tall, dark-haired, dapper man. His white shirt appeared as fresh as it had the first time we'd met, his purple vest and black jacket showed no signs of age or the dirt from his travels since then.

"Mister," I said, "you're right. So why don't we make a deal? You keep that news to yourself. And you go away."

"What's your part of the deal?"

"I keep my mouth shut and let you work this town for a while longer."

"Didn't I hear word you'd died?" he asked.

"And that's the way I want it to be," I said. I allowed myself to giggle. " 'Course, it's a shame I can't share the story."

"Try me. It's obvious you're busting to tell."

I gave it time to seem like I was considering it. I burped. Reminded myself to keep my voice slow with the false dignity induced by whiskey. "Since we are a considerable distance from Laramie. . . ."

"Remember," he said, "I can't tell anyone your secret. Otherwise you'd tell mine."

I knew then I had him convinced I was drunk. He was speaking to me as if I were a child.

"Sure," I said. I burped again and hoped I wasn't overdoing the stomach gas. "I went to sleep in my own bed. I woke up in a coffin at the undertaker's. Of course, I didn't know it when I woke. It was dark and I had to push my way out. Good thing the undertaker hadn't nailed the lid down."

I shook my head with indignation at how poorly I'd been treated. I reached for the empty whiskey bottle, stared at it as if realizing only at that moment it was empty, and I continued.

"I hopped out. A crazy idea hit me. Why not fill the coffin with dirt? It'd be a great trick to play on my friends, walking into my own funeral." I giggled again. "A real great trick."

"Absolutely," he said. "So why didn't you play it? Why didn't you walk in on your own funeral?"

"Nope. Not after I got to thinking how it would be the same old thing again. Friends who—" I interrupted myself to swallow back a burp "—friends who keep trying to drag me away from places like this. So I left town."

I grinned and stretched my arms out. "End of story," I said grandly. I clutched the edge of the bar for balance. I giggled again. "Maw was right after all. I *was* late for my own funeral."

With that, I turned the other way, and I took my hat from where I'd set it on the chair. I carefully swung my feet away from the bar stool and tested my balance as I stood. I grabbed the empty whiskey bottle and held it close to my chest.

"Where are you going?" he asked me.

"Next town," I said. "Where people don't know me."

"That's a ways, isn't it?"

"My horse ain't had no whiskey," I told him. With that, I began to depart the saloon. I walked with precision, the way a man would walk if he were thinking about how to walk, and left behind the man with one brown eye and one blue eye.

****

I waited again. This time, however, it was well to the side of a campfire, some six hours later, some ten miles out of Rock Springs. I sat easy, rifle in my lap, my back against a pine tree, and all of me well screened by the lower boughs. I had a good view of my bedroll beside the campfire. I'd filled it with clothes, and in the flickering darkness, it truly appeared as if I were sleeping in it.

I fully expected the old bedroll trick to work. The man I waited for was a man of alleys, saloons, and hotel rooms. The wisdom of the night he'd learned in those places would do him little good here.

A wind blowing from the northeast had brought clouds

and cold. There were few of the night sounds of animals above the keening of the wind coming across the plains and up into this hill. I resisted the temptation to rub my hands or to shift to stay warm. With no moonlight or starlight, and with the wind to mask sounds, he would be upon the camp before I saw him, and I did not wish to give him the slightest warning.

My waiting was easier, because even if he hadn't believed I'd been drunk, I still expected him. I'd gone through those efforts in the saloon, however, because it would simplify things if he were less guarded on his approach. While his appearance alone would still most of my doubts, I wanted to discover what he would do if he believed I were vulnerable. The more certain I could be about the course of action I'd chosen, the easier it would be on my conscience.

He arrived as the flames of the campfire were dying to bright embers. He was smart enough to approach into the wind, reducing any sounds he made stepping on twigs or brushing against branches. He moved with the stealth of a wolf, detaching himself from the shadow of a large tree, and if the cold and hatred hadn't made me so alert, it would have seemed as if he'd simply sprung into existence on the circle of flattened grass around my fire and bedroll.

He had a shotgun, and he didn't pause or hesitate. Simply brought it to his shoulders, aimed down the barrel at the middle section of my bedroll, and pulled the trigger. Twice. To deliver twin roaring explosions and belched flares of fire from his gun barrel.

My horse stamped and snorted and pulled at the rope halter. I took advantage of that distraction and of the aftershock of noise and rolled forward onto my stomach, bringing my rifle up as I did so. His back and shoulders filled most of my rifle sight. I thought briefly of pulling the trigger myself, but I was not an executioner.

"Drop the gun!" I yelled. *If he swung it toward me, if he ran, maybe then I could allow myself the satisfaction of shooting....*

He dropped the gun.

"Now flat on your belly."

He hesitated. I swung my rifle slightly wide of him and fired. It was better than an explanation of why he should listen. I levered another bullet into the breech. The sound was clear, even with the wind. He dropped to his knees then stretched forward on his belly.

"Feet spread. Hands on your back."

He obeyed. Only then did I rise to my feet. I set my rifle down and took my Colt from its holster. In close, I wanted the freedom of movement. This was not a man I intended to underestimate.

I moved to him, then slung my handcuffs from a belt loop. I pressed the barrel of my Colt against the back of his head, and with my other hand, cuffed his wrists behind his back.

"Legs together."

I took another pair of handcuffs from another belt loop and cuffed his ankles together. I grabbed his left shoulder and pulled him over onto his back. I frisked him. Found a knife in an ankle sheath. Derringer rigged beneath his right sleeve. Another derringer in his waistband.

He remained silent, refusing to show fear or bewilderment. It only underscored his deadliness.

For my part, I remained silent too. Visions of slaughter at the Sioux camp and at the blue-coat camp kept rising into mind. I heard Nathaniel Hawkthorne's earnest voice as he handed me the letter before his death. I worried if I unleashed my anger through words, it might begin a rush of rage and the cowardly beating of a man helpless to defend himself—when I already had too many reasons not to respect myself.

I took some rope from where I had readied it earlier on a nearby branch. I made a noose, dropped it over his neck, rolled him back onto his stomach, threw the other end of the rope over a higher branch and snugged it, just slightly, giving him only enough slack to breathe if he didn't move. With more rope, I made another noose, dropped it over his feet, threw the end into another branch, and snugged it to raise his ankles a couple inches from the ground.

It satisfied me that he would live through the night, his face pressed into the dirt, helpless to move his hands or his ankles, helpless to roll to either side.

Then I grabbed the remains of my bedroll, wrapped it around myself, and made myself as comfortable as possible. Let him shiver as I slept. I wasn't man enough not to enjoy the thought of his discomfort.

FORTY-ONE

THE NIGHT'S CLOUDS BROKE sometime during the hours of my sleep, and I woke when the sun hit my eyes. The cardsharp was where I'd left him—helpless and trussed on the other side of the fire's ashes. Dawn showed what he wouldn't have seen during his approach in the darkness. Our camp was perched on the rounded top of a dry-grass hill among widely scattered and sparse pine trees.

While I found dry branches among those pines and cracked the wood over my knee to shorter pieces, he didn't beg, didn't complain. He continued to watch me in silence while I rekindled the fire and started a cup of coffee to brew.

After I was satisfied with those arrangements, I splashed water on my face from a canteen. I moved to my saddlebag and found a roll of red cloth, unfurled it, and hung it like a flag at the end of a long pole. I jabbed the pole into the ground. It leaned but did not fall. The cloth flapped lazily. While the clouds had departed to leave the sky unsmudged, some of the wind had remained.

When I returned to the fire, the coffee was bubbling. I poured it into a mug and set the mug on the ground to let it cool. I stepped over the trussed man and loosened the ropes which held his ankles and neck. He sagged face down with relief but still said nothing.

I took him by the collar, dragged him to a nearby tree, and rolled him onto his back. His hands were still cuffed behind him, his ankles still cuffed together, but I handled him with care. This was a tough man, and I had no doubt he was waiting for the slightest carelessness on my part.

"Might as well sit against the tree," I told him, and hauled him up by the shoulders. "It's why I moved you here."

He did—and stared upward at me. One brown eye. One blue eye. White shirt no longer fresh. Matted dirt and strands of dead grass on his black jacket.

I stared back until he blinked and looked away.

Then I went for my mug of coffee and returned with it. The first sip was too hot to taste, but the warmth felt good moving down, reminding me of the whiskey I hoped never again to use as refuge.

"Within the half hour," I said, looking down on him, "you'll be riding away without me."

"This is a trick to get a confession?"

"Have something to confess?"

He spat at me. I saw it coming, however, as he sucked his cheeks in, and I stepped aside.

"I'm not particularly interested in a confession anyway. Won't do me any good." Coffee in one hand, I swept my other to indicate the broad view of the rolling hills and grassy plains below. "There's no one nearby to overhear what you might tell me. In court, it would be your word against mine, and without a witness, no judge would convict you on what you might say to me. As a matter of fact, even how you tried to shoot me in my sleep last night would be my word against yours."

I paused for coffee. A few grounds had bubbled into the liquid, and I thoughtfully chewed on them before speaking again, remembering what I'd learned from studying law books over the winter. "Another reason you should believe I'm sending you on your way," I said, "is there ain't enough proof to convict you based on evidence or material witnesses. Except for me, anyone involved is dead or gone, and you were hundreds of miles away from the scene of the crime you paid for. Court and jury ain't the place for you."

I moved back from him and squatted on my haunches to watch his face better. "More important to me," I continued, "you don't need to confess. I already know most of what happened."

"Really." He said it flat, like he didn't care.

"Yup. You can change your name, but you can't change your eyes."

I watched him more over the edge of my cup as I tilted it back. "Theodore Rudolph Hawkthorne," I told him after a few more sips. "Remaining and only heir to the Hawkthorne millions. Convenient, wouldn't you say, Nathaniel's early and unexpected death?"

"If you say."

"Let me think out loud," I said. "You're out west anyway and hear Nathaniel's soldiering in Laramie. You stop by for a brotherly visit, discover his commander likes to gamble. That's definitely convenient, for a self-avowed, family black sheep who prefers to make his living at the card tables instead of learning how to run the Boston factories."

My coffee mug was nearly empty, and I had to return to the fire for more. Upon my return, I squatted comfortably and continued. "Colonel Crozier was just one more pigeon for you. I want to think the best of you, Theodore. I want to believe the plan didn't occur to you until *after* you played in one of the colonel's private games. I don't want to believe you went in hoping to win so much he'd be forced to do you a favor instead of paying his debts. What was it?"

He shrugged.

I shrugged too. "You're right. It matters little in the face of it. The end result is he owes you. Maybe you present your request to the colonel so it seems like you're only asking him to help Nathaniel, to put Nathaniel on a safe expedition to give him seasoning, seasoning that won't hurt Nathaniel's military career, especially if he's put among soldiers so bad Nathaniel looks good in comparison. How's that so far?"

"Astounding." He grinned maliciously. "For a drunk, truly astounding. Crozier was so eager to help, he decided to send along a green lieutenant too."

"But what you really wanted was a death. Nathaniel's. Once the expedition was set, you approached Mick Burns and Two Hats, the scouts you knew would be on the expedition. Their job was to make his death look like an accident. The perfect murder. It would never be connected to you."

"You handcuffed me to listen so I could be impressed with all this?"

"Not much to be impressed with. Mick Burns told me most of it. Once I knew your brother was the target, all I had to ask was who would benefit most. Took a couple of telegrams to Boston to get the rest of it. Got the information from a detective agency. Found out you were the only heir. Found out how much you stood to gain. Found out you had expensive tastes in wine, women, and gambling. Found out your father sent you on your own until you reformed your ways. Found out you weren't hard to miss, not when they said to look for a man with different colored eyes."

A couple of crows let the wind bounce them to the tops of nearby pines. They bobbed up there and cawed derision down on the two of us.

"Once I heard about the eyes, it made sense why you took so much effort to get rid of anyone who might trace you to the expedition or the murders. The slightest whisper of a man with a brown eye and a blue eye could sour the inheritance. Burns told me the only times you met him was at night, and you had your hat down low. To hide your eyes, right? As for the meeting you and I had in Rawlins—"

"Probably didn't remember much," he sneered.

"—you had such keen interest in what I might say at the inquest. And I realized the two men you sent after me hadn't shown up to kill me until shortly after that meeting. For I'd mentioned murder, and you couldn't risk letting me testify."

I was conscious of the red flag somewhere not far behind the two of us.

"Once I knew who to look for, I knew I wouldn't have to look far. I sent a few more telegrams out, up and down the lines of towns along the rails, asking other lawmen to tell me if and when a man with your eyes appeared. Someone like you needs to be around people. Saloons. Wild women. Drink. And where cowboys throw down money at poker. I also figured you'd wait some time to go back to Boston, maybe make a big show of surprise to find out Nathaniel had died in the course of duty. So it didn't surprise me when word of you eventually got back to me."

The crows tired of their scolding. I watched them drift away with the wind.

"The two men you sent after me—they're the ones who ran down Colonel Crozier?"

"I told the fool to meet me," he said. "I told him we had to be in the hills where no one could see us together. He was so afraid of what might come out in the inquest, he bought the story."

I nodded. "Then you killed both of them later?"

"They pushed me for more money."

"Of course," I said. "Two Hats shotgunned in my office, a Sioux camp dead, an expedition wiped out—what's a few more murders?"

I stood, and threw the last drops of coffee from my mug.

"Why me as scout?"

"What?" he said in mock surprise. "You don't know everything?"

"Why me as scout?"

"Why not? Burns was nervous you'd be after him once you found out it was Two Hats killed in your office. He said once he got you up in the north country, he could take care of you too. So I asked Crozier to hire you on."

I felt tired and old.

Theodore Rudolph Hawkthorne continued his mocking tone. "Heard enough now, marshal? Enough so you can feel good about killing me?"

I didn't reply.

"I asked around about you earlier," he said. "Straight shooter and all that. Someone like you would never dream of killing a man in cold blood. What if you couldn't sleep nights or look yourself in a mirror?"

"If I wanted you dead, I would have killed you last night. I had plenty reason then, watching you shotgun the bedroll you believed was me."

"What do you want then?"

"I got it last night. You came following. You tried to shoot me. Only a guilty man would have done that. All I wanted to know with certainty was whether you were guilty."

His face twisted with scorn. "You're the one who said no judge would hang me. If you're not going to do anything, why the effort?"

"Sun Dance," I told him.

"Sun Dance?"

"The Sioux. They're together, spending the required days of ritual to prepare for the annual Sun Dance. You know what a Sun Dance is?"

"No. And don't care much either."

I took my eyes off the plains below and directed my gaze back to the man with one brown eye and one blue eye. "The braves skewer the skin and muscles of their chests with large slivers of wood, tie that wood to leather lace, and dance for hours while suspended from a thong attached to a Sun Dance pole. They dance until they rip the skewers loose. The vows they take during a Sun Dance are sacred to them."

"So?"

"All the braves who want war, and too many of the peace

advocates will be swearing revenge for what happened on the expedition. If they dance the Sun Dance, whatever retaliations happening now will look like a friendly barn dance compared to the war they'll start."

I looked back down the hill and saw what I'd been expecting for a while.

"Get to your feet," I told Theodore.

He smiled insolence.

I grabbed his collar and pulled him up. I pointed at a dozen distant riders approaching our hill.

"Between getting the telegrams from Boston and finding your whereabouts," I said, "I had time to send word to Red Cloud, one of the Sioux chiefs. I made a deal."

The riders were closer now, recognizable as warriors by the silhouettes of eagle feathers worn on their heads, by the war shields and spears they carried. For the first time, a flicker of fear crossed Theodore's face. He hid it again by forcing his face into a mask.

"See," I said, "Red Cloud believes if you are brought before the Sioux, and turned over to them, it will appease those who seek revenge. These braves here have been watching for the red flag to know I had the man whose punishment would satisfy them."

The Sioux were closer now, faces more than shadow, the drumming of their horses' hoofs audible.

"You can't just let them take me." His voice held the first traces of desperation. "You're a marshal. You can't just break the law."

"I see no other way. I can't bring myself to shoot you; a court won't convict you."

I smiled briefly. Cold. A reflection of the anger I carried and expected to carry for quite some time. "I'll be sending a letter to your folks, letting them know how unfortunate it was for you to be waylaid by Sioux hostiles. Much as that letter might hurt them, it won't be near the pain of them finding out you had your brother killed, their only other child."

I smiled again. "In the letter, I'll let on you died quick and painless because, for all I know, you actually might die that way instead of by inches and over days."

I paused. "But if you're a gambling man, place money once you get back to their camp, you'll die as slow and hard as a man can die."

The Sioux warriors crested the hill and began to slow their horses. One of the horses was riderless.

Theodore shuffled backward a few inches. He understood why the horse held no rider. "Figure on a week of travel," I said. "It'll give you time to think about all the people who died just to give you a chance at that money. Two Hats. More than forty Sioux women and children. Over a dozen soldiers. The colonel, the two men you hired to kill me. All told, close to sixty people. Dead because of you."

The lead Sioux warrior dismounted. He greeted me in sign language, his face bronzed and expressionless.

I pointed at Theodore, and the warrior nodded.

"Could I have some coffee?" Theodore asked. His voice broke. "I'm cold. Real cold. It would be nice to have some coffee before I went."

I grabbed the pot and poured it on the ground at his feet. "Fresh out," I said.

I nodded again to the Sioux warrior. He took the man with one brown eye and one blue eye by the elbow and roughly pushed him toward the horses. Less than a minute later, they rode away, taking him as I had promised.

I went back to the fire and sat for a long time, staring at the embers until they became ashes, cold and gray.

EPILOGUE

NO BRIDE could have asked for a better day to wed, blessed by a rare windless early afternoon, and double blessed by cloudless July sunshine. Back here in Laramie, it seemed like three decades had passed instead of three months since finding a dead man in my office.

Although the ceremony was not scheduled for another half hour, a scattered crowd of people in knots of twos and threes had begun to form outside the front doors of the First Methodist Episcopal Church, all of us encouraged to congregate early by the favorable peace of such a fine summer day.

Most of the faces around me were familiar. Jake, of course, in a dark suit, his hair gleaming with the grease he'd used to keep his cowlicks laid back. Doc Harper, the stern angular lines of his face gentled by the occasion, and him smiling occasionally during his conversation with Jake. I'd nod whenever I met eyes with those around me, but for the most part, I was content to watch silently and listen to the ebb and flow of murmured conversation, enjoying as I was a precious sense of belonging to this community.

I busted into a full grin as I saw the Chinaman approach.

His wife followed several steps behind, her head bowed and covered by a full scarf of rich, red silk. Behind her, in a line of descending size, marched their four solemn children, and all formed a procession of ducklings behind the Chinaman.

He caught my grin, and I hurried to meet him.

"Mahshaw," he said, his head bobbing with his jerky half-bow, "Mahshaw Keaton! It warms my hat evly day to see you arrive."

Which I silently translated to mean it warmed "his heart every day to see me alive."

"Nice to see you could attend," I told him. "Along with your lovely wife and children."

She raised her head briefly, allowing me to see the hint of a smile in her exquisite doll face. Although I'd never be able to prove it, I was fully convinced she knew English as well as any school marm.

"Mahshaw, you shine up good," he said, pointing at my bow tie.

It reminded me I didn't feel so good, starched up in a white shirt and a newly purchased suit.

"Big day," I told him. "Worth the sacrifice."

A whimpering at my feet drew the Chinaman's eyes downward.

"Ho, ho," he said, "this one belong to you?"

I shared his glance, casting a look of disgust at the ungainly black puppy bumping his nose against my polished boots.

"Only until I find someone to take him," I said. "Suzanne gave him to me last night. A wedding gift. When I went to leave the house today, he started yipping so bad I finally decided to let him follow."

The puppy shuffled over to sniff at the Chinaman's feet.

"Marshal Keaton!"

This was a strident, harsh, female voice. The Chinaman looked past my shoulder, half bowed a quick good-bye, and led his wife and children in the opposite direction, leaving the puppy to watch after them, his tail wagging.

"Marshal Keaton!"

I knew who it was before turning. Millie Stickney. A town gossip with an uncanny resemblance to a determined buffalo. Her presence here almost offset the blessings of sunshine and no breeze.

"Marshal Keaton!"

She was pushing people aside in her charge to reach me. I thought of taking the puppy in my arms to save it from a stomping which would surely kill it, then decided if he was too stupid to dodge such obvious danger, I didn't want to be bothered with him anyway.

" 'Afternoon, Mrs. Stickney. Nice day ain't—"

"Don't give me that, Marshal. I saw who you were with. Just like you to spend time with a heathen slant-eye. Probably your idea to have him and his lice-infested brood stop by, wasn't it? And don't think I've changed my mind since yesterday when I told you God would not intend for a wedding like this. No two people could be set so far apart, and it makes me ill to think of such an unnatural union."

I felt the puppy take cover between my legs. This woman would seem like a mountain to him, her broad, chunky body covered with layers of petticoat and dress down to her ankles, the volcanic thunder of her voice hurting his tender ears.

"With all respect, Ma'am, since yesterday I haven't changed my mind either."

"But as town marshal, we expect you to set an example. All the ladies in the auxilary are up in arms over this proposed union, and I am here to represent their view. Mark my words, I fully intend to answer when the preacher calls for lawful objections."

"We had this discussion yesterday, Mrs. Stickney. It—"

"And I'm disappointed you learned so little from it, Marshal." She began to puff her face as she fed on her anger. "Why—"

"Samuel, a few words?"

I nodded at Doc Harper with gratitude. His quiet question

had easily cut through the indignant rise of her voice.

She glared at him, grabbed the sides of her long dress, hitched the dress and petticoats, and marched to the front of the church where she could wait to get the seating of her choice as soon as the doors were opened.

"Thanks, Doc."

We both stared after her, then exchanged glances and both shook our heads in unspoken agreement of aggravation.

Doc let a few quiet moments pass.

"Well?" I said.

"Nice day for a wedding," he replied with the same neutrality I'd used.

"Yup."

"You all right being here? I mean, you and Rebecca—"

"It's not what I expected," I said.

"Life rarely is."

"Yup."

We both lapsed into silence again. As Doc had guessed, my thoughts had wandered back to territory I could not avoid in light of this day's events.

Red Cloud had been true to his word following the departure of Mick Burns, Sitting Bull, and the other Wicasa Yatapickas that afternoon among the Sioux. He'd found Rebecca and sent her back to the tepee where I paced tight circles with a dry mouth and a heart which seemed to flutter and shake like an old man's hands.

Although she stepped fully inside the tepee and let the flap fall into place behind her, she stood close to the entrance as if she were a doe on the edge of a clearing, ready to flee at my slightest move.

I checked my impulse to take her into my arms. She was so painfully close to me. Two steps forward and I could breath in the soft perfume of hair, hold her firm against me, and lose my sorrow and pain and love and fear in the comfort of the woman who had held me on a hillside and whispered love promised to last forever.

Instead, I felt like I was watching her from across a chasm too wide to leap, a terrible sensation more agonized because across the tepee I could see so clearly the dark braids on the shoulders of her tan leather dress, see so clearly the curves of a face which haunted my memories, hear so clearly her hesitant, whispered greeting.

"Please don't make this difficult," she said.

Difficult? That terrible, agonizing sensation began to crush the shaky fluttering of my heart.

"I don't understand," I said. "You heard what I told Sitting Bull. You know it was Mick Burns behind it. Can't you believe that what happened with the blue-coats was not my doing?"

"I knew as you rode up you were not guilty of leading the blue-coats to the massacre," she said, eyes on the ground. "Remember? I know your heart. And love you."

"Love." I clutched at the single word. "Not loved."

"Never will I stop loving you," she said. "Never will I deny it."

I took my first step toward her.

"Please no," she said. "I could not bear to hold you. Not if it means letting go. And it will."

"Why?" I pleaded. "Why? We can leave here together. There won't be a day we're not together."

Her sudden tears ripped at my soul. "Samuel, my love, you're wrong. There won't be a day we're together. And I wish it were not so."

There was a finality in her trembling voice which rooted me to the ground.

"Remember the brave who offered ten horses for me?" she asked.

I did. Only now it didn't seem funny.

"I am his wife," she said, her voice so low at first I wasn't sure she'd spoken.

I shook my head. "No. You said life among the Sioux would be a prison. You said you wanted me. You said—"

"Samuel, I am now married. And I cannot break my vow."

I began to comprehend she was not lying. I tried to speak, but I was unable to croak out any sound.

"Please forgive me," she whispered. "Worse than not having you was the thought of knowing you would die to the warriors who tracked the blue-coats.

"They were going to kill you along with all the other soldiers." She began to sob, and her breath left her in half-hitches strangled by tears. "Can't you see? I bought your life."

I did see. I bowed my head in my hands.

"He agreed to take you away from the camp, agreed to deliver my note," she continued. "In return, I promised myself to him."

I moaned as I understood further. Every night as I fought to find sleep, she would be held by another man. Yet how could I lash out at her, find fault for her decision? If she loved me as I loved her, her heart would be torn at the prospect of giving me life and freedom to find another.

"Oh dear God," I said. To Him. Not her. Because she was gone, the tepee flap still quivering, as she ran through the camp away from me and the pain we shared. I rode away from the Sioux camp within the hour, unable to bear the thought of her so near with infinite chasm between us.

An old cowboy once told me that memory rides a quiet horse, taking you to the tops of high hills with long sweeping views. Well, this quiet horse would be riding until the day I died, with a view so pretty it would always pain my heart. And today, while that horse rode so quiet in my mind, I would be walking up the church aisle with another woman. Doc's hand was on my arm. "Sam?"

I looked down at Doc's hand. Realized my arm was rigid, my fists clenched. I took a breath.

"Don't worry about me, Doc." I tried a grin. "Shoot, I already turned down celebration drinks from a half dozen cowboys."

Organ music rose above the quiet conversations around us. Someone had swung the church doors open. People began to move toward the church. Doc and I and the clumsy, black puppy remained where we were.

"Turning down a whiskey," he said. "Is it getting any easier?"

"Some. But it seems like the urge for a drink is never far away."

He nodded. "You might recall I once told you I lost my family to the bottle, that the urge never ends."

Yes, he had once told me. He hadn't spent much time in discussion of the details, and I hadn't pressed him, for by then I'd already heard the rumors of a successful practice abandoned back East.

"Why is that, Doc? The craving?"

"Let me try these thoughts on you, Sam. Because as you might imagine, I've spent long hours wondering the same thing myself."

The puppy whined for attention. I picked him up. I wrinkled my face and pulled my head back as he tried to lick my neck and chin.

"The way I figure it," he said. "We're born with a soul, as surely as we're born with a mind and body. Nothing in thirty years of doctoring has shown me different."

The puppy gave up on licking and settled his chin on my arms.

"When you understand we all have souls, you have to wonder about purpose, and as near as I can tell, our purpose is to go home. And it's a powerful calling, Sam. We don't understand it, but it's an instinct of the spirit on its journey toward God."

He stopped and frowned, trying to sort his thoughts. "Think of it as a God-hunger, built into each one of us. See, we all want to go back to Eden, and because the soul is brought to life in our tired, worn bodies, our souls must cross a long, hard desert called life. Our soul grows or perishes, depending on what we do crossing that desert. What He gives us along that journey to fill that hunger is love."

I scratched the top of the puppy's head, then realized

what I was doing, and stopped. Stupid dog.

"When love isn't there, Sam, we try to fill the terrible yearning for God. With anything. Money. Women. Booze. Or we try to deny the God-hunger. With hatred. Evil. Revenge."

He removed his wire-rimmed glasses and polished them. When he raised his eyes to mine, I saw sadness. "There's moments when a man drinks he gets that warm peace to fool him into thinking the hunger has ended, like he's on the far side of the desert." He smiled. "I think that's why they sometimes call drink a spirit. Those of us who hurt and can't take the pain want a shortcut across the desert."

He put his glasses on.

Jake called us from the doorway of the church. "Sam, Doc, quit your gabbing and get your carcasses inside."

I looked across to Jake. Doc and I were the only ones still outside in the sunshine. Millie Stickney stood at the door beside Jake, waiting, I was sure, to harangue me on my moral ineptitude to be involved with this wedding.

I set the puppy down and waved acknowledgment at Jake. I noticed Doc smiling down on the puppy, and a sudden suspicion crossed my mind.

"This critter your idea, Doc? I can't see Suzanne deciding it on her own, not with her thoughts on this wedding."

He coughed.

"'Fess up." I said.

"Didn't think it would hurt for you to have something to warm your heart, something you knew wouldn't leave you or hurt you."

"Hmmph."

Jake was waving with his good arm. "She's ready and waiting, Sam. Come on!"

"Tell me, Doc," I said. Jake and Suzanne could hold tight another minute. I felt uncomfortable with this sort of talk and knew it'd be a long while before Doc and I got to ground like this again. "Why didn't you start on love again? You've had time to remarry."

He paused so long, I wondered if I'd pushed too far. "Ever noticed my long hours?" he said. He stared down the street away from the church, away from my eyes. "No one to blame but myself for losing my wife and family. What I should still be giving to them is what I try to give to folks who need doctoring. It doesn't make my regrets any easier, but it stops me feeling sorry for myself and reaching for a bottle."

"Sam! Doc!" It was Jake again.

Now I was glad for the distraction. Doc had given me plenty to ponder. He'd also removed the distance between us, distance which had been gnawing on me since the night I'd angrily pressed a gun to my head at his invitation.

"Ready, Doc?"

He answered by stepping toward the church doors. I followed, the puppy trailing me, tugging and snarling at my pants leg. A lot of folks took their dogs to church, and I knew Jake would keep an eye on it for me.

Jake was inside the shadows of the church when we arrived. Millie Stickney, however, hadn't moved. Doc got past her, but she stepped to block me. Over her shoulder, I could see Suzanne in a wedding dress, anxiously staring back at me.

"Marshal, she's a dance hall girl." Millie Stickney said it loud enough for Suzanne's benefit, loud enough that folks in the back rows just beyond Suzanne turned their heads our direction with curiousity. "You can't take her up the aisle."

"No?"

"Not to let her marry a preacher you can't. She's obviously used the tools of the devil to turn that young man's head. The ladies of our church won't permit such a scandal."

"Fact is, I can take her up the aisle and I will. Even if stepping around you means going an extra mile." I looked her up and down. "Which it appears it might."

Her face darkened to puce. I'm guessing her anger kept her from reacting to the puppy as it gave up on my pants legs and snuffled and burrowed beneath the bottom of her long dress.

"Remember, the vote for your position is coming up," she said. "And my husband's on town council. He'll hear about this."

"He has my sympathy, Ma'am. Now if you don't mind."

I stepped to the side, hoping I wouldn't have to push Millie Stickney from my path. Past Suzanne, at the front of the aisle where the stained glass windows let a shaft of rose-colored light fall upon the pulpit, I saw two preachers waiting. One to perform the ceremony. The other to marry Suzanne as soon as I took her arm in place of her father and led her to the front of the church.

"Yes, I do mind," she said. "And I'm doing what the Lord called me to do by —"

She shrieked. And actually jumped, sending the puppy scuttling and yelping. She shrieked again and her double chin dropped downward as she strained to peer at her ankles. I followed her eyes. She was lifting the hem of her dress and hopping from foot to foot in an awkward dance.

Because the bulk of her body blocked her view, I probably saw and understood it first. The hosiery around her fat ankles was dark with wetness. A small, spreading puddle between her ankles gave mute testimony to the puppy's most recent activity.

"Perhaps the Lord was trying to deliver another opinion," I said. I'm not sure I managed to hide my grin.

I stepped past her, whistling. I extended my elbow to let Suzanne take it, and we began to walk up the aisle to the swell of organ music.

The church doors slammed behind us in the wake of Millie Stickney's departure.

The puppy ambled up the aisle in front of us, and Jake reached down for it, then took his seat in a nearby pew with the puppy in his arms.

I decided I could really like a dog with such good instincts. First thing I'd have to do was find a name for him.

Don't miss a single story from the Ghost Rider Series!

In the rough-riding tradition of the great American Western, the Ghost Rider Series brings you all of the excitement, drama, and energy of life on the frontier. The vivid world of Samuel Keaton comes alive in *Morning Star, Moon Basket, Sun Dance,* and *Thunder Voice.*

Look for them at your local Christian bookstore.

VICTOR BOOKS

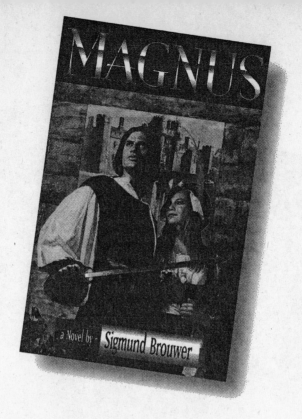

Enter a medieval world of ancient secrets, an evil conspiracy, and a mysterious castle called Magnus.

The year is 1312. The place, the remote North York Moors of England. Join young Thomas as he pursues his destiny—the conquest of an 800-year-old castle that harbors secrets dating back to the days of King Arthur and Merlin.

You'll find *Magnus* at your local Christian bookstore.

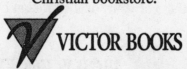

VICTOR BOOKS